NO SUCH THING AS A SECRET

AS A SECRET

A Brandy Alexander Mystery

Shelly Fredman

authorHOUSE™

1663 LIBERTY DRIVE, SUITE 200
BLOOMINGTON, INDIANA 47403
(800) 839-8640
WWW.AUTHORHOUSE.COM

First published by AuthorHouse 06/25/05

ISBN: 1-4208-4381-8 (sc)

Printed in the United States of America
Bloomington, Indiana

This book is printed on acid-free paper.

For Rosebud and The Ace

This book could not have been written without the support of the following people:

Marty Schatz
My friend and editor. Thank you for countless hours of consultation, commiseration and coffee. *"Marty, we need an adventure!"*

Corey Rose Fetzer
The sweetest kid on Earth, who went without meals so that her mother could hole up in her bedroom and write, and, who rescued said mother, every time she had a computer-illiterate moment.

Franny Fredman
Thanks, Mom, for being my biggest cheerleader.

and **Dudley Fetzer**
Whose unconditional love, support, good humor and infinite patience are a constant source of strength to me. *To our long and happy life together.*

Special Thanks to:

Judith Kristen
A wonderfully talented author who so generously shared her knowledge and resources with me.

Akram Ibrahim
I appreciate your patience. You're a gem to work with!

And to:
Susan Jaye, **Dana Pupkin**, **Meyera Robbins**, **Julie Sayres, Sandi Sherman, Amanda Silver** and **Debbie Swartz**—Thank you all for taking the time to preview my book. Your input, enthusiasm and encouragement were so appreciated.

Chapter One

My name is Brandy Alexander. Swear to God. I wish I were kidding, but I'm not. What were my parents thinking? Apparently, that naming me after a cocktail *and* a porn star would somehow enhance my life. They've always wanted the very best for their little girl. My mother remains fascinated with the cleverness of attaching Brandy to Alexander, "which co-incidentally is our last name," as if I could have somehow missed that bit of family trivia. I love my parents despite their oddness. Or maybe because of it. I thought about this as I wended my way through the Philadelphia Airport terminal, trailing bits of silver foil from the two hundred Hershey Kisses I'd consumed during my five-hour flight out of L.A. I'm what you'd call a reluctant traveler and chocolate calms my nerves. It also clears up acne, prevents colds and builds strong bones, so I eat as much as I want and feel really good about it.

Even at six in the morning the airport teemed with activity. I'd taken a night flight—the only way I could fly nonstop. I'd been awake the entire time, just in case

1

the pilot needed me for some reason. Although the bag of corn nuts they'd provided midway over Tulsa *really* filled me up, I was still hungry. I stood in the middle of the food court, debating the merits of eating a cheese steak at the crack of dawn and decided it was a good thing. Then I hopped in line behind a woman with a gigantic ass and rethought my decision. The woman was holding the hand of a sleepy three year old with very wet pants.

"Didn't Mommy say 'Go potty' before we left the plane?" She harped in a voice that could cut glass.

"A bit late for that, eh?" I thought I'd muttered under my breath, but apparently not. She whipped around and shot me a dirty look before turning back to her kid, who was, by now, standing knee deep in urine. I guess the no sleep thing was really catching up to me, because that yellow puddle just cracked me up. I was still laughing as a familiar voice called out to me. "Yo, doll face." My friend, Johnny Marchiano, all five feet, three inches of him came striding forward dressed in fashionably autumnal rust and gold. He wrapped his skinny arms around me for a surprisingly strong hug, and then stood back and eyed me critically.

"You go out in public lookin' like this?" I glanced down at my jeans and "travel sweatshirt" feeling slightly ashamed.

"Is that any way to greet your best friend? I haven't seen you in forever. Tell me I look amazing."

"You look amazing," he said, rolling his eyes. Johnny and I are the same age—twenty- eight, but he was born an Alter Kocker, that's "old geezer" in Yiddish. I picked up my carry-on bag and swung it over my shoulder.

"So, what are you doing here? I thought Paulie was going to pick me up." Paul is my brother. He's two years older, tons nicer and infinitely better looking.

"We drew straws," said John. " I lost. I mean won!"

"You love me," I said, throwing an arm around him. "You couldn't wait to see me. Admit it." I kissed him, big, wet and sloppy on his thin cheek.

"Eeewww!" He said, and wiped his face on his designer sleeve. Smiling, I headed for baggage claim.

It was definitely weird being back. I hadn't set foot on east coast soil since the day I boarded the plane for Los Angeles, over four years ago. I'd left the South Philadelphia neighborhood I'd grown up in, heartbroken and disillusioned after the demise of an intense, ten-year relationship, determined to put time and distance between me and the source of my pain. I missed my friends and family like crazy, but they made their yearly pilgrimage to southern California, and we'd meet sometimes in Vegas or Florida. Last year my parents retired, bought a condo in Boca and now spend winters there.

I work for a local news station in L.A. I'm the hard hitting reporter who brings you up to date coverage on "How to Turn Your Bedroom into a 'Boudoir,'"or "Ten Things You Should Know About Termites." My grad school journalism professor would be so proud. It's a stupid job but it pays well, and it's as close to investigative reporting as I've gotten, thus far. Anyway, it was a terrific excuse for not coming back to visit. It usually worked. But not this time. *The voice on the other end of the line meant business. "I'm gettin' married."* The voice belonged to Franny Di Angelo, one half of the Hell raising DiAngelo twins, my best girlfriends from the neighborhood. She informed me of her plans in her typical, no nonsense way. *"No, you don't know him... He's okay...yeah, I love him... you gotta come in for the wedding, you're in it, and I'm*

3

not takin' no for an answer...don't give me any shit, I'm your best friend..." So, that was that. She really didn't have to say it. I wouldn't have let anything scare me away from Franny's wedding, not even a six foot one inch cop with a crap load of heartache and my name written all over it.

"So, how're ya doing?" John asked, knowing me only too well.

"Fine. No problem," I lied and he let me.

"Well, you look great, apart from that whole "anti-fashion statement" thing you've got going on."

"Thanks, I think." I was going to make up something about seeing Brad Pitt in a restaurant wearing white after Labor Day, when suddenly John stopped walking and grabbed me by the arm.

"Listen," he said, sidling closer to me. "Don't look now, but see that guy over by the water fountain—the one in the tan jacket?" *Oh, goody, we're going to play "Celebrity Look Alike!"* I studied the man for a nano second.

"Okay, I've got it. Wayne Knight."

"Who?"

"You know, Newman, from Seinfeld. Hellooo," I nudged John, who hissed back at me.

"First of all, he doesn't even come close to looking like Newman and secondly, we're not playing Celebrity Look Alike."

"We're not?" I asked, disappointed. *Some homecoming.*

"No. I think that guy has been following me."

"Really?"

"Yeah. I noticed him down in the parking lot."

"Maybe he thinks you're cute. Maybe he likes you."

"Shut uh- up!" Johnny shoved me, two handed, palms flat against my shoulders, but I could tell he was flattered.

"So what do you want to do about it?" I asked, my nosy nature starting to take over. We could reverse the tail, start following him around."

"Okay, settle down there, Harriet the Spy. We're not even sure he's following me."

"Settle down? You're the one who brought it up in the first place." We would have spent the next fifteen minutes arguing about it, as was our way, when the point became moot. The little soggy pantsed kid from the airplane ran headlong into the guy's arms, followed by the woman with the big butt. A happy family reunion ensued. John cast a nervous glance around and shrugged.

"What's going on, John?"

"Whatdya mean?"

"Well, you seem on edge, and—Oh, here's the luggage carousel," I interrupted myself, my ADHD kicking in. I stationed myself next to a burly man wearing a Philadelphia Eagles ski cap. He looked like he lifted cars for a living, so I figured he'd come in handy when my suitcases came around. I was planning on a two-week stay, which naturally meant I'd packed enough for two months.

Twenty minutes later I tossed the last of my suitcases onto the floor.

"Can you *believe* that guy standing next to me? Asked me if I'd mind grabbing his eighty-pound duffel bag. Said he had a bad back. Bad back my—John?" *Where'd he go?* I found him just outside the sliding glass doors, hovering over a sleeping homeless man who was blanketed in old newspapers. John carefully lifted the newspaper off the man's head, folded it neatly and tucked it under his arm. He then reached into his pocket, took out his ever-present Purelle and scrubbed his hands.

"John, if you wanted a newspaper that badly I'd have given you the quarter."

"Very funny. And FYI they're fifty cents now."

"What is going on with you? You're acting so weird." The homeless man shifted in his sleep.

"Not here," John whispered dramatically, sweeping the area with his eyes. He looked so silly I wanted to laugh but somehow felt he'd be hurt, so I just handed him three of my six bags and said, "Lead the way." Once outside the terminal, John put down the bags, opened up the newspaper and pointed.

"Okay," I said, scanning the article, "I agree public transportation is an important issue, but do I really have to be kept abreast of it now?"

"Not that—*that*!" He stabbed his index finger at the headshot of a young man who looked to be in his late twenties. "Who is he?" I asked.

"You mean, who *was* he." The light changed and we made our way across the street, towards the parking lot.

"I don't understand," I said, shifting the weight of my bags from one hand to the other. "What happened to him?"

"His name was Konner Novack. He was killed, four nights ago. Or more accurately, murdered."

"Ooh." I shuddered. "I'm sorry. But what does that have to do with you? Did you know him?"

"In a manner of speaking."

"You mean you"—

"No! Does he look like my type? *Please!* The man had *sideburns!*"

"Okay, so how did you know him?" John did another slow scan and turned back to me.

"I'm really not supposed to talk about this to anyone."

"Says who?"

"The police. I'm sort of working with them." He announced this last bit of information almost proudly.

"You know you're dying to tell me," I said, which was all the prompting it took.

"Alright, so here's the thing. Last Saturday night I went to my friend, Daniel's thirtieth birthday party. It was held at this pretty outrageous gay club downtown. Daniel asked me to be the official photographer for his party." John is an incredible portrait photographer. He used to work for a studio but recently began freelancing. "I came home that night and I couldn't sleep, so I developed the pictures. So the next day, I'm watching the news, and they show a picture of this guy. He'd been found floating face down near Boathouse Row. He'd been badly beaten, and he appeared to have been strangled. Well, he looked really familiar to me, and then it dawned on me where I'd seen him. So I started going over the pictures of the party, and sure enough, he was in a few of them."

"He was a guest at the party?"

"No, he was in some of the background shots, sitting next to some other guy. Well, I freak out thinkin' that maybe the guy he was with could be the murderer, so I decided to call the police." In answer to my unspoken question, John added, "I didn't call Bobby. He's been out of town." At the mention of Bobby's name I felt the old familiar pangs. Homicide detective, Robert Anthony DiCarlo, had been the love of my life since I was fourteen years old. We grew up together. For ten years we were soul mates, partners in crime, and eventually, lovers. He *was* my life, the person I trusted more than anyone else in the world. And then he left me.

Sensing my shift in focus, Johnny waved a hand in front of my face. "Brandy, snap out of it! You can whine about your crappy love life later. I could be in trouble here."

"Sorry. So what happened next?"

"Well, like I said, I called the police and talked to the cop who's in charge of the investigation. I told him about the pictures, and he said he'd come over to collect them. About a half hour later this plainclothes detective shows up at my door. I explained to him how I came about having the pictures, and he asked me a few questions, like, did I have any other copies, and did I show the photos to anyone. I told him that I had just developed the shots and hadn't had a chance to show anybody. He said that was good, because these investigations are very sensitive and discretion was of the utmost importance." John shrugged. "He was being super cautious. You know, making sure there are no leaks in the investigation that could come back to bite him in the ass. There's been a lot of press lately about corruption within the police department."

"When isn't there?"

"True, but you know how accusations come crawling out of the woodwork during election years. Makes it hard for the incumbent mayor to concentrate on winning his next post when he's so busy defending his current one."

"So, you think the allegations are bogus?"

"Hell, no," John replied, cheerfully. "I'm just saying that with all the watchdog agencies in this town, a cop couldn't take a crap without it being analyzed by four different commissions."

You really couldn't blame them. The Philadelphia Police Force has a long history of scandal, involving internal and external corruption. These scandals range from graft to extortion, police brutality and perjury. Ever since the 1995 39th District scandal, in which six officers were convicted of robbing and framing a multitude of suspects, a host of task forces and oversight commissions were created to oversee the Internal Affairs Division.

I digested all that John had told me. "So, what happened after he took the photographs?"

"Nothing. He told me he'd be in touch. And he warned me again not to speak to anyone else about it, and then he left."

"So, if that's all that happened, why the paranoia?"

"Well, that's the thing," Johnny replied, dragging my bags onto the curb. "Maybe I *am* just being paranoid, but for the past few days I could swear I'm being followed."

"John, the guy in the tan jacket has a kid with an incontinence problem. I don't think he has time to follow you around."

"Shut uh-up." John's answer to most of my "Life Observations" is to tell me to 'shut uh-up.' But this time he was serious.

"You really are scared, aren't you?"

"Yeah, I am. I just have this really creepy feeling that I'm being watched. Two days ago, I even thought someone had been in my apartment."

"Was anything missing?"

"No. There were just some things out of place. No one would have noticed it but me." Now there was an understatement. John is an obsessive-compulsive neat freak. An improperly placed pillow could put him in a funk for days.

"And then yesterday I noticed a black SUV parked a few buildings down from my place. As I went to cross the street it started moving, and I swear it tried to run me over. I didn't think much of it at the time. Just figured the guy was drunk or else a really bad driver. But then I saw the same SUV again, parked at my gym." I didn't want to ask him how he knew it was the same car, when half the east coast and all of the west coast owns black SUVs. We reached the entrance of the parking lot, and Johnny began searching around for his car. About forty black SUVs blocked his view. "I'm parked up there," he announced, missing the irony.

John has a brand new BMW, which he calls his "baby." In an effort to keep his baby dent-free, he carefully selected the most deserted spot in the lot. Just as I thought I'd have to call a cab to get us there, we heard the squeal of approaching tires.

A car came barreling out of nowhere. It was an old Ford, battleship gray. It was missing a headlight, which gave the impression that it was winking at us, as if to say, "If I run you down, you know it's all in good fun." I knocked John sideways, falling on top of him. We rolled out of the way as the Ford slowed to a crawl and stopped, inches from us. As Johnny and I struggled to an upright position, the car door creaked open. I could feel John's ragged breath in my ear. He grabbed my hand, ready to flee our assailants. In the next instant, two shriveled, old nuns climbed out of the car. They must've been about a hundred years old apiece. One had a cane, which she used to poke us with.

"Are you kids alright?"

"I think so." My arm throbbed where I'd landed on it.

"I'm so sorry," said the other nun. "We just rented this car from Drive a Jalopy. I'm not used to all the modern conveniences." By the looks of her, a rumble seat would've passed for a modern convenience.

"Forget about it," John told her, relief etched on his face. "No harm done."

"Hey." The one with the cane peered at me, through imitation Ray Bans. "Aren't you that reporter from the Early Edition News in L.A.? We *love* you. Don't we love her, Alice? That piece on sexy lingerie was a real eye-opener."

"I'm so glad you like our show," I replied, slightly dazed.

"Is it true Brian Murphy wears a toupee?" Brian Murphy is the lead reporter on our show and an incredible narcissist. He once held up a live newscast for five minutes while he flossed his teeth.

"Yes, it's true," I said. "Write to him and tell him how natural it looks. He'll really appreciate that." After extracting my autograph and a promise to "do lunch" when we got back to L.A., Our Ladies of the Death Mobile ambled back to their car. "So," I said to John as they drove off, "Do you think they're the ones who broke into your apartment?"

"Shut-uh-up!"

John swung onto the I-95 and headed south. After assuring him that no, I did not think he was crazy, and yes, I had faith that the Philadelphia police force would keep him out of harm's way, he relaxed into his leather seat and turned the radio up full blast. I amused myself with the newspaper John had swiped off the sleeping, homeless guy.

"Oh, this is interesting. I read aloud.

Mayor Vows to Clean up City

Taking a page out of former New York mayor Rudy Guiliani's book, Philadelphia mayor, Bradley Richardson has pledged "a return to 'family values' for the city of brotherly love." Richardson, an outspoken conservative, has targeted many local establishments that cater to the fringe population. At a recent press conference the mayor stated, "Families deserve a decent place to raise their children. There is no room in our city for drug pushers, prostitutes, or perverts."

I stopped reading. "Is this guy for real?"

"Afraid so. He ran a very successful family values campaign, and he's not about to get off the gravy train any time soon. Personally, I think the mayor doth protest too much."

"What do you mean?"

"Oh, you know those super repressed types are always so conflicted. I wouldn't be surprised if he went to bed at night with a bible tucked under one arm and a copy of Male Hustler under the other."

"All that angst must make for a very crowded bed."

Twenty-five minutes later, we were almost home. I swear I could smell the melted Cheez Whiz calling to me from Pat's Steaks at Ninth and Wharton. Signs of Halloween began springing up on every porch. The closer we got to my old neighborhood, the more festive it became. Skeletons, Jack O'Lanterns and ghosts greeted passersby with macabre cheerfulness. People in these parts take their holidays very seriously. We passed Saint Dominic's church, where my mother had been baptized, and Manny's Delicatessen, where my father had his own religious experience over lox and bagel—his way of getting in touch with his Jewish roots. My dad is what he refers to as a cultural Jew and what my mom calls a Jew of convenience, meaning he's not big on schlepping to the synagogue on the high holy days, but he has a vested interest in the meals that come afterwards. When my brother and I came along, my mother laid quick claim to our immortal souls, and, before my dad could say "gefelte fish," we were launched into the world of Roman Catholicism. Well, fair's fair. Mom did do all the legwork by going to church every Sunday. To that end, when I was six I was trundled off to Saint Dom's for a proper parochial school education. I lasted there about two weeks. At first, I loved all the pomp and circumstance, the uniforms, the statues. But being the curious kid I was, I began to ask questions when things didn't make sense to me. I didn't know my questions would throw the teachers into such a tizzy. I just assumed everyone else wanted to know exactly how immaculate conception worked and where Mary's husband fit into the scheme of things. I hadn't quite gotten the concept of blind faith yet. It wasn't long before I'd worn out my welcome, and the nuns suggested I might be better suited for public school.

Paulie, at eight, had fared worse than I did. After going just one day, he'd decided he hated parochial school, and he began showing up for class in a yarmulke he'd found in the back of my father's drawer, with the words "Coen Bros. Mortuary" stamped on the back. After a week of this, it was suggested that he too would be better suited elsewhere. I felt a little disappointed. I'd really looked forward to my first communion. I'd already gotten the dress, a lacy white frock with matching gloves. I decided to go ahead with the communion anyway, and invited all the neighborhood kids to my backyard to "watch me get married to Jesus." As this was a wedding of sorts, I urged them to bring gifts and enticed them with cake. It was a lovely affair. Being a somewhat enterprising child, I also enjoyed a profitable, if not entirely kosher, Bat Mitzvah.

"Okay, doll face, you can open your eyes." We were standing on the porch of my parents' home, the house I'd grown up in. The houses in my neighborhood are cramped, narrow, brick structures called row homes. They are linked together by common walls, the better to hear your neighbors and be able to keep tabs on them. Many of these houses were built in the nineteen thirties. People were shorter then, I suppose, and didn't require as much space. There's a trend in some of the more upscale South Philly neighborhoods to buy the house next door and knock down the adjoining wall. This is not the case on my block, where limited income and tradition prevail. My house is at the end of the block, on one of the few streets that have an actual, albeit miniscule lawn.

When we exited the car, Johnny insisted that I close my eyes as he led me up the three short steps to the front door. Nostalgia washed over me as I breathed in the smell of my neighborhood. Four years is a long time to be gone from a place you love. I heard some shuffling, and then, "Surprise!"

My eyes flew open, and I was engulfed in a sea of arms. My brother, Paul, scooped me up and hugged me breathless. Over the top of his curly, dark hair I could make out the faces of the twins, Franny and Janine. Franny, definitely not a morning person, was wrapped in a ratty, old, pink robe. On her feet were oversized Homer Simpson slippers. Janine was still in her waitress uniform, having just gotten off the night shift at the 24 Hour Diner. My favorite uncle, Frankie, was there too, and his girlfriend, Carla Marie. It was seven thirty in the morning, and they were all there to greet me.

"Yo, Paulie, let her down so the rest of us can see her," yelled Uncle Frankie. As Paul lowered me to the ground I gazed around at my friends and family. Emotion beat the life out of any sarcastic cover-up comment I could utter. Emotion won hands down, and I burst into tears.

"You guys..." I gulped. "You didn't have to...you're just the best!"

"Hey, did you really think you could sneak back into town without the Welcome Wagon? Come here, honey." Uncle Frankie folded me up in his massive arms and kissed me on the top of my head. "I know you talked to your parents, but they wanted me to tell you again how sorry they are they can't be here for you. What with your dad's leg being in a cast, it's gonna be awhile before he can travel." My dad joined a bowling team in Boca, last week. Two days later he tripped over his bowling ball and broke his leg. I get my stellar coordination from his side of the family.

"Okay, my turn." Carla nudged Uncle Frankie aside and clasped me to her ample chest. My nose caught in her lacquered hair and I nearly choked on the fumes. Carla's a hairdresser, and she makes the most out of the discounts she receives on hair products. Carla and Uncle Frankie met a few years ago at an AA meeting. She's thirty-seven, three years younger than my uncle. Until I came along to usurp the position, Frankie was considered the lovable screw up of the family. Twenty years younger than my mother, he grew up with the benevolent disinterest of older parents, who loved him, but just didn't have a lot of energy to devote to their "little surprise package." By the time my uncle turned thirty, he'd been married and divorced twice, served a little time for B&E and was headed in the general direction of Hell in a hand basket. But Carla changed all that. He's absolutely devoted to her.

We trooped into the living room, everyone talking at once. Franny flashed me her engagement ring, a Princess cut diamond the size of a grapefruit. Her fiancé, Eddie, is in the jewelry business and obviously does not ascribe to the theory that less is more.

"Janine thinks I should have chosen something more subtle." She made a face at her sister. "What the hell do I want subtle for? I've waited my entire life for this sucker."

I smiled and hugged her. It was quite a stretch. Twin auburn haired goddesses, Franny and Janine stand 5' 9" in their stocking feet. I'm 5' 4" in two-inch heels.

"The ring is perfect," I said. "So when do I get to meet Eddie?"

"Tomorrow night. We're having a little blowout at Paul's club. It's Oldies Night."

My brother is part owner of a small dance club in downtown Philly, off Market Street. He plays a mix of live local bands and canned music. Paul plays the saxophone. When he was twelve my parents had started him on lessons, thinking it would help boost his self-confidence. Growing up, my brother had a royal stutter. As a kid he was the butt of merciless jokes, (made mostly by me) but he kept it under control with the overuse of certain illegal substances (you know those wacky musicians!). It's pretty much gone now and only reappears when he's super tired or stressed.

"Frankie, Paul, take Brandy's bags upstairs. Janine and John, come help me in the kitchen." Franny, the group's leader, disappeared into the other room as Paul and Frankie carted my bags up the narrow staircase to my old bedroom. Franny is an organizational freak. She manages a small law office in Center City. Before Fran started working there, the place was "going under," but Franny whipped the office into shape in no time and now they run a thriving business. Of course, everyone's deathly afraid of her, which is exactly how she likes it.

I plopped down on the couch, exhausted, and began to survey the room. Everything looked exactly the same, not a plastic flower arrangement out of place. My mother prides herself on two things, good cooking and good taste. While it is a well known fact among family members that she has neither, no one would ever dream of letting her in on the general consensus. She makes two meals, dry chicken and overcooked pasta, and she has the decorating sense of Martha Stewart on Acid. Colors clash, knick knacks abound and shag carpeting reigns supreme. As far as my mother is concerned, if God had meant for her to put fresh flowers on the table, He never would have invented plastic. The house is a monument to Kitsch, and I love every chatcha in it. The house used to belong to my grandparents. My grandfather died when I was four, and my grandmother couldn't bear to stay here without him. So my family moved in and she moved into a duplex, a few blocks away. That's how I met Johnny. His family lived on the other half of the property. I have vivid memories of our first encounter. I was sitting outside on the little porch swing, kicking my feet high out in front of me. Johnny emerged from his apartment and sat down next to me, uninvited. Neither of us said a word for several minutes. We just sat there, swinging our legs. Finally John spoke up.

"You're ugly."

"So are you." Ah, trading insults, the universal language of love. And that was the start of a lifelong friendship.

I leaned back and closed my eyes. Carla arranged herself on the couch, next to me.

"I ran into Bobby at the Italian Market," she said, without preamble. My head shot up so fast I thought it would fly right off my neck.

"Oh?" *Breathe, Brandy. Keep it light.* "I thought he was on vacation."

Carla shrugged. "He's back. He asked about you."

"That's nice." *Oh my god, he asked about me!* "What did he say?" *A perfectly reasonable question.*

"He said, 'How's Brandy?'"

"Hmm…" *Nice touch. This "faux casual" is really fooling Carla.* "And what did *you* say?"

"When?"

"When he asked about me. What did you say back?"

"I said you went on safari and were eaten by a gazelle, and then *he* said, "Oh, that's too bad, Zimbabwe's lovely this time of year." *I think she's on to me.*

"Brandy, I love you, sweetheart, but this phony nonchalance isn't fooling anyone. It's been four years. You've got to come to terms with your feelings for that man."

"You're right," I sighed, slumping forward on the couch. "I know I'm being ridiculous. So, really, how is he?" Carla shrugged.

"Truthfully, I don't know. For a guy who just got back from a vacation he didn't look too well rested."

"What do you mean?" Carla shifted in her seat and began picking at her left pinky nail. A bit of bright orange nail polish chipped off and fell onto her blouse. She flicked it away.

"Damn. That's what I get for using the store brand."

"Carla!"

"Oh, sorry, honey. I don't know, he just didn't seem himself. When I think about it, he hasn't seemed himself in a long time. Oh, he still jokes around, still has that devilish grin, but he's been real distant lately, and I get the sense that he's not real happy. Personally, I didn't think his marriage was going too well, but then he announced that he and his wife and the baby were going on vacation…" She looked up at me with compassionate, mascara-laden eyes. "Are you sure you want to hear about him, honey?"

"Yes." *No, not sure at all.* "Carla, when Bobby and I broke up, it almost killed me. But I always knew he never meant to hurt me. You said it yourself, I've got to come to terms with my feelings for him and move on. I've run away long enough."

"Since when did you become so emotionally mature?"

"Since I started watching Dr. Phil. *What?* It gets really slow at work in the afternoons."

I wanted to pursue my questioning about Bobby, find out more about his shift in personality, but Paul and Uncle Frankie chose that moment to reappear back down the stairs.

"I see Mom and Dad haven't touched your room since you moved out," Paul observed. They've still got your Julio Inglasias poster hanging on the wall."

"That is *not* my poster. I think Mom put it up when she was going through 'the change.'"

An hour and a half later, the various members of my Welcome Wagon had taken off, either for home or work. We had stuffed ourselves with lox and bagels and homemade cannoli. Now, I just wanted to curl up in my own little bed and take a nice long nap.

I was being chased by a herd of man-eating gazelles. They were bearing down on me, and I couldn't outrun them. Just as I was about to be devoured by a particularly aggressive one, Julio Inglasias appeared and began singing to them in Spanish. That seemed to calm them, and they all went to sleep and began to snore. The snoring became louder, more insistent. I sat up and looked around, groggily. Julio winked at me from the wall on the other side of the room. The phone on the bed-stand continued to ring.

"Hello?"

"Hey, Sweetheart. How's my girl?"

"Dad! I'm fine. How's your leg?"

"Not so bad. Everyone in the complex thinks I broke it water skiing."

"Why's that?"

"Because it sounds a hell of a lot better than tripping over a bowling ball." He let out a hearty guffaw, and I laughed along with him. My dad has a knack for adjusting reality to suit the image he has of himself. It's one of his most endearing traits.

"Lou, let me talk to her." My mother grabbed at the phone.

"Just a minute Lorraine, I just got on." A five- minute discussion ensued about whose idea it was to call in the first place, during which time I climbed out of bed, brushed my teeth and washed my face. My mother won.

"Honey, how was the flight? Did you meditate, like I told you?"

"Yeah, mom. Worked like a charm."

"I knew it would. It's supposed to be very calming. I heard it on 'Oprah'". My mother worships at the Oprah Altar.

"I miss you, baby."

"I miss you too," I said, automatically.

"So, what are your plans for the day?" I checked the clock on the bed-stand. Ten thirty a.m. Great. That brings my total hours of sleep in the last two days up to "one."

I eyed my bed, not bothering to suppress a yawn.

"I don't know yet, Mom. The meditation was great and all, very refreshing, but I'm still a little tired. I thought maybe I'd go back to sleep. *Take the hint. Please, take the hint.*

"Oh, honey, you really should get out and see what they've done to the neighborhood, since you've been gone. The Costellos got an awning, it's so garish, and the new neighbors in the Lipskys' old house just remodeled. Oh, and I hear St. Dom's is having a Halloween Carnival. I wish I could be there with you now," she ended wistfully. Somewhere in the back of my throat a lump was forming, and I began to miss my mommy in earnest.

We talked for another fifteen minutes, about Franny's wedding and the psychological effects it will have on Janine. My mother thought she recalled an "Oprah" about twins and wedding-sibling rivalry. Then, with great reluctance, she said her goodbyes.

"Mom, I love you. Kiss daddy for me."

I tried to get back to my nap, but it was a fruitless effort. Maybe I was having a delayed reaction to all the chocolate, but suddenly I was wide-awake. I laid in bed, staring up at the ceiling at the Kurt Cobain poster I'd stuck up there when I was fifteen. I can't say I was a huge fan, I just thought he was cute. That started me thinking about people I didn't like but thought were cute, and those thoughts segued into people I like and think are cute, but I wouldn't want to sleep with, which made me think about Johnny, who is very cute in an Italian elf sort of way but not exactly the stuff female fantasies are made of. Then I began thinking about Johnny stumbling onto a police investigation. Some people have all the luck. I've waited my entire life to sink my teeth into something like this, while John just snaps some pictures in the wrong place at the wrong time and suddenly he's swapping doughnut recipes with Philadelphia's Finest. It is *so* not fair. Then, I thought John could introduce me to the cop in charge of the murder investigation, and we could work shoulder to shoulder to solve the crime (me and the cop, not me and Johnny) and we'd fall in love (again, me and the cop, not me and Johnny) and get married, and we'd become this dynamite investigative team, a sort of Nick and Nora for the new millennium, and...*Okay, get a grip. We haven't even been introduced yet.*

I glanced at the clock. Eleven a.m., which would make it eight o'clock in L.A. The morning news would be in high gear by now. My segments are generally pre-taped, but I do get to go on the occasional shoot. Real high profile stuff too, like The Burbank High School Spelling Bee Championships, or a freak snowstorm in Crenshaw. I honestly don't know what they'd do without me to cover these world-changing events. Feeling pretty high on myself, I called my boss to see how they were faring without me. One of the P.A.'s, a nineteen year old UCLA student name Jeannie, answered the phone.

"Hey, Jeannie, it's Brandy."

"Oh hi, Brandy. We miss you." *Sweet kid.*

"Thanks. Is Gail in?"

"Yeah, but we've got our hands full right now."

"Oh? What's up?"

"A big fire broke out in an apartment building, down town, and according to our sources it may be the work of a serial arsonist."

"No kidding!" I said, salivating at the assignment. "So, is Brian out covering it, or is he still home, flossing his teeth?" I chuckled good naturedly to let Jeannie know I was just joshing old Brian.

"Actually, Brian's home with the flu, and Mark's covering a murder-suicide in Echo Park, Connie's investigating the noxious fumes on Fairfax, so that just leaves me!"

"You!"

"Yeah," she gushed. "Can you believe it? I'm going out on an honest-to goodness assignment—something important, and life changing. I just can't believe my incredible luck." *She stole my assignment, the Bitch!*

"Oh, listen, Brandy, I've got to run. I'll tell Gail you called."

"You do that, Jeannie. Oh, and Jeannie" —

"Yes?"

"Break a leg."

"Thanks, Brandy!" I slammed down the phone, furious. Three years! I've worked my ass off for these people for three years! Squeezing into a phone booth with sixteen sorority sisters for a segment on "Campus Antics," walking eight, yapping mutts at a time to bring our audience the "true L.A. dog walking experience," eating sushi on Sunset, masquerading as a Mariachi on Cinco de Mayo, and I've done it all without complaint. But this time they've gone too far! Somehow, my righteous indignation failed to recognize the fact that I was three thousand miles away when the arsonist decided to get match-happy. It's not that I begrudged Jeannie her big break, (okay, I did, but I didn't *want* to begrudge her, so that should count for something.) It's just that I wanted to make a difference in the world. I knew I was capable of much more than the puff pieces I was doing, and I wanted a chance to prove it. It was time to take stock of my life, but I wasn't sure how to go about it. Finally, I reached into my bag and extracted the last Hershey's Kiss. When in doubt, eat more chocolate.

Chapter Two

Sam's Italian Deli makes fantastic hoagies. They're crammed with every kind of Italian cold cut imaginable, plus provolone, Swiss, tomatoes, onions, shredded lettuce, oregano and generously doused with olive oil. There are lots of restaurants sprinkled around the L.A. area touting "authentic Philly hoagies," but no self-respecting native Philadelphian would be caught dead eating one of those glorified subs. If you asked a Philadelphian what the difference is, they probably couldn't tell you. Some would say it's the rolls. Others might argue over cuts of meat. A few may chalk up the superiority of a hoagie made in Philly to old-fashioned city pride, but on one thing they would all agree; you can't take the hoagie out of Philly. And Sam's hoagies are among the best.

I've known Sam all my life. I went to elementary school with his kids, and his delicatessen's been a neighborhood fixture for a long as I can remember. In Philadelphia, especially in the older neighborhoods lots of "Mom and Pop" type stores are located on residential streets. Sam's store is on the corner of 9th and Christian.

He and his wife live in the apartment above, where they'd raised five kids in very tight quarters.

I walked the eight blocks to his store. As I entered, the most wonderful aroma besieged me; garlic, fresh bread, Romano cheese. Sam was behind the counter, sneaking a cigar. He cast a furtive glance around when he heard the chimes go off in the door, signaling a customer. Then his eyes settled on me, and he did a double take as recognition set in.

"Brandy! How are ya, Sweetheart?"

"I'm fine, Sam. How are you?"

"Can't complain, doll. Who'd listen?" He snorted congenially, and I laughed along with him. We'd been having the same conversation since I was a little girl. "So, your mother tells me you're a big television star out in Los Angeles." My mother exaggerates.

"Pretty big."

"Do you know Mannix?"

"Uh, no. Unfortunately, he's dead." Sam shrugged. Disappointment loomed in the air. "But I know Regis Philbin." Actually, I don't technically know him. I sat next to him in a restaurant once. Sam brightened considerably, my t.v. star status remaining intact.

"So, how long are you in town for?"

"Two weeks."

"Oh yeah, I heard you were coming in for the DiAngelo kid's wedding."

In Philly, we're all "kids." You could be fifty years old, with grandchildren, but if you're younger than the person who's talking about you, you're a "kid."

"How's Mrs. Giancola? Sam is Sam. His wife, Dolores, is Mrs. Giancola.

"She's fine. Went back to school after Gracie graduated high school. She's getting her degree in dental hygiene."

"That's wonderful," I said, but my mind was really on the deli case. Sam stubbed out his cigar and rubbed his hands together.

"So, the usual?" Four years and he still remembered.

A half an hour later I left Sam's with a double cheese and salami hoagie in tow. While Sam worked his magic inside the store, I scooted around back to say hello to his son, Vincent. Vince and I were an "item" when we were eight. That is, until he tried to French kiss me and I bit him. Somehow, we managed to overcome our romantic past and remain friends. I found him in back of his parents' house, his legs sticking out from under a nineteen sixty-three Alpha Romeo. A Z-28 was parked next to it, in various stages of dismemberment. I grew up in a neighborhood of gear-heads. If the guys weren't working on cars, they were talking about them, or racing them, or occasionally, stealing them, as in the case of Ronnie Torino, an otherwise upstanding citizen of our block.

"Yo, Vincent," I called, lapsing into the vernacular. "What does a girl need to do to get a hug around here?" Vince scooted out from under the car and blinked into the sunlight.

"Hey! I heard you were back in town." The omnipotent neighborhood grapevine strikes again. He wrapped his grease-stained arms around me for a warm hug.

"Sorry," he said, wiping a smudge off my cheek. Then, he stood back and eyed me appreciatively. "Wow!" he wolf-whistled. "You look great."

"Thanks," I blushed. As a kid I carried around a fair amount of extra poundage. It was sort of a badge of honor with me. At family dinners, my grandmother would comment on Paul's finicky eating habits. "Now Brandy, she's the GOOD EATER. She'll eat anything you put in front of her. Won't you, dear?" Then I'd beam like an idiot and stuff half a pot roast down my throat, just to ensure a place in Grandma's GOOD EATER Hall of Fame. Fat Aunt Doris was a "good eater" too. In fact, she was such a good eater she died of heart failure at forty-six.

I left Philly with "baby fat" still clinging to my post-pubescent hips. But four years in body-conscious L.A., three of them in the public eye, gave me the impetus I needed to shed the extra pounds. I am by no means skinny, but I no longer resemble a Cabbage Patch Kid on steroids, either.

"Still working for the D.A.'s office, Vin?" Vince is an assistant district attorney.

"Yeah, and it's been nuts, lately."

"How come?"

"Ah, some gay guy got whacked about a week and a half ago. There aren't any leads, and the asshole cop who was supposed to be in charge of the investigation decided to take a vacation the day after this guy turns up D.O.A." My heart lurched.

"Bobby?"

"You got it." Vince grinned. "He's back now, and he's catching a rash of shit for his little impromptu disappearing act." Vince and Bobby are long-time friends, but there's always been a rivalry between them. Physically, Vince takes after his dad, husky build, wide, flat nose, and a receding chin that disappears into his neck, while Bobby is nothing short of gorgeous. He's got the best of his Irish-Italian ancestry: piercing blue eyes, dark wavy hair, and the lean, muscular body of a middleweight boxer. As a teenager it was hard for Vince to watch girls fall at

Bobby's feet. So whenever Bobby screwed up, (which was often, in those days) Vince really made the most of it.

As much as I would have liked to hear more about Bobby, something else Vince had said caught my attention even more.

"You said there are no leads?"

"Yeah, why?"

"Oh, but"—I was thinking about Johnny's pictures and the detective's admonitions not to tell anyone. "Nothing. It must be frustrating, that's all."

I ate my sandwich on the walk home, my conversation with Vince turning over in my mind. Why would Vince say there weren't any leads in this murder investigation? What about John's photographs? And why would Bobby just take off like that? As a kid, he was rebellious, angry, even a little dangerous at times, but never irresponsible. What could have been so pressing that he'd up and leave at such a vital time? It occurred to me that I was spending an inordinate amount of time thinking about an ex-boyfriend who had clearly moved on in his life. The man had a wife and baby, for God's sake, while *I* had a goldfish. At least I *did* have a goldfish. Turns out that bits of raw hamburger meat are a real treat for dogs, but not so much for goldfish.

I reached the front door and turned the key in the lock, just as the phone started ringing. Wiping the grease from my sandwich onto my jeans, I picked up the phone on the fourth ring.

"Hello?"

"Did you have a nice nap?" John inquired. At least I thought it was John. The connection was lousy.

"I couldn't sleep, so I walked down to Sam's for a hoagie."

"Meat or cheese?" I hesitated a moment too long. "You had salami, didn't you?" He accused. Recently, John has become a vegetarian and a pain in the ass along with it.

"Well, I didn't enjoy it, so it doesn't count."

"Liar."

"Hey, listen," I said, changing the subject, "I had an interesting conversation with Vince Giancola today."

"Why would you speak to him? Why? Why?"

"Okay. Not your favorite person."

"He's a Neanderthal! Or have you forgotten about the time he turned me upside down and shoved me in the trash-can!"

"We were ten. People change, and besides, he said he was sorry. Anyway, let me tell you what he said." John cut me off, abruptly.

"Tell me later. I'm on my way downtown. I've gotta get Fran's wedding gift and I wanted to know if you wanted to come along." The connection began to crackle, furiously.

"I want to come!" I shouted.

"Damn crappy phone. Make that a wedding gift and a new cell phone."

Franny and Eddie were registered at a half-dozen stores in Center City, and John was determined to schlep me to every blessed one of them.

"How will we know when we see the perfect gift if we have nothing to compare it with?"

"They're all the perfect gift," I reasoned, "or else she wouldn't have put them on her bridal registry. We could have purchased any one of six thousand items by now, all hand picked by Franny."

"Jeez, if I had wanted to go shopping with a guy I would've asked Paul to come along."

"What's that supposed to mean?" I said, barely containing my urge to knock him into tomorrow. Johnny rolled his eyes so far they almost fell out the back of his head.

"I mean it's very butch not to enjoy shopping. Get in touch with your feminine side, sweetheart. You'll be a much better woman for it." This time I didn't even try to fight the urge. I whacked John a good one.

"Ow. I think you broke my arm."

"I did not. Quit being such a baby." I was heading on thirty-two hours without sleep and my patience was wearing thin.

"Okay," John relented. "If I buy you a Starbucks will you go to one more store?"

"Coffee *and* those little chocolate grahams?" John nodded.

"Deal."

We strolled through Rittenhouse Square, counting the number of people talking on their cell phones. One very loud woman wearing too-tight overalls was having a fight with her boyfriend. She kept shouting, "you asshole, you asshole. I should have thrown your sorry ass out a long time ago." A silver haired society matron was making plans to meet her lawyer, for lunch. Young and old, rich and poor co-mingled in the October sunshine. I drank it all in, happy to be back. The leaves had turned a magnificent array of autumn colors, yet the air was still warm.

"Indian Summer," said John.

"In L.A. we call it Native American Summer."

"You're shittin' me."

"No, I swear. Some Chumash filed a law suit to have the phrase legally changed."

"You are so shittin' me."

I laughed and John threw a companionable arm around me.

"I really miss hanging out with you."

"Me, too."

"So, now can I tell you about my conversation with Vince?"

"If you must." We were seated at a window table in the Barnes & Noble café, where they "proudly serve Starbucks coffee." I knew I'd regret having caffeine this late in the afternoon, but I was so tired I could barely keep my eyes open.

"Okay," I said, settling in. "So I ask Vince how's work and he says things are nuts because of this murder case that's going on."

Konner Novack?" John asked, suddenly interested. I nodded.

"Wow. So what else did he say about it?"

"Well, this is where it gets weird. He said that Bobby was supposed to be in charge of the investigation, but he all of a sudden leaves town, and Vince *also* says there aren't any clues in the case. I'm paraphrasing, but that's the gist of it."

"No clues? I hand that cop eight by ten color glossies of the probable killer and they say there are no clues?"

"Weird, huh?" We sat there for a moment; John sipping his latte, me with a "red-eye" clenched firming in my hand.

"Maybe the pictures just didn't pan out," John concluded.

"In that case, you should ask for them back. Your friend Daniel will want them."

"It's no big deal," John shrugged. "I've got copies."

"But didn't you tell the detective you didn't have any copies?" John looked at me like I'd grown another head.

"Don't you remember how long it took to get your bike back after it was stolen? It sat in the evidence room for three months. You think there's any way I'd hand over all the copies? I put them on my I-Mac. The password is 'brassiere,'" he added, giggling. I would have told John to grow up, but that word makes me giggle too.

"So, what do you think's up with Bobby?"

"Haven't got a clue. But you could ask him. He'll be at Paul's club, tomorrow night, for the party." This last part was said very quietly, I suspect to soften the impact of his words. I felt my stomach tighten at the mention of his being there.

"Bobby's coming?" I squeaked. *Of course he'd be there. Bobby has been a part of the gang for as long as he's known me.*

"Franny had to invite him. Bobby's the one who introduced her to Eddie in the first place."

"It's okay," I said, with a bravery I didn't feel. "He'll be at the wedding. I may as well get it over with. Actually, I'm looking forward to seeing him." John grinned.

"You are so full of shit." I shrugged.

"Flatterer."

We settled on a pair of Waterford "toasting goblets," which weren't even on the registry lists. As soon as Johnny saw them he declared them "the perfect gift," instantly negating three hours of hard shopping labor.

Johnny and I listened to Motown all the way home, except for a brief interlude with Springsteen. We rolled the windows all the way down, and I hung my head out the window, shouting out the lyrics to Born in the USA and getting them mostly wrong.

John parked in front of my parents' house and turned off the engine.

"I had fun today."

"Me too. Just like old times."

"So what are your plans for tonight?"

"Frankie and Carla invited me over, and Paul asked if I wanted to catch a movie, but to be honest, I think I just want to stay home. I need to." John nodded his head in understanding. That's what I miss most about living in L.A. I've made some good friends out there, but no one who really *knows* me. It was a luxury to not have to explain myself all the time.

"Bran, be careful, okay? The past is a nice place to visit, but I don't think you'd want to take up permanent residence there. Call me if you get lonely," he added, leaning over for a hug.

"I will. Thanks." I climbed out of the car and watched as John drove off. As I opened the door, something caught my eye. A black SUV cruised down the street, picking up the pace as John rounded the corner. Impulsively, I jotted down the license plate number, although I wasn't sure of its accuracy. I've had to wear glasses since I was twelve, but I never do. "Five billion black SUV's in America," I laughed to myself. "They can't all be following Johnny."

I sat cross-legged on my bedroom floor, elbow-deep in my memory box. Actually, it's more of a memory closet. I'm a clutter freak. I can't throw away a thing, as evidenced by the old movie stubs, the fourteen year old pack of cigarettes, the toothpick that Franny had salvaged from the cafeteria trash can, that had been sucked on by a boy I LOVED, but whose name I can't remember. "Journey" pumped through my old tape deck. I grabbed my hairbrush and began belting out the tunes. "Don't stop belieeevin' Hold on to the feelin." I looked "hot" in my Calvin Klein panties and sports bra, sashaying all over the bedroom with my fake microphone. I leaned into my brush and got a mouthful of hair. Ewww.

The phone interrupted my concert, for the third time tonight. The first call was from Franny, breaking the news about Bobby.

"It's fine," I reassured her. "Johnny told me...don't worry about it. I'm *so over him*...no, I don't want to be fixed up with Eddie's cousin, but thanks for asking." Call number two was from Paul.

"I forgot to tell you, the keys to Dad's Le Sabre are in the kitchen drawer, next to the sink."

"I don't want to drive the Le Sabre."

"Why not?"

"It's maroon."

"It's burgundy. What's wrong with burgundy?"

"Burgundy isn't metallic blue."

"But my Mercedes sports car is. I see where this is going."

"Come on, Paul. I'm only in town for two weeks. You've got two other cars. You don't even drive the Mercedes."

"That's right, I don't!" He said, pointedly. "That car is a classic."

"Oh, fine. I'll drive the old lady car." Paul sighed.

"I'll drop off the Mercedes, tomorrow. Bu-but if anything ha-happens to that car" —

"It won't, I promise." Did I mention that I love my brother?

My third interruption came in the form of John. I lowered the volume on the tape deck.

"What are you listening to?"

"Led Zeppelin," I lied.

"You are not. I'll bet it's 'Journey'."

"Okay, it's 'Journey.' What of it?"

"What a trendy little eighties girl you were."

"Oh, you should talk. I seem to recall a certain someone's fascination with Don Johnson from Miami Vice. You died your hair blond and made your mom go out and buy you those tight, pastel-colored t-shirts and a linen sport jacket. No wonder you kept getting beat up at school."

"I was so friggin' fashionable," John said, remembering. "They were all jealous."

"They were," I agreed. "So, what are ya, checking up on me?"

"Maybe."

"John, it's not like I have a terminal disease or anything. I'm just feeling a little nostalgic, that's all."

"In that case, I'll let you get back to your reminiscing. Just promise me you won't break out the "Kiss" records."

"I promise."

"Hey, while I'm thinking about it, do you want to take a ride with me to Atlantic City, on Saturday? I'm meeting Joel Mishkin at nine a.m. He's been bugging me forever to take him out on my boat."

"That sounds great! I could drop you off at the Marina, and then I'll cruise the casinos while you guys do your little nautical thing."

By the time I hung up with John it was after eleven p.m. I was tempted to take the phone off the hook, but since everyone I'd ever known from the Greater Philadelphia area had already called, I figured it wouldn't ring again. Just then, the phone rang.

"Hello?" I detected a slight hesitation, and then a woman's voice.

"Is Bobby there?"

"Bobby who?" *Click. What the hell was that all about?* I hit "Star 69" and waited for the "mystery woman" to pick up the phone. After fifteen rings it became clear that she wasn't going to.

"Well, that's interesting," I said aloud, because I was starting to get a creepy feeling, and it helped to pretend someone was there with me. "What do you think of that?"

"I really couldn't say." After a good talking to, I convinced myself that it was a wrong number, nothing more.

God, I was tired. I turned off Journey, checked the locks on the doors, and threw on a pair of sweats and an old Temple U t-shirt I'd found in the closet. Then I flicked on the bathroom light, turned off the overhead, crawled into bed and immediately fell into a dreamless sleep.

Chapter Three

"Jerry or Kramer?"

"I don't want to play."

"Come on," Franny coaxed.

"Okay," I sighed, "Jerry."

"Kramer or George?" That, from Janine.

"Ooh, tough one—George." I picked up my glass of single malt and took a healthy swig. Janine knocked back her third Rolling Rock and slammed the bottle on the table, signaling for another.

"Ross or Chandler?" She said.

"Joey."

"Not an option."

"Oh, like the other ones are?"

"Okay, okay. Ooh, I've got one. Gilligan or The Skipper?"

"Doesn't my reality suck, enough? Either give me a decent fantasy choice or I quit."

We were sitting in one of the back booths at Paul's club, playing "Who would you rather *do it* with?" We had to disqualify Johnny Depp, because everybody wanted to do it with him, and it was making the other contestants feel bad. At least, we thought they'd feel bad if they knew, which we believed was an actual possibility. We were really drunk. I drained my glass and sat back, debating whether to order another. Paul ambled over and slid into the booth, next to me. He eyed my empty glass and chuckled softly.

"Having fun?"

"Yep!"

The place was packed. Paul's club is a throwback to another era; red leather booths, blue velvet walls, a small stage overlooking a rectangular dance floor and a killer sound system. The club plays an eclectic mix of music, which attracts a varied clientele. There's everything from Salsa, to Big Band, to Heavy Metal and Alternative. But Friday nights are reserved for Classic Rock and Motown. Years ago, Paul had his own garage cover band. They played all the oldies as well as classic artists like Otis Redding, Al Green, and Aretha. I used to sing backup, occasionally taking the lead when a female voice was needed. He reminded me of this now.

"Ya know, the old band is here."

"*Get out!* Kenny? Chris? Taco?" We didn't know from politically correct back then. We just knew the guy ate *a lot* of tacos. "Hey, where are they?"

"Out in the parking lot, unloading their equipment. Franny and Eddie wanted some live music. By the way," Paul added, looking around, "What'd ya do with Eddie?"

"He's in the back room with John, playing pool. He took off as soon as we started drinking."

"Smart man. So anyway, Sis, we're going to need some female accompaniment here, and it looks like you're it."

"You are nuts if you think you're gonna get me up on that stage," I said, with as much dignity as one can muster through a single malt haze.

"What's a matter, you chicken?" Low blow, Paul. He knows I can't stand to turn down a challenge, even a stupid one.

"Grow up, big bro. I'm not getting up there and making an ass of myself. No friggin' way." I looked to Franny and Janine for support, but they busied themselves, guzzling a new round of drinks. If I didn't know any better, I'd swear they were in on it.

"Fine," Paul said, too easily. "Mindy Rebowitz is here. I'll ask her." Talk about your low blows! Mindy Rebowitz was my nemesis all through high school. She was the one who ratted me out when I went "undercover" in the Boys' locker room to check out an allegation that they had saunas and a wet bar in there. She was the one who stole my history test and drew little penises on it and then slipped it back on the teacher's desk when he wasn't looking. I was suspended for a week. And Mindy was the bitch who started the rumor that I'd had a sex change operation! The only reason people believed her was I had allergies, which made my voice unusually deep for a girl. I hated Mindy Rebowitz with a passion, and didn't Paul just know it!

"When do we go on?" I sighed. Paul flashed a triumphant grin.

"Thirty minutes."

It was ten p.m. and the club was jammed to capacity. I cast my eyes over the crowd, silently wishing everyone would realize it was way past their bedtime and go home.

"Are you sure Bobby isn't coming? I mean I really, really need to know before I get up there on stage."

"Look," Franny shouted over the noise, "I'm only telling you what Eddie told me. He said that Bobby called him about an hour ago and said he was still at work, and it didn't look like he was going to be able to make it to the party, after all." Relief and disappointment battled it out in my colon.

"Ya know I was kind of looking forward to meeting the little woman." Did I say that out loud? I sounded like my Grandpop Max.

"The 'little woman!' Hah! That's a good one." Franny cackled hysterically and tossed back a tequila shooter. I quickly followed suit, squirting lime juice all over my arm. "Well," Fran continued, "*I* like to call her Miss Congeniality. She's just a peach of a gal!" That got me laughing so hard I nearly toppled off the barstool. We had given up our comfy booth to the "paying customers" and were now seated precariously at the bar. "Ya know," Franny whispered conspiratorially into my ear, "I don't like to talk trash about anyone," which set us off on a new round of guffaws. "You know me. If I can't say anything nice…" I nodded my head, solemnly.

"You are the soul of discretion."

"But I gotta tell ya, that bitch hasn't said word one to any of us the entire time she's been married to Bobby. I think the only reason they eloped was so she wouldn't have to invite us to the wedding. Do you think I'm pretty?" She asked suddenly, thrusting her upturned face into mine. With her make-up pooling around the base of her eyes, she looked like a besotted raccoon.

"You're gorgeous. Hey, you're not going to try and kiss me or anything, are you?"

"Eddie says he loves me because I'm *so pretty.*" Please, God, don't let me be as drunk as Franny.

The band was onstage, warming up; Kenny on drums, Chris, on guitar, Taco on keyboard, and Paul on his old, beat up saxophone. I tried to climb down off the stool, but my legs couldn't find their way to the floor.

"Okay! I can do this," I said, giving myself a much-needed pep talk. "It'll be fun." I pushed myself off the stool and bumped smack into Mindy Rebowitz. I had hoped she'd gotten really fat over the years, but she looked the same as always, only now I was seeing two of her. Her bouncy, bottle- blond hair framed a perfect heart shaped face.

"Well, well, if it isn't Brandy Alexander. I haven't seen you since high school graduation. How are things out in La La Land?" That was the trouble with Mindy. She said things like La La Land. She really made me want to puke.

"Couldn't be better." I casually draped my arm over the bar for support. "So, how have you been?"

"Great," she gushed. Did you know that Terrence and I have just had our second?" Their second *what?* I must have looked puzzled, because she clarified right away. "Our second *baby.* Another girl. Terrence says she's the image of her mommy." Oh goody, Spawn of She-Devil.

"Congratulations. You must be very happy." All of a sudden I had to pee, really badly. I straightened myself up and prepared to walk away. "Well, Mindy, it was terrific seeing you" —

"So, have you seen Bobby since you've been back?" Shit.

"No, I haven't. Listen, Paul's waiting for me. I really have to go."

"Of course," She said, with a smug little smile. I wanted to slap it right off her face "I imagine it's still hard for you."

"You can imagine anything you want, Mindy," I said, through a smile of my own. "Personally, I don't have time to reflect on other people's lives. I'm too busy living one of my own." She stared at me, open mouthed, as I spun around, cross-legged and hobbled off to the Ladies' Room. Half way across the club I could hear Franny snickering.

"Bran-dee! Bran-dee!" The crowd was chanting my name as I exited the bathroom. While I was in there I tried to gussy up a little. The only time I ever wear make-up is when I'm on-air. But after my run-in with Mindy, I decided it wouldn't kill me to look a little more presentable. I ran into Janine coming out of one of the stalls.

"Hey, lemme have some mascara, 'k?"

"Sure. You feeling okay?"

"Swell. How 'bout some lip gloss?" Janine searched her pocketbook.

"Nope, no lip gloss. But how about this?" She held up a tube of blood red lipstick to the light.

"Perfect." I began to apply it to my mouth, making big red loops that extended far beyond my lip lines.

"Here, let me do that. You look like Lucy Ricardo." Janine grabbed the lipstick out of my hand. "Now," she said, appraising her handiwork, "What are we going to do with your outfit?" I looked down at my jeans and sweater. They seemed fine to me.

"What's wrong with my outfit?"

"Nothing, if you're going camping with the girl scouts. But you're a rock and roll princess, now. You've got to look the part." She reached into her huge black bag and extracted a tube top that wouldn't fit a Barbie doll. "Here, put this on."

"Janine! I couldn't squeeze my *neck* through this thing, let alone the rest of me!" She gave me a withered look.

"Brandy, you have been wearing jeans and a t-shirt since you were seven. It's time to branch out. Now get in there and change, and then we'll figure out what to do with your hair." Uh oh.

Ten minutes later I stared at my reflection in the bathroom mirror. Florescent lighting not withstanding, I looked good! Janine had somehow managed to tease my poker straight hair into some kind of "do". My bangs flopped lazily across my forehead, emphasizing my eyes. She had gone a little overboard with the eyeliner, which gave me a weird, sort of Vampira look, and the tube top clung to my chest like a second skin. All in all the effect was rather sexy. I smiled coquettishly in the mirror. Damn, I'm hot.

I strolled confidently out the door, unaware that a long strand of toilet paper had attached itself to the heel of my shoe. Some people are born to nerdiness, while others have it thrust upon them. In my case, it's a little of both.

"What you want, Baby I've got it. What you need, do you know I got it, All I'm askin' is for a little respect."

The band was on fire! We'd torn through all the old standards and thought we'd end the set with Aretha. The audience, made up mostly of neighbors and long time friends, responded with wildly enthusiastic hoots and hollers, calling out our names, begging for encore after encore. That last shot of tequila I'd consumed just before climbing on stage was a real confidence booster. Taco hugged me hello and whispered something dirty in my ear—something to do with the tube top and if he wasn't married. I laughed, feeling truly relaxed and happy for the first time since I'd been home. From somewhere out in the audience a male voice called out, "Strut your stuff, Baby." I strained to see who it was. Jimmy Donopolis gave me the "thumbs up," and I blew him a kiss in return.

"Lookin' good, Brandy," he shouted. People were dancing and swaying to the beat. My voice rose to a wail, and I began to bump and gyrate like I never had before. Tina Turner could have learned a thing or two from me. The crowd was reeling and so was I. I had no idea I was such an exhibitionist! By the end of the song the entire club was on its feet, whooping and shouting out the lyrics. The last note sounded and Kenny and I collapsed in each other's arms. We took our bows as the crowd roared their approval. The whole thing was entirely thrilling.

After a few minutes the noise died down, and I slowly began to focus on the crowd below me. Franny and Eddie stood arm in arm, talking animatedly to some guy standing next to them. Eddie slapped him on the back and then did one of those fake boxing moves that guys do. The guy dodged and laughed. Then he reached around Eddie to kiss Franny on the cheek. And when he did, my heart fell right out of that tube top, onto the floor.

He was more beautiful than I'd remembered. More rugged. Sadder, older, leaner. He looked up and our eyes locked onto each other. A slow smile spread across his face, and I felt a familiar "rush" somewhere just below my belly. *Fuck. This can't be happening.* How long had he been there, watching me? "Oh, God," I groaned, inwardly. During "Natural Woman" I'd bent down to adjust the mic and my left boob popped out of the tube top. I was so drunk it took a full minute to realize I was paddling with one oar out of the water. No *wonder* the man was smiling! I flushed with embarrassment and glanced away. Then an idea occurred to me. A wild, hopeful idea. Maybe this wasn't happening at all. Maybe this was one of those recurring dreams, where you show up at high school naked, and to make matters worse, you have a term test, only you haven't been to class all year. I pinched myself to test my theory. Ow! *Fuck.* "Okay," I thought, taking a deep breath. "This is not exactly the reunion I'd hoped for, but hell, I'm a professional. I'm trained to handle any situation, with grace and composure. I can salvage this. Meeting his gaze once again, I pushed my sopping wet bangs off my face and returned the smile.

"Bobby. How good to see you." I took a step forward and promptly fell off the edge of the stage, knocking myself out.

Shit. My head hurt. I opened my eyes and found five pair staring back at me.

"I'm fine." I tried to sit up but everyone was crowded around.

"Should I get a doctor?" I recognized Janine's voice through the ringing in my ears. "Larry Mitchell's here. Maybe he should look at her." Larry Mitchell is a veterinarian.

"Here, let me do it. I'm trained in emergency procedure." Bobby whipped out a tiny flashlight from his key chain and leaned over me. His smoky blue eyes peered intently into mine. "Brandy, can you sit up?"

"Of course I can sit up." Ow.

"Here, look into the light."

"Guys, this is so unnecessary. Really, I'm fine."

Bobby flashed me another smile. "Humor me." I sat stock still while he gently prodded my forehead with his fingers. A lump was beginning to form over my right eye. I guess I should have been concerned about a possible concussion, but I was too busy enjoying the feel of his hands on my face to worry about a little thing like brain damage. He leaned in closer. I could feel his breath, warm on my neck, and I shivered involuntarily. I closed my eyes and let the sensations wash over me.

"Um, Brandy?"

"Hmm?" I responded, dreamily.

"Could you open your eyes? I want to see if your pupils are dilated." My eyes flew open. Oh my God. Here I am practically having an orgasm, and all the poor guy wants to do is check for vital signs. I felt like a colossal idiot.

I pushed Bobby's hand away and sat up. *Shit. Double shit!* Mindy Rebowitz was striding towards us, her husband, Terrence, in tow. "Are you alright?" She asked with exaggerated concern. "When I saw you fall off the stage, I thought, 'that poor girl. How will she ever live it down?'" Concussion, or no concussion I struggled to my feet and planted my hands squarely on Mindy's shoulders.

"Live *this* down, why don't ya?" I gave her a solid shove, and she landed on her big, post partum ass. I half expected Terrence to spring to her rescue, but he just stood there trying not to crack up.

"Bobby," Mindy screamed. "She attacked me! You saw it happen." She looked from Fran, to Paul, to Janine, to John. "You're all witnesses. I want her arrested!" Fran, Paul, Janine and John all started mumbling at once about having something important to take care of, and they scurried off in different directions.

"Relax, Mindy," Terrence said, extending a hand to his prone wife. "You've been begging for it all evening." Wow, Terrence grew *cajones* while I've been gone. Very impressive. He winked at me and dragged Mindy away, leaving just Bobby and me.

"Alone at last," Bobby joked.

"Where's your wife?" I blurted out. What is *wrong* with me? Emotion flickered across Bobby's face, but I was too slow to read it. Anger? Sadness? "I'm sorry. That was rude. I-I just thought she'd be here."

"She's out of town." All signs of joking were gone.

"Oh. Well, that would explain why she's not here." I caught an almost imperceptible sigh before he answered.

"Yeah, I guess it would."

"So, I guess congratulations are in order—I mean, on your wife and baby."

"Thanks." I nodded my head as if he'd just said something quite remarkable. We stood there for a moment, silently appraising each other. I wondered if he'd noticed my weight loss. I wondered if he liked it. I wondered if he was happy in his marriage, how long it took to get a Mexican divorce, and if he asked me to come home with him tonight, what my answer would be. I wondered if Jesus was judging my musings and finding me wanting as a Christian. Maybe the Jews are less judgmental. Hah! The sound of his voice stirred me out of my reverie. "So, how have you been?" He asked. *Lonely, frustrated.* I gave a quick scan over that all too familiar body. *Horny.*

"Great! I have a job I adore, tons of friends; the weather in L.A. is to die for. What's not to love about my life?" Who *is* this woman, and why doesn't she SHUT UH-UP!

"I'm happy for you, Brandy." He flashed me that old familiar smile, and for a brief moment I felt a pang so deep I couldn't breathe. I struggled to regain my composure.

"Well, what about you?" I asked, ho-hoing like some demented Santa on crack. "Lots of changes in your life, I hear."

"You could say that." Oh Christ, I'm not ready for the "I'm deliriously happy with my wife and child" speech. I just prayed he didn't whip out the family photos. I waited a beat. When he didn't elaborate, I quickly went in search of another topic. I looked down at my shoes, adjusted my top and cleared my throat a few times. When I looked up again, he was still there. This was just too weird. How could we be so awkward with each other? There was a time when we knew everything there was to know about one another. We shared it all—our hopes, our dreams, our fears, our first orgasms involving another person. Well, at least *I* did. Is this really the same guy who used to eat Chinese food, naked, off my stomach? This really sucks! It's taken me four years to screw up the courage to face him again. I'd dreamed about this moment since I'd first gotten on the plane. I was going to knock his socks off with my ravishing beauty, my daring wit and my newfound sophistication. I'd make him sorry he'd ever left me. My fantasies definitely did not include long, uncomfortable silences, and a yearning to rip his clothes off and pin him to the floor in a mad, passionate embrace. *He* was supposed to feel that way about *me*. The silence stretched out for what seemed like hours. And then, just when it seemed like it couldn't get any worse, it did, in spades. After the band had left the stage, a D.J. had taken over, and was playing audience requests. Bobby was gearing up to make a polite exit and I was trying to beat him to it. And that's when we heard it—the unmistakable strains of "Bobby's Girl."

" I wanna be Bobby's girl, I wanna be Bobby's girl, that's the most important thing to me." My hands flew up to my face.

"I didn't!" —

"Neither did I!" —

"This is so" —

"Who would" —

The answer came to us, simultaneously. "MINDY!" We stood there, paralyzed, as those dopey lyrics ran on and on. Somewhere in the background, someone snickered.

"Uh, listen, Brandy. I've got to go. It was good seeing you."

"You too, Bobby." I extended my hand to shake his, and he reached around for a hug but stopped midway when he realized I wasn't planning on full body contact. Then I felt bad because he looked embarrassed, so I tried to make it look like I was planning to hug him all along. I reached out and we bumped heads awkwardly, and we ended up in a half-assed embrace, which I made worse by over compensating with a friendly goodbye kiss on his cheek. Only he moved, and I ended up grazing his neck instead. How pathetic is that!

The gang took a taxi home, because we were all too drunk to drive. Franny tried to grill me about Bobby, but I pretended to fall asleep, complete with fake snoring. I wasn't about to pour my heart out in front of Eddie and the cab driver. The cabbie turned out to be a hell of a nice guy from Saudi Arabia. He and Janine exchanged phone numbers.

When I got home I walked straight upstairs to the bedroom. I didn't bother to wash my face or change my clothes. I just turned on the bathroom light, threw back the covers on the bed, snuggled under the blankets and cried myself to sleep.

Chapter Four

Note to self: I am not a Waring Blender and therefore, should not act like one.

I woke up with the Mother of all hangovers. Mixing Tequila, single malt and club soda seemed like a festive idea, last night, but in the clear light of day it just seemed really, really wrong. I turned my head carefully, lest it fall off and roll under the bed. The clock said "six thirty a.m." Oh my God. I'd been asleep for less than four hours, and Johnny was picking me up in thirty minutes. Whatever possessed me to agree to an early morning trip to the Jersey shore? I picked up the phone and dialed his number.

"You're not crapping out on me."

"How'd you know it was me?"

"Who else would it be?"

"I'm tired." I whined.

"You can sleep in the car."

"But, I don't feel well. I could end up getting sick all over the Beemer." That made him pause, but he was back in the race before I'd taken my first victory lap.

"So, you'll hang your head out the window. We're driving downwind. No backsplash."

"You are so gross!"

"You're the one who brought it up in the first place, Sunshine." I flipped him the bird.

"You just gave me the finger," he huffed, indignantly.

"No, I didn't." *How did he know?*

"Look, it's a long drive, and you promised to come with me."

"I didn't exactly promise," I sulked. "Oh, alright. Give me an extra fifteen minutes to hop in the shower."

"That's my girl," John said, significantly cheered. "Just take some hair of the dog and you'll be fine."

"Screw 'hair of the dog.' Bring me chocolate."

I swore to myself that I would not look in the mirror, but morbid curiosity got the better of me. I tiptoed into the bathroom and sneaked up on my reflection. EEEEK! Turning on the shower full blast, I peeled off last night's outfit and jumped in. I immediately felt lighter as five pounds of ruined make-up slid off my face and down the drain. I washed my hair twice, removing all traces of Janine's hairspray. Then I climbed out and toweled off and spent the remaining five minutes trying to blow dry my hair into some sort of style. It refused, and rather than get into a big fight with it, I let it hang straight to my shoulders, per usual. My hair is so impossible to style they almost considered making me wear a wig at work. But the producer, a very sweet kid of twenty-two, said he thought it looked sexy. At twenty-two, everything looks sexy.

I had just climbed into my jean jacket when a horn tooted outside. I grabbed my bag and my keys and headed out the door.

My parents' neighbor, Mrs. Gentile, glared at me from her front porch as she bent down to collect her newspaper. She and my mother have had a running feud for the past twenty-odd years. It all started when my mother bought a ten foot inflatable Santa one Christmas, to put out on the lawn. Mrs. Gentile said it dwarfed her manger and was an affront to Baby Jesus. My mother tried to reason with her, citing the fact that my father, being Jewish wanted to join in the festivities with a non-denominational, yet universally recognized symbol of joy and generosity. Mrs. Gentile called my mother's explanation a "heathen crock of shit" and stuck to her guns, literally. At three o'clock in the morning, shots rang out in our normally peaceful neighborhood. The police arrived ten minutes later, to find Santa dead on the lawn. No charges were pressed, but the incident put a damper on neighborly relations that to this day have yet to be repaired. Every year at Christmas, my mother makes a big show of dragging out the ten foot Santa, complete with a huge bandage strapped over his heart. It causes Mrs. Gentile no end of grief.

We headed toward the bridge. Traffic was light, this time of morning. Most of the older people in the neighborhood were home, puttering around the house and garden, while the younger ones were still in bed, recuperating from their Friday night out on the town. I yawned a big yawn, wishing I were one of the ones still in bed.

"Here," Johnny said, sweeping a hand over the console. "I figured you'd need this." He handed me a large double shot mocha, which I gratefully accepted. I took my first sip and breathed a satisfied sigh.

"You're a good man, John Marchiano."

"That's not what you were saying thirty minutes ago."

"Thirty minutes ago I was undernourished. Now, I am thoroughly content and all is right with the world."

"Uh huh. Until the caffeine kicks in and you go into hyper overdrive. Brandy, you really ought to think about a more nutritionally balanced life style."

"Have you been watching 'Discovery Health' again? Those Diet Nazis don't know what they're talking about, trying to ruin everything that's good in the world." I drummed on the console for emphasis.

"Damn, It's starting already. I knew I should have ordered you a decaf."

"I'm fine." I opened the window and hung my head out, enjoying the crisp, October air. In L.A. we have two seasons. Summer and Not Summer. There's no discernible difference between the two, but we like to pretend that there is. A black SUV passed us on the right, and I gave the driver a hearty salute. He didn't wave back. Not a morning person, I guess. The SUV reminded me of the murder investigation that John was involved in. I stuck my head back in the car, and started to ask him about it but was interrupted by the strains of an old Green Day CD.

"Okay," John said, adjusting the volume to a tolerable roar, "Are you ready to talk about what happened between you and Bobby last night, or do I have to wait until you've thoroughly discussed it with Fran and Janine first?"

"Sorry," I said, sheepishly.

"That is so totally sexist, you know."

"It's not," I protested. Franny would kill me if I didn't talk to her first. Besides, there's nothing to tell." John gave me a sideways glance.

"Uh huh."

"Really, John. We exchanged pleasantries. It was very anti climatic. I don't know what I was so afraid of, all this time."

"So, you didn't feel anything for him then."

"No." He studied me for a beat.

"You're lying."

"I'm not lying."

"You're lying."

"Fuck you. I'm not lying. Will ya keep your eyes on the road? You're going to get us killed."

"Fine," he said, dragging his eyes back to the hiway. "I'll wait until you've had your little girlfriend chat with Franny, but then I want details." I sighed.

"Deal."

Traffic was beginning to pick up. We passed a couple of tour buses filled with senior citizens, on their way to the casinos. Their little gray heads peaked over the tops of their seats like fluffy clouds. "That's so sweet," I said, pointing to a group sitting at the back of the bus.

"Don't let those old people fool you," John said. "They look all innocent and vulnerable, but just try to horn in on their 'lucky slot machine' and they'll kill ya. They're like rabid dogs when it comes to their nickel slots." The black SUV appeared again in my side mirror, but stage one of the caffeine high—warm and fuzzy, had begun to wear off, and I was entering phase two— impatient and grumpy. This time I didn't wave. I put my feet up on the dashboard and John tossed me a death ray.

I took them down again and began pawing through his CD collection.

"Are we there, yet?" I asked, holding up some Coltrane for inspection.

"Jesus, Brandy, will you quit touching everything? You're like a little kid."

"I'm endearing."

"Is that what they call incredibly annoying, in L.A.? I would have thought that being in the public eye would mellow you out a little. You know, get rid of some the rough edges."

"They think I'm refreshing. Hey, we're here! I can smell the ocean."

It was eight forty five a.m. when we pulled up to the marina. Joel was already there, waiting.

"Okay, out you go," I said, anxious to scoot into the driver's seat.

"Swear you won't drink coffee while you're driving. This is real Corinthean Leather." I didn't bother to tell him that there's no such thing as Corinthean Leather, that it's just a marketing ploy. I just swore on a stack of invisible bibles that I wouldn't spill anything on it, or drive over thirty-five mph and he handed me the keys. "Come back at eleven. We should be done by then and we'll go to brunch." John watched me as I carefully backed the car out of the parking space. Then I watched him in the rear view mirror, as I burned rubber out of the lot. "Only kidding!" I yelled back at him. No need to give the guy a heart attack.

I cruised down Brigantine Boulevard until I reached Trump Marina. There it stood, in all its tacky splendor, calling to me to squander my money in its hallowed halls. "Sounds good," I thought. I parked, and wandered around aimlessly for a while, stopping to watch a man in a powder blue jogging suit play blackjack. He had on a wide brimmed cowboy hat that shielded his face, and he never said a word. He just nodded and gestured whenever he wanted more cards. I found him fascinating. After five minutes I got tired of watching him, so I wandered around some more, looking for just the right spot to amass my fortune. "This one looks like a winner," I thought to myself as I settled on a quarter slot machine.

Ten minutes later I was out of money, so I headed for the boardwalk. Even in mid October, the boardwalk draws a crowd. I watched as a toddler wobbled along, chasing a flock of pigeons. Her arms spread wide, she did this little stomping thing with her feet. Then she dove into the flock, headfirst, laughing and screaming. Her mother grabbed her and tried to get her back in her stroller. The little girl struggled valiantly, but the mother was bigger and she won, in the end. I vowed that if I ever had a kid I'd let her chase pigeons until she dropped.

I walked along, perusing the tourist stores. I stopped in one and bought an aquamarine baseball cap for a dollar that said "Atlantic City" on the brim. I tried it on. It looked pretty good so I got one for my friend Michele, in L.A. and one for John, too, only his was the deluxe version. It came with a little plastic propeller on the top with the words, "Keep Kool" embossed on the front. John would never wear it, of course, but I figured it would make him laugh. After that, I got back in the car and headed back towards the Marina. Traffic was backed up for about half a block. I stuck my head out the window to try to see what was tying things up.

I inched my way closer as a police car roared past me. "Must have been an accident," I thought. "Wow, must have been a *big* accident." Police cars littered the parking lot. A roadblock stretched across the entrance, and a dozen cops milled around, securing the area. Oddly, there was no sign of damaged vehicles. I sat there in the all-consuming traffic, staring out towards the ocean, my eyes drawn to a strange light in the water. "HOLY SHIT." My stomach lurched at the sight before me. A few miles out, a boat, or what was left of it was completely engulfed in flames. Several rescue boats had encircled it, but their efforts were in vain. My hands began to shake, and I could barely keep control of the wheel. I pulled to the curb and turned off the engine, parking in a red zone. "Johnny will be so pissed if his car gets towed," I thought idly before bursting into tears. For in that moment I knew, without a doubt, whose boat had just been blown to bits. I flung open the car door and threw up.

Officer Luke Taylor wrapped a steadying arm around me, as I sobbed into his handkerchief. He was about sixty years old, with steel gray hair and a chin like Tom Selleck. Handsome and dignified, but I bet he could really kick ass if the occasion called for it. He waited patiently while my tears subsided and then he nodded to the rookie cop who stood beside him. "Ma'am," coaxed the younger officer, "You say there were two men on the boat?"

"Yes," I whispered, not trusting my voice. "John Marchiano, and Joel Mishkin. The boat belonged— *belongs* to John. How could this happen? How?" I began to cry again, in earnest.

"I wish we had the answers for you," Tom Selleck said. I knew he wasn't really the movie star, but it made me feel better to think he was. "We won't know anything until there's an investigation. My guess is a faulty fuel tank". He shifted me to his other arm. "Is there anyone I can call for you?" He asked, kindly. I had been answering questions for the past half hour. What was my relation to the people on the boat? Where do they live? Do they have any next of kin? I had questions of my own. *Why are you standing here like a yutz asking me questions, when you should be out there, rescuing my friend?* I slumped against the car in a fit of exhaustion. "I need to call my brother."

"Paul's voice, fuzzy and distant warmed me through my cell phone. I knew I'd woken him up, but he greeted me with his familiar comforting words.

"Yo, Brandy, what's up, kiddo?" Battling a new round of hysteria, I filled my lungs with air and forced the words out of my mouth. "There's been an accident." I could hear Paul suck in his breath as he fought to remain calm.

"Are you alright?"

"I'm fine."

"Wh-what about J-John?"

"I don't know about John," I wailed, totally losing it. "Nobody will give me any answers. I dropped John off at the Marina, and he and his friend went out on the boat. When I went back to pick him up, the boat was on fire. It exploded and, and" —Officer Taylor took the phone from my ear and spoke quietly into the phone. "Your sister needs you. How soon can you be here?"

Officer Taylor stayed with me until Paul arrived. He had sent "the baby" as I came to think of the young cop, out for coffee and doughnuts, and we sat in the parking lot munching on Krispy Kremes. He kept my back to the ocean, so that I couldn't see the police activity, and he kept me talking. About Los Angeles, what it was like living in a "world of glamour," a million questions I'm sure he had absolutely no interest in knowing the answers to. This dear stranger was determined to keep my mind occupied while we waited for the Calvary to arrive. When we had exhausted the subject of Hollywood Lives, he brought out pictures of his sons, twin boys. They were handsome, like their father, around thirty years old. One was a cop, like him. The other one was an investment broker. The cop had a girlfriend, but the broker was up for grabs, and "quite a catch," in case I had any girlfriends who might be interested. I thought about Janine, and gave Officer Taylor her phone number to pass along to his unattached son.

A shadow passed over us and I looked up. Paul stood in front of me, and next to him was Bobby. He looked worn out and sexy as hell, and I immediately felt guilty for noticing that when John could be—no, I refused to go there. I got up and immediately felt the tears well up in my throat again. Paul took me in his arms and held me tight. Bobby stuck out his hand and introduced himself to Officer Taylor. They walked off to the side as Paul held me. "Why is Bobby here?" I sniffed.

"I c-called to t-t-ell him what happened, and he offered to drive J-John's car back. I thought maybe he could get m-m-more information out of the cops." He took a deep, painful breath. "Ya know, pro-professional courtesy." I nodded, squeezing his hand. Bobby and Officer Taylor walked back over to where Paul and I were standing.

"Brandy, I'm sorry I can't give you any more to go on right now. Like I told your friend here, there just isn't anything to tell yet. The search and rescue team are still out there..." He left the rest unspoken, but it didn't take a rocket scientist to know how a less sensitive man would have finished the sentence.

"Thank you for staying with me, Officer Taylor."

"Luke," he smiled. "Now you be sure to tell that girlfriend of yours to expect a call from my son." I nodded, barely able to keep myself together.

"And Luke, as soon as you hear anything…" He looked at Bobby, and then back to me.

"I'll be in touch."

I drove home with my brother while Bobby took the Beemer. Paul pulled up in front of our parents' house and parked. "You get some sleep, kiddo. I'll call Franny and the rest of the guys."

"What are you going to tell them?" Paul looked pained.

"That John is— that he's, ya know" —

"We don't know that for sure, Paul. They haven't found a body. They're still looking," I screamed. I knew I was scaring him, but I couldn't help it. I wasn't going to accept anything as fact until the search was complete. Paul unbuckled his seat belt and opened the car door. "What are you doing?"

"I'm coming in. I can't leave you here like this."

"I'm fine," I barked and immediately regretted it. "I'm sorry, Paul. I'm just tired." He studied me for a moment, realizing my need to retreat into myself. Even as a little girl, when things went wrong I'd go into denial mode, secluding myself until the storm passed.

"Promise you'll go lie down?"

"I promise."

"Call me later."

"I will."

I tried to fall asleep, but as I closed my eyes, the sight of the burning boat kept pressing its way into the forefront of my brain. Soon, the tears started again and I cried until there was nothing left but dry, heaving sobs. The phone rang and I ran for it, praying it was Officer Taylor with news of a miracle about Johnny. The machine picked up before I could locate the handset. Franny's voice, solemn and strained echoed in my ear.

"Brandy, you're probably sleeping—maybe not. It's okay. You don't have to talk now. But call me later." There was a slight hesitation before she added, "I love you, Bran. Call me." Franny's not the most demonstrative person in the world; in fact, terms of endearment really embarrass her. She would sooner call someone she loves a four letter word than to admit that she has tender feelings for them. Her message really touched me. I'd call her back when I knew I could talk without breaking into tears every five seconds.

I wandered into the living room and turned on the radio. As long as I was up, I decided to make myself something to eat. It was almost six and I hadn't eaten anything all day besides a cup of coffee and a Krispy Kreme doughnut. Johnny was right. I needed some balance in my diet. *Johnny.*

I made my way into the kitchen and began poking into cabinets. I found a stale package of TastyKakes chocolate cupcakes and a can of tomato soup. I opened the cupcakes and rummaged through the refrigerator for milk. No milk. Feeling more sorry for myself than I ever have in my life, I opened the soup and poured the contents into a pot. The congealed paste really cried out for milk, but since I didn't have any, I heated up the paste and ate it right out of the pot, not bothering to transfer it into a bowl. I was getting off on how pathetic it all was, when there was a knock at the front door.

I got up and walked through the dining room, glancing at myself in the beveled mirror that hung over the china cabinet. I barely recognized the image that stared back at me. Outside of work I've never been a fashion maven, but this was going too far, even for me. Two red- rimmed slits surrounded by puffy skin passed for eyes. My hair hung in strands, a huge tomato paste glob of soup stained the front of my Bart Simpson sweatshirt, while my knee poked through a hole in my jeans. I looked exactly the way I felt, and I felt like shit. "Love Hurts" blared through the radio speakers. *No duh.* I approached the door. "Who is it?" I asked, as the knocking continued.

"Bobby." My stomach did that leaping around thing and I pulled open the door. The look on his face told me everything I didn't want to hear. I opened the door wider, and he came in without a word. *"Love hurts, love scars, Love wounds and mars"*

He started to say something, but no words came and he shook his head silently. Suddenly, he grabbed me and pulled me close to him. I didn't try to fight it. I needed to feel his arms around me. I pressed my face into his chest and I could feel his heart beat as we stood there, bodies locked in a tender embrace. He backed me into the room and we swayed together in time to the music, barely moving, letting the words envelop us. The tears started to flow freely now. His arms tightened around me, and I felt his lips brush the top of my head. We stood that way until the song ended and then, abruptly, I pulled away from him. He watched in silence as I wiped my face with my sleeve. I noticed with grim satisfaction that I'd left a tomato soup stain on the front of his leather jacket, and I wondered what "the little woman" would say about it. Finally, I spoke up.

"You heard from Officer Taylor." A statement, not a question. Bobby nodded. I sat down cross-legged on the couch and waved my arm vaguely in his direction, indicating he could sit too. I did not want to have this conversation. I did not want Bobby standing in front of me, telling me things I already knew. In that moment I hated him more than I ever had before.

"They've suspended the search for today. It got too dark. They're going to resume it tomorrow, but I get the feeling they think it's a waste of time."

"A waste of time? Try telling that to Johnny's dad. Assholes." I added, bitterly.

"Bran, you saw for yourself. There was nothing left. No one could have survived an explosion like that."

"Well, even if they can't find" —I couldn't bring myself to say it.

"The bodies?"

"Yeah, even if they can't, won't they still look into what caused the explosion?" I looked up at Bobby and saw the abject misery that was etched on his face. Bobby loved Johnny, too.

"I mean, did he say how the fire started?" I asked, softened by my realization.

"It's too soon to tell. The assumption is a faulty gas line, but it will take some time to get the official word on it." I nodded absently, until my nods automatically started going in the other direction, and I was shaking my head, no, no, no! "It wasn't a faulty gas line," I said, with sudden clarity. "Bobby, that explosion was no accident." Bobby slumped down onto the couch, his long legs crossed at the ankles. His heart was breaking for his missing friend and now he had a hysterical woman to contend with. Well, tough. "Did you hear what I said? I think that fire was set intentionally. I think someone was out to get John."

"Who?" Bobby asked, incredulous.

"I don't know," I admitted, and what I do know, you're not going to like."

"Okay, spill it." Bobby sat up, cop face in place. I took a deep breath and started at the beginning. I told him about John's friend's birthday party, about how John had recognized the murder victim from the pictures he'd taken and had contacted the police.

"Why didn't he come to me?" Bobby demanded.

"You were on *vacation,*" I said, pointedly. His eyes flashed with pain. *Why do I keep doing that?* "Look, there was nothing you could have done. You didn't know John was going to come up with evidence in a murder. Anyway, he called the police station and some cop came over to talk to him."

"Did you get a name?" I thought back to our conversation.

"No. He just said it was the guy in charge of the case."

"Then what?"

"Then the cop took Johnny's pictures and thanked him for his help. Oh, and he warned him not to talk about it to anyone. He said it could really screw up the investigation if any information were to leak out."

"Did you see a copy of the pictures?"

"No. This all took place before I got into town. He just told me there was a shot of the murdered guy and some guy seated next to him. They looked like they were on a date."

"Brandy, I still don't see how we go from John taking some pictures that may or may not have had something to do with one murder, to him being the target of another one."

"I'm getting to that. When John picked me up at the airport he was acting all jumpy and weird. Then he told me that since he'd given his statement to the police and handed over the pictures, strange things had begun to happen."

"Like what?"

"Like he felt like he was being followed. And he thought someone had been in his apartment. And someone almost ran him over."

"He *felt* like? He *thought?* He *almost?* From this you conclude that John's on some kind of cop hit list? Jesus, Brandy, have you completely lost your mind?" When he put it that way, the man had a point.

"Okay," I conceded. "But there's something else. A few days ago I ran into Vince Giancola. He started complaining about work, per usual, and he mentioned this murder case. Then he said it's been frustrating because there isn't any evidence. I'm paraphrasing, but he clearly said there weren't any leads. I started to ask him about the pictures, but John wasn't supposed to have told anyone about them, so I kept my mouth shut." Bobby was quiet for a moment, his face unreadable. I watched the muscles in his jaw tighten and release.

"This doesn't make any sense," he said finally. "Why would the police stonewall the D.A.'s office about the evidence? They usually share what they know."

"I don't know. And how do you explain the fact that John hands over the pictures, and then all these weird things start happening?"

"What things?" Bobby exploded. "You said yourself that John wasn't even sure anything was happening. Christ, Brandy, you haven't changed one iota since the day I met you. You were always looking for THE STORY. You had more conspiracy theories than the History Channel. What happened to John was an accident. A tragic, senseless accident. But that's all it was."

"It figures you'd say that. Cops always watch each other's backs. Code Blue, isn't that what they call it?" Low blow I know, but I was royally pissed. Bobby stood up, enraged. An angry blue vein popped up on the side of his neck, and began to throb as he fought for control over his emotions.

"I think you've been watching too many reruns of NYPD Blue," he growled low in his throat.

"No, just reading the newspapers."

"What about the newspapers?"

"They're full of stories about police corruption. It must be very tempting for a cop on a limited income to pick up some extra cash," I added, casually.

"Is that what you really think of me?" he asked, in a tight, quiet voice.

"No. I'm sorry. I'm just..." I shrugged my shoulders, too tired to finish my thought.

We stood there, looking at each other, the silence building to deafening proportions. I wanted to apologize for real, to take back every agonizing innuendo, but Alexander stubbornness reigned supreme and I willed my mouth shut.

"Look," he said, finally, blowing breath out of his mouth in a sharp burst of air. "I'll ask around. I'll talk to the primary in charge of the investigation, and I'll take a look at the pictures. But I'm warning you, Brandy, stay out of this. We're not in high school anymore. There's more at stake than a week's worth of detention."

"Thank you," I replied, softly.

"For what?"

"For taking me seriously." He relaxed a little, and a glimpse of the old Bobby reappeared.

"I've always taken you seriously." The look that accompanied that statement could have populated a small country. I blushed and stood up, pushing him towards the door. "You throwing me out?"

"Looks like it."

He arched his eyebrows, and I wondered if he knew how seductive that was. I ignored him the best I could, along with the skittering in my stomach. I opened the door. "Call me as soon as you know anything. And, um," I added, almost in a whisper, "I really am sorry about what I said before. I didn't mean it." Bobby nodded briefly. Message received.

"Don't forget what I told you," he admonished, back to being a cop again. "Let me handle this. I don't want you getting involved." He stepped through the threshold and I slammed the door shut behind him. *Fat chance.*

Chapter Five

He must've gone straight from my house to the police station, because an hour later the phone rang.

"It's Bobby."

"What did you find out?" I tried to concentrate on his words and not the longings his voice stirred in me. I sensed a slight hesitation before he answered.

"Dead end on the photographs. The guy the victim was with checked out. Had an airtight alibi for the time of the murder. Listen, Brandy" —

"Can I have the pictures?"

"What?"

"Can I have the pictures?" Sheesh, I thought that was plain enough.

"What do you want them for?"

"I don't know," I answered, honestly. "I guess because they were a part of John. Maybe I'll give him to his friend, Daniel. The one who he'd taken them for." Again, I felt the slightest hesitation before he answered.

"Sure, but it could be awhile before they release them."

"I thought they were worthless."

"Yeah, well, you know how cop stuff works. I'll get them to you as soon as I can."

"Thanks," you lying bastard, I added, under my breath.

"So now that we know that there was nothing incriminating in the photographs, maybe you're ready to put this whole crazy idea of John being murdered to rest?" It was a question, but it seemed more like an order.

"Sure, Bobby. And thanks for getting back to me so quickly on this."

"Listen, if John's dad decides to uh, have a memorial service or anything" —

"I'll let you know. Thanks again for your help today." I hung up the phone and sat staring at it for a while. It had been four years since the last time Robert DiCarlo had lied to me. He stunk at it then, and he stinks at it now. The question is, "Why is he lying?"

It was eleven p.m. and I had long given up the idea of getting any rest. Maybe I didn't need sleep. Maybe I was some sort of Sleepless Wonder you find on display at Ripley's Believe it or Not, on Hollywood Boulevard. School children could come visit me and point. I was really losing it. Bobby's visit had left me feeling confused, angry and frustrated. His phone call only served to exacerbate those feelings. An overwhelming sadness settled in my heart and refused to budge. I knew I should call Johnny's dad, but I just couldn't bring myself to do it. I vowed to call him first thing in the morning. Who knows, maybe overnight Johnny would reappear, refreshed and invigorated after his five-mile swim back to shore. Then I wouldn't have to call his father. Goddamn it, Johnny, how could this happen?

My mother called me at eight, asking me the same thing. She'd seen it on the news, along with footage of the burning boat.

"Mom, I don't have any answers for you. I just don't know."

"I'm sorry, sweetheart. That boy was like a brother to you—speaking of which, is Paulie there with you?"

"No, Mom. He's at the club." Life goes on.

"Do you really think you should be alone?"

"I'm *fine*," I said, barely containing the exasperation in my voice. She's just trying to be helpful, I reminded myself.

"Do you want me to fly home? Your father would be okay alone for a few days."

"No!" I said, a little too vehemently. "It's just that, you know" —

"I know," said my mother. "You like to weather these storms alone."

"Listen, Mom," but she was already off in another direction.

"You'll never guess who I saw at the airport this afternoon, while I was picking up your Great Aunt Rose."

"Who?" I said, knowing she'd make me guess anyway.

"Go on, see if you can guess. You'll never guess." Oh Jeez.

"Jack Baumgarten."

"Who?"

"You know, Jack Baumgarten, our old neighbor."

"Brandy, don't be ridiculous. The man has been dead for twelve years."

"Oh. I give up. Who?"

"Bobby DiCarlo's wife and their precious little girl."
My heart stopped.

"Brandy?"

"Yes?"

"Good, you're still there. Anyway, I called out to her—what's her name again? Something Puerto Rican, I can never remember, but she didn't stop to talk. She had luggage so I guess she was in a hurry to catch a plane. Between you and me," she added in a whisper, just to make sure Bobby's wife, "what's her name" didn't hear, "she's not the friendliest." My mother's musings were starting to give me a headache. I clicked the receiver, twice.

"Mom, it's 'call waiting'. I'm expecting an important call from L.A."

"Sweetheart" —

"Sorry, Mom, I've got to take this. I'll call you tomorrow." I threw kissy noises her way and hung up the phone. It was only after I'd replaced the receiver that I remembered that my parents don't have call waiting, and she probably knew that. Oh well, I had bigger things to worry about, like what was Bobby's wife doing in Florida? Does she have relatives there? Was she on her way home? Is that where they went on vacation, and why didn't she come home with Bobby? Did she get on the phone with him and say, "Guess who I saw at the airport today? That girl you used to date's pushy mother. She said hello to me. Of all the nerve!" Yeah, I'm sure that's just what happened, because everyone's life always revolves around me. Note to self: work on being less egocentric.

"Janine, it's Brandy. Can you talk?"

"No problem. Hey, Chrissy, take this plate over to the guy in the mohair sweater, will ya? And watch it, he bites." Turning back to the phone she said, "Bran, I'm sick about Johnny. And Fran's really worried about you. Have you called her?"

"Not yet. I want to, but I just can't yet."

"I understand." Franny and Janine look identical, and they're both tough as nails, but that's where the resemblance ends. Franny's a big "psychology" fan, and she always wants people to talk about their feelings. Frankly, that's not my strong point, even on a good day. Right now I needed some practical help, from someone as impulsive as I was. Enter Janine.

"Listen, I know you just started your shift and all, but do you think you can get out of work, tonight? I have to talk to you about something, and it can't wait." *It* could wait. *I* couldn't.

"Why don't you come down to the diner?"

"Well, this is more of a-a mission, of sorts."

"You're being awfully mysterious, Brandy."

"Yeah, I know. I'll explain it all when I see you." I had no doubt that Janine would be there. Thirty minutes later, there was a knock on my door.

Janine stood on the steps, breathless, as if she had run all the way from work. She was still in her uniform, a pink nightmare complete with nametag. The nametag said "Madge."

"Who's Madge?" I asked.

"My alter ego." She came in and sat down on the couch, not bothering to remove her jacket.

"How'd you get out of work?" I asked.

"I quit." She shrugged. "*What?* It's not like they're gonna miss me. I was a really shitty waitress." For about a year now Janine has been on a quest to find the perfect job.

After she had graduated college, she became a court reporter, until she developed Carpal Tunnel Syndrome. One of the law offices she worked for helped her sue the court-reporting agency, citing some kind of negligence or other, and she walked away with a tidy little sum in workers' comp. In the past year, Janine has tried her hand at various enterprises, including handsome cab driver, meat packer and Mary Kay sales representative. She says she's going to gather all this experience and write a best selling book about it. "Okay," she started, "How are we going to play this? Are we talking about John or not?" I shook my head, loving her. "Ya know, Fran would say you're in denial."

"That's why I invited you to this party instead of Franny."

"What's up?"

"It's a long story." I told her everything, up to and including the latest phone call from Bobby.

"And you don't believe that story about the pictures turning out to be worthless."

"No, I don't. I know there's some kind of connection between those photographs and what happened to John. I just have to get my hands on them."

"Boy, you don't ask for much, do you? Bran, you know I'd do anything for you, but breaking into the police evidence room?" She blew out a long whistle, shaking her head. "I'm good, but I'm not that good."

"Janine," I laughed, for the first time in what seemed like years, "I know you pride yourself on your manual dexterity with locks, but even I'm not crazy enough to suggest you try it out at the police station. I need to get into Johnny's apartment."

"Oh. Why?"

"Because I just remembered something he'd told me a few days ago. He'd lied to the detective when he'd asked John if there were any other copies of the pictures. John told me he'd stored them on his I-Mac. Then he said a bunch of technical stuff that I didn't understand, but I know you're good with that kind of thing. He even told me the password. Brassiere." I waited for the inevitable guffaw from Janine. "I need to do something, Janine. Maybe this is just a wild goose chase. Maybe Johnny's death was nothing more than a horrible accident, but in my gut I feel there's something more. Are you with me on this?" Janine stood up and began to walk into the kitchen. "What are you doing?"

"Getting my tools."

We parked around the corner from John's apartment. John lives in a quaint, one-story building on a beautiful tree-lined street in Center City. It's about twenty minutes from my parents' house. We stood now, outside John's place, screwdriver, flashlight and butter knife in hand. I don't know what all that girl did, but inside of a minute we were standing inside John's foyer. The smell of his favorite air freshener hit me as we walked in, and I bit my lip to keep from bawling all over the newly waxed mahogany floors.

"Should we turn on a light?" Janine stage whispered to me.

"Probably not. Technically, some people might consider this 'breaking and entering.'" We fumbled around in the dark, guided by the faint glow of a dying flashlight. I really had to upgrade my tools of the trade, or I'd be the laughing stock of all the other burglars.

"Okay," said Janine, once we'd become acclimated to the darkness, "Where would John keep his lap top?"

"You look in the bedroom. I'll poke around out here in the living room." Janine hesitated.

"What's wrong?"

"I don't know. It feels creepy being here so late at night, in the dark, with John being, ya know." I knew.

"Well, the sooner we access the pictures, the sooner we can leave." Janine stood her ground.

"You come with me."

"No, you big baby. Just go. We're wasting time." Reluctantly, Janine headed for the bedroom, taking the meager light with her. I began to survey the room. There were some magazines on the coffee table in front of the couch but no laptop. I quickly scanned his bookshelves and the surface of the small, Cherry wood, roll top desk, a recent acquisition and Johnny's pride and joy. Nothing. Why couldn't John be the type of guy who leaves everything lying around on the floor? It would make things so much easier. I opened the hallway closet and started feeling around on the floor. Vacuum cleaner, rain boots, emergency kit, small attaché case—Bingo! "Janine," I whispered, hoarsely, getting to my knees. "I found it." And then I *heard* it. A distinct scratching at the door. Janine had locked the door behind us as we came in. Now, someone, or some *thing* was methodically picking away at the lock. *Oh my God, Oh my God!* I grabbed the case and scrambled to my feet just as Janine wandered back in.

"Did you call me?"

"Oh my God, there's somebody here."

"Where!"

"There!" I jerked my head towards the door as Janine stood rooted to the spot. Then simultaneously, we leaped into action.

"Hide!" We hissed, and bumped smack into each other.

"Here" —

"No, here." We danced around one another, slapping each other out of the way, like Curly and Larry, without Moe to tell us what to do. The door opened just as we scrambled out of sight behind the couch. Two intelligent adults and that's where we chose to hide. We may as well have stood in the middle of the room with our eyes closed, shouting 'you can't see us.' We'd really have to work on this cloak and dagger stuff. Obviously, neither of us was very good at it.

Someone entered the apartment, someone a lot better prepared than we were for nighttime surveillance. A strong beam of light swept the living room, running over bookshelves and under the coffee table. Janine and I squeezed our hands together, willing the intruder to leave. "Please don't look behind the couch, please don't look behind the couch," I chanted silently, to the tune of Nom mi oh ho reng ga keo." I did a segment for the show on Pop Buddhism once, and this chanting thing really seemed to work. The footsteps came closer and my heart erupted in a wild jungle beat. I put my hand to my chest, willing myself to stay calm. Suddenly, I caught a glimpse of a boot as it hesitated in front of the couch before striding past us on its way to John's darkroom. A familiar, black, leather boot, the kind that looks really cool with a black leather jacket. *Shit! What in world's fuck is Bobby doing here?*

As Bobby disappeared into the darkroom, I silently signaled Janine to get up. We tiptoed across the floor, into the hall closet. I no longer felt that our lives were in danger, but I still didn't know why Bobby was there, and I'd be hard pressed to explain why we were. We waited impatiently, breathing in the mothballs that overwhelmed the closet. I needed to sneeze in the worst way, but I felt too ridiculous getting caught in such a sit-com manner. So I pinched my nose until little red dots began to appear before my eyes. After an eternity, we heard footsteps again, heavier this time, padding back across the floor. A small, nearly silent "damnit" accompanied the footsteps. The front door opened and closed quietly behind him.

We waited a moment to make sure he wasn't coming back, and then we bolted out of the closet. "I think I just peed myself," Janine said. She stuck her hand between her legs. "Yep, I peed myself." I was glad we'd taken her car instead of Paul's Mercedes. "I've never been so scared in my life," she continued, as she walked into the bathroom. I followed her in and sat on the tub while she stuffed toilet paper down her pants. "I thought that guy was going to kill us."

"Janine," I said, interrupting her. "That guy was Bobby."

"What?" She screeched.

"Shh. It was Bobby. I saw him." Janine finished up her business and left the bathroom, with me trailing behind her.

"Well, he's got some nerve breaking in here like that. He could've given me a heart attack."

"Yeah, he really should've been more considerate of the people who were breaking in before him." The absurdity of the situation caught up to us, and we erupted in laughter.

"Shh!"

"No, you shh!" Frayed nerves and relief over not getting killed made us laugh even harder.

"What was he doing here anyway?" Janine asked, when we'd finally gotten ourselves under control. "He was obviously looking for something."

"The pictures." I surmised. He spent a lot of time in the darkroom. What else could he have been looking for?"

"But, why? Oh my God, Brandy. You don't think Bobby's in on the whole murder thing, do you? No, that's crazy," she answered herself in the same breath. "But maybe he's trying to protect his cop buddies. Maybe whoever is involved figured out there was another set of pictures, and sent Bobby to find them. Maybe" —

"Maybe we'd better open this file and then get the hell out of here before anyone else decides to break in here, tonight." I couldn't begin to answer Janine's questions, and I had a thousand more of my own. John had seen something in those pictures, even if he didn't know exactly what the significance was. And now he was dead because of what he'd seen. I did not believe Bobby had anything to do with John's murder. I knew it like I knew my own name. But somehow, he was involved in this whole mess, and I fully intended to find out how involved he actually was. Janine was not exactly on the same page.

"Well, case closed," she stated with finality.

"What do you mean, 'case closed'? I'm just getting started, here."

"Well, it just occurred to me that, assuming John was killed because of something he'd seen in the pictures, if word gets out that we've seen the pictures, the same thing could happen to us."

"So, what's your point?"

"My point is I don't want to die."

"Which is why you're gonna keep your mouth shut about the photographs. Janine, believe me, it's not on my agenda to get myself killed anytime soon, either. But we made a lot of progress here tonight, and I'm not backing off."

"But, what if we end up finding out something about Bobby that we don't want to know?"

"We won't." I said, and silently prayed I knew what the hell I was talking about.

We left the windows down on the ride home, because it smelled a little "gamey" in the car. The night air invigorated me, which did not bode well for a good night's sleep. It was after one a.m. when Janine pulled up in front of my parents' house. She offered to stay with me, but I insisted she go home. Sooner or later I would have to face my demons; I may as well start now. We agreed to keep silent about what had happened tonight. There were too many unanswered questions. The fewer people who knew about our little escapade, the better.

"Ya know," Janine began, as I opened the passenger door. "I hate to admit this, but I kinda had a good time tonight. Oh, I know that sounds awful, given the circumstances and all, but Christ Brandy, we used to have fun. It seems like the day you left town, everybody grew up."

"That's me, Peter Pan." I smiled ruefully and hugged her. Clutching the hard copies of Johnny's pictures to my chest, I climbed out of the car and walked into the house.

Chapter Six

I woke up to the sound of rain hitting the gutter pipes; huge, fat drops that scuttled down the window like roaches on their way to breakfast. I snuggled under the covers, unwilling to give up the warmth of the bed. Yawning, I leaned over to look at the clock. Ten thirty a.m. "Oh, no," I groaned and sat up. "I don't believe this. I've slept half the day away." In actuality, I'd only been asleep for about three hours. After Janine dropped me off last night, I went upstairs and took a shower. I let the steaming hot water pound away at my aching muscles until my skin pruned up and the hot water ran out. "This had to be the longest day in history," I thought, as I pulled a cozy sweatshirt out of the drawer and yanked it over my head. On the front it had a picture of a kitten rolling around with a ball of yarn in its paws. Bobby had bought it for me for my fifteenth birthday, and my mother had saved it all these years. My mother never throws away a thing. I took out some sweatpants too, and climbed into them, then I headed back into the bathroom to brush my teeth. It was two thirty in the morning and entirely too quiet. I walked back down the hallway, singing the theme song from the television show, Friends, and I wondered if it was on in syndication, somewhere. That started me thinking about how fun it would've been to be written into the show as some quirky new character—maybe Phoebe's eccentric cousin. I guess everyone has his or her way of coping with stress. For Paul, it's stuttering, while I pal around with fictional characters. I was lonely and I thought I might cry again, which I definitely did not want to do, so I tried to go to sleep. Half an hour later I turned on the light and took out the photographs.

I'd given them a cursory look in the car, but now I spread them out on the comforter, willing them to speak to me. I decided to categorize them. "This must be Daniel," I decided, gazing at a close-up of a drunken, smiling man in a party hat. Daniel and his date. Daniel chugging beer. Party guests. Okay, here we go. It was hard to tell who was an actual guest, and who was merely a bar patron. I looked at the next few shots—well, not that hard. Daniel's friends looked like your average, upscale gay guys, slumming in one of the seedier parts of town, while the 'regulars' looked, well, *icky.* Infectious disease kind of icky. Porn City, with a Capital P. I studied the atmosphere shots. Men in leather. Men in chains. Men in men. *Ooh, more than I need to know.* I could not imagine germ phobic John getting close enough to any of these people to snap a picture. He must've used a zoom lens. One picture in particular caught my eye. A young man sporting a dog collar was seated at the bar. Konner Novack. I recognized him from the newspaper article. Next to him sat another young man with light brown skin and short, spiky hair. Konner had his hand on the other man's knee. They were laughing. "What had Bobby said? The guy he was with had an airtight alibi for the time the murder had taken place. I sorted through the other shots. Two more of Konner. They were blurry, but I could still make out his face, smiling, enjoying life, not a care in the world. Suddenly, I was irrevocably sad. Konner Novack, someone's son, perhaps someone's lover was dead. What kind of a person could willfully end someone's life like that? A chill ran through my body; a chill so profound it actually made my teeth chatter. I gathered up the photographs and stacked them neatly on the bedside table. Then I tucked the comforter all around me, and for the second night in a row I cried myself to sleep.

I stared at the blank poster board in front of me, unsure of where to begin. I selected a black marker from the Crayola eight- pack and drew a line down the center of the board. On the left of the line I wrote **Things I Know** in big, bold letters. I chose another color, and on the right hand side I wrote **Things I Don't Know.** Then I sat back to admire my handiwork. I'd bought the poster board and markers at the Seven-Eleven, a few blocks away from the house. While I was there, I also picked up some milk, cheese, eggs, cereal, TastyKakes and a Score Bar. The produce didn't look too promising, so I passed on that. Okay. Maybe I'd better eat something first, to get the brain in optimal working order. I made a cheese omelet and washed it down with a chocolate cupcake. That taken care of, I concentrated on the business at hand. **#1,** I wrote confidently, on the left hand side. **Konner Novack is dead**. On the corresponding line to the right I wrote, **Who killed Konner Novack?** On the left I added, **John's photos reveal something**, and across from it, **What do they reveal? The police are involved in a cover-up**, on the left. **Is Bobby a part of the cover-up?** appeared on the right. On the left, **John is dead,** and on the right,

Who killed John? I put down my marker and reviewed what I'd written. I picked up my marker again, and under **"Things I know,"** I wrote **I am an idiot**, accompanied on the right by **I don't know SHIT!** UUNNHHH! This was getting me nowhere. I put my head down on the dining room table, resting my cheek against the smooth, maple surface. I awoke ten minutes later to the sounds of a ringing bell. Feeling dazed, I got to my feet and stumbled towards the kitchen, grabbing the phone just before the machine picked up. "Hello?"

"What the hell is wrong with you, breaking into John's apartment in the middle of the night, and why didn't you ask me to come along?"

"Oh, Hi, Fran. I guess Janine told you, huh?"

"Well, she tried not to, but you know Janine. She never could keep a secret. It's genetic," Fran added, in defense of her sister.

"So, what exactly did she tell you?"

"Everything."

"Everything?"

"I can't believe you'd leave me out of the loop, Brandy."

"Well." I wracked my brain for a reasonable response and came up empty, so I tried a diversionary tactic. "You have so much on your mind, what with the wedding and all. I didn't want to add to your pressures." *Or mine.*

"About the wedding," Franny interrupted, "I think we should call it off."

"Franny, no!"

"Not the ceremony, just the reception. Without John there it wouldn't be right."

"Now, you listen to me, Francine Elizabeth Mary Ellen DiAngelo. You will do nothing of the sort. That is the last thing John would want, and frankly, we all need this wedding! It's beautiful, and life-affirming, and—and all that crap." She didn't say anything for a beat, but I heard her blow her nose in the background. "Hey, are you crying?"

"Of course not," Franny sniffed. "I've got a cold."

"You are so crying."

"Well, that stuff you said about my wedding being so beautiful, and life-affirming and all."

"Oh. Well, it's just that I've never known you to be so sensitive."

"Yeah, well, I've never been pr" —She stopped, just a hair too late.

"Oh my God," I shrieked, "you're pregnant!"

"SSHHHH! You want the whole damn neighborhood to know?" The thought of Franny "with child" was mind-boggling. I feel suffocated riding in the same elevator with anyone under the age of twelve. This news was huge.

"So, how do you feel about it?" I asked, tentatively.

"Well, at first, it was a shock. There is no way I felt ready, and the truth is," she added, quietly, "I'd decided not to have it. But then yesterday, hearing the news about Johnny"—Her voice trailed off for a moment, and I could hear the tears welling up. "I'm just glad it wasn't too late to change my mind."

"Oh, Franny, that's wonderful," I said, meaning it. "Who else knows—I mean, besides Eddie. Eddie does know, right?"

"Of course he knows, and he's thrilled. I mean we were planning on having kids. Maybe not this soon, but ya know, this is right for us. But swear you won't breathe a word to anyone. My mother thinks I'm a virgin." I suppressed a laugh as she added, "I haven't told a soul, except you."

"What about Janine?"

"That big mouth?"

"Oh, right. Well, it goes both ways, Fran. You can't tell anyone about what I've been up to in regards to John."

"Don't worry, not being able to keep a secret is only genetic on my dad's side of the family. Fortunately, I take after my mother." We hung up after Franny extracted a promise from me to keep her updated on my investigation. That would be easy. Apparently, I suck at investigating.

I was on my way back to the dining room when the phone rang again. "Yo," I chirped, figuring Franny had forgotten to tell me something.

"Brandy?"

"Yeah?" I was caught off guard by the male voice on the other end of the line.

"It's Vince Giancola."

"Oh, hey, Vince. What's up?"

"My dad just told me about John Marchiano, and I know you guys were really close, so I wanted to, ya know, offer my condolences."

"Oh," I replied, touched by his efforts. "That's really thoughtful of you."

"Yeah, well." South Philly men are so comfortable with verbal displays of affection. I waited a beat. He didn't say anything else, and I didn't know what else to say, so I was all set to hang up, when an idea occurred to me.

"Listen Vince, I'm glad you called."

"Yeah?" He sounded surprised, and *something else… hopeful?*

"Yeah, there's been something I've been meaning to ask you." It really bothered me that he didn't seem to know about John's photographs.

"There's something I've been meaning to ask you too," Vince interjected, with a jaunty little chuckle. Very coy. Very un-Vince.

"Oh? What's that?"

"No, you go first," he teased.

"Okay," I started, a little thrown off by his weirdness. "Um, something you said the other day" — Vince cut me off in a rush of words.

"Look, why don't you meet me for a drink, later on. I have to go into work for a while, but there's this little bar and grill around the corner from my office. We could grab some dinner, catch up on things, maybe reminisce about the good times you, me, and John had in high school." *Oh my god, the little weasel is asking me out. He is capitalizing on my grief over John to date me! I decided to go for the jugular.*

"And which good times would those be, Vince? The time you dropped him head first into the trash can, or the time you "pantsed" him in front of the entire Girls' Basketball team?" There was silence on the other end of the line, and for a minute I thought he'd hung up. Finally, he spoke up.

"I was a first class jerk back then. You don't know how often I've wished I could go back in time and keep myself from doin' that kinda shit." He sounded so sad I decided to forgive him. Besides, I was getting hungry again.

"Dinner sounds good. Give me the address." I jotted it down and told him I'd see him at five.

Paul's Mercedes is a 1975, 450 SL, a two seater sports car convertible. It is gorgeous. Well, I would be too, if I were as pampered as this set of wheels. He keeps the car encased in plastic. It only sees the light of day twice a year, once in the summer, to remove the hard top, and again after Labor Day, to stick it back on. If the car could talk I'm sure it would say, "Thank you, Auntie Brandy, for setting me free." I rode around for a little while looking for a place to park. Finally, I pulled into a spot, off Arch Street. It was a tight fit and the front fender stuck out just a smidge, but not so's you'd notice. Carefully, I checked the street parking for Tow Away Zone signs. Seeing none, I locked up and headed for the restaurant.

I was early, so I thought I'd take the time to reacquaint myself with the city. The air had turned cooler, so I buttoned up my coat, an old navy blue pea jacket someone had left in my parents' hall closet, eons ago. It smelled like wet dog, but it was warm. I guess I should have packed warmer clothes for the trip, but I didn't have anything appropriate. There's not a huge need for a lot of cold weather clothes in Los Angeles. I began to stroll down the tree-lined street. Late afternoon sunlight filtered through the last remaining leaves of giant maples, casting a golden glow over the city. I stopped to examine a huge pile of fiery red leaves crowding the gutters. It looked so inviting I jumped right in, kicking up the heels of my hiking boots, in utter childlike abandon. I was enjoying myself immensely, when my foot came in contact with something squishy. Too late, I remembered that I'm not in L.A., where pooper-scooper laws are considered the eleventh commandment. I looked down at my shoes. They were covered in dog poop. Eewww. Furiously, I began scraping the bottom of my shoes along the curb, using the leaves like toilet paper to wipe the tops. I succeeded in wiping most of it off, although a bit got smeared into the shoe leather. By the time I finished cleaning up, I was late and had to run a block and a half to the restaurant.

It took a few minutes for my eyes to adjust to the dimly lit room. The ambiance of Henry's Bar and Grill was white collar casual; wide leather booths, candles on the table, hardwood floors. I suspect they did the bulk of their business during the week, catering to the business lunch crowd. It was fairly empty on this early Sunday evening. Vince was seated at the bar. He wore a soft, black pullover sweater and dark gray slacks. He looked nice. I glanced down at my standard issue jeans and wished that I'd taken the time to dress up a little. Oh well, the dog doody added that little something extra. I walked over to where Vince sat, a big smile plastered on his face. As I got closer, the smile faltered and then disappeared altogether, to be replaced by a look of puzzlement and finally, disgust. "Christ, Brandy, you look like Hell." He sniffed the air. "And why do I smell dog shit?"

"Well, that's a lousy thing to say," I sputtered. And then I caught sight of myself in the mirror, behind the bar. Aaahhh! Five days of minimal sleep and untold grief had turned me into a monster. A red-eyed, sallow-cheeked, scraggily haired, dog shit smelling freak. I'll bet he was sorry he asked me out now! The thought did little to pacify me. Suddenly, the tears started to fall with no signs of stopping.

"Oh, man, I'm sorry. I didn't mean it. You look swell. Really."

"No, I don't," I sniffed. "I look hideous. You said so yourself." The host, a fresh-faced young girl in her late teens, approached us, oblivious to the unfolding drama.

"Will you be staying for dinner?" She chirped. Vince looked at me, afraid to venture an opinion. I weighed my options. Go home now and eat Cheerios, or stay and make Vince pay through the nose for that crack about my appearance. I nodded briefly to the host, and she showed us to our table.

Vince settled into the booth while I veered off in the direction of the bathroom. Vince's remark had hurt. He was right, I did look like hell, but he didn't have to be so blunt about it. The florescent lighting did nothing to bolster my flagging spirits. I ran a comb through my hair, washed my face and cleaned my shoe. It helped a little, but I still looked like the "Bride of Frankenstein's" unattractive sister. I *really* needed to get a decent night's sleep!

When I got back to the table the waiter was there. I ordered a steak, medium rare, with big thick fries on the side. Everything was a la carte and Vince was paying, so I also got a salad, soup and steamed broccoli. I didn't plan on eating the broccoli. I just figured the smell would camouflage anything untoward left on my shoe. Vince ordered a steak too, and a bottle of Merlot. He poured me a glass and I chugged it down in three quick gulps. The wine mellowed me out a bit, and I sat back in the booth, relaxing into the plush leather seat. I looked over at Vince. He's not a bad looking guy, actually. He's got nice, even, white teeth, soft brown eyes and two pinchably chubby cheeks. He smiled tentatively at me and I smiled back, basking in the glow of the wine.

"You okay?" He ventured.

"Not really. I'm sorry about before."

"It's alright."

"No, it's not. It's just—I haven't been sleeping. This thing with John has really gotten to me." Vince reached across the table and grabbed my hand, giving it an awkward pat. The waiter chose that moment to arrive with our meal, and I silently thanked his impeccable timing. I extracted my hand from Vince's and fell to eating.

Halfway through his steak he looked up at me. I'd torn through a bowl of French Onion soup, a mixed green salad, three fourths of my filet and half a loaf of sourdough bread.

"Is something wrong?" I asked through a mouth full of French Fries. He shook his head as if he couldn't quite believe his eyes.

"Where do you put it all?"

"Huh?" *It must have been my scintillating conversation that drew him to me.*

"This." He gestured at the buffet set before me. "How can you eat so much and not look like a baby beluga?"

"I don't eat like this all the time," I explained, defensively. "Besides, I work out." *Ha!* I waited a beat to see if God would make me choke on my fries for being such a big fat liar. Nothing happened, so I kept on eating. The truth is, I don't actually work out. I joined a gym. Big difference. I joined because my friend, Michelle had told me that former World Wrestling Federation Champ, turned movie star, Dwayne "The Rock" Johnson was a member of her gym. She happened to know I have a tiny crush on The Rock—the life size poster in my bedroom may have given it away. Anyway, I decided it would be better to become an actual member, rather than stake out the parking lot and look like a stalker. I spent half a month's salary on non-refundable dues, only to be informed by Michelle that, oops, she'd made a little mistake, it wasn't The Rock, after all, but some guy named Vin Diesel. I am now the proud owner of six hundred dollars worth of workout clothes and absolutely no intention of using them.

We finished our dinners and the bottle of wine, and then waited for the waiter to bring the dessert menu.

I selected a chocolate mousse and some decaf. Very sensible.

"Vince," I began, as I dove into the mousse, "Remember I said on the phone that I needed to ask you something?"

"Shoot."

I launched into my story about John and the photographs, leaving out a few details, like, I think he was murdered and the entire Philadelphia Police Force is in on it.

"Let me get this straight." Vince sat up and leaned forward on the table, his palms resting on the surface. Suddenly, he was no longer the neighborhood nebbish, surreptitiously asking me out. He was a prosecuting attorney, and he was pissed. "You're telling me that John handed over these pictures to the police and nobody fuckin' bothered to inform the D.A.'s office?" I guess that answered my question. He stabbed at his cheesecake, took a huge bite out of it and washed it down with a swig of coffee.

"Is it possible they checked out the photos, but they didn't think they amounted to anything?"

"Anything's possible. I swear, these guys wouldn't recognize their own butts if they weren't attached to them." Vince sat back and eyed me critically. "What's your interest in all this?"

"What do you mean?"

"I've known you a long time, kiddo. You're holding out on me. What is it?"

"Are we talking D.A. to concerned citizen, or friend to friend?"

"Depends." Wrong answer. I shook my head.

"I just thought it was weird, that's all." He gave me a look that said he knew there was more to it than that, but I was in no mood to give anything away. I decided to throw a little guilt his way and see what he did with it. "I just think that if the police can't use the photos, they should be given to John's friend, Daniel. John would've wanted him to have them." It had the desired effect. Vince promised to talk to the investigator and get back to me. He finished his coffee and signaled the waiter for a refill. I held out my cup as well, forgetting that I'd cut myself off from the high-octane stuff.

"Man, this case has been a bitch and a half," Vince grumbled.

"How so?"

"The mayor's getting squeezed from all sides. The Conservative Right —the folks who probably finance his campaign are up in arms that these freaks are allowed to walk the city streets. I'm sure most of them think Novack got just what he deserved. Now, the Gay Rights activists are screaming bloody murder, no pun intended, saying the mayor isn't doing anything to protect "alternative lifestyle" citizens." He laughed, mirthlessly.

"And what do you think?"

"I don't think anyone deserves what happened to that poor bastard."

"So, what's the mayor going to do? How does he manage to placate two such diverse groups?"

"The mayor is praying the voters bump their collective heads and develop group amnesia. He just wants this stinking mess to go away." I couldn't see that happening. Philadelphians are tenacious buggers. "I gotta tell ya," Vince continued, "this is wreaking havoc with his re-election plans, and who knows what it could do for his bid for governor."

Vince offered to walk me to my car, but I told him it wasn't necessary. I wanted to do a little window-shopping before I went home. We stood outside the restaurant together, his arm draped amiably over my shoulder. It had turned cold, and a wind was beginning to kick up. My coat was unbuttoned, and I could feel the night air work its way inside. Vince took his arm from around my shoulder and buttoned the top of my jacket. A protective, brotherly gesture.

"Thanks," I smiled.

"Any time, kiddo."

"Vince, tell me the truth, was this like a *date* tonight? I mean, when you called, were you asking me out?" Vince snorted loudly, shaking his head.

"Christ, you're a pistol."

"You didn't answer my question."

"Okay, I guess I did kinda have it in mind to ask you out. *Well*," he added, embarrassment etched on his face, "you looked really hot when I saw you the other day, and—Ah, Bran, you know I've had a crush on you since the third grade. I figured, what the hell."

"Well, now that you know what a glamour queen I really am..."and let my appearance finish the sentence.

"I'd ask you again in a New York minute."

"Thanks, Vince." I kissed him on the cheek and we hugged, a big gumbotz embrace.

"Don't forget to call me."

I walked back to Paul's car feeling optimistic about my dinner with Vince. He would find out about the pictures, and I'd finally be able to lay that question to rest. I was thinking so hard about our conversation that I must have walked right past the car. I started to backtrack but stopped when I realized that I was practically back to where I'd started and there was no sign of it. Frantically, I raced back towards to the restaurant, searching up and

down the street for the Mercedes. I rounded the corner
and relief flooded through my body as I spotted it. A split
second later I let out a blood-curdling scream as I realized
it was driving down the block without me. The goddamn
car was being towed! I sprinted off in pursuit of the tow
truck, waving my arms around like a pinwheel to try to
get the driver's attention. "Hey," I shouted, "Stop!" My
voice carried about as far as the length of my outstretched
arm. The tow truck kept on barreling down the street, out
of sight. This can't be happening! What am I going to do?
Paul is going to kill me. Worse, he'll be *disappointed* in
me. How could I let this happen?

I sat on the curb and whipped out my cell phone.
After three rings, it picked up.

" Uncle Frankie, it's Brandy. I need a little help."

It took Frankie twenty minutes to locate me. I sat on
the curb, a cold, forlorn mass of guilt. Paul had trusted
me with his car and I screwed up, big time. I don't even
know why I'd been towed. Well, maybe I'd been sticking
out a "smidge" more than I'd thought. Frankie pulled up
alongside the curb and crooked his finger at me. I hopped
into the cab of his silver Ford F150 and we took off for
the impound lot.

"Thanks for coming to get me, Uncle Frankie."

"Any time, Midget Brat." Midget Brat. That's what
he used to call me when I was little. It was only fitting
that he use the term, now. At the moment I felt like about
five years old. I looked over at my uncle as he drove
along, one massive bicep draped along the back of the
seat cushion. Uncle Frankie manages a boxing gym
down on South Street, and he works out daily. He's in
amazing shape. Frankie could have been a professional
boxer, but too many years of hard partying curtailed

any dreams he may have had in that direction. Now, he spends most afternoons working with kids on the edge, giving them hope for their futures, a place to go, someone to listen to them. I met Bobby at my uncle's gym. He was sixteen and had just moved from Chicago, into the neighborhood. God, he was angry in those days, and he had good reason to be. He'd lost his mom only a few weeks before. She'd been killed by a drunk driver. His dad had left when he was four. After the accident, Bobby was shipped off to Philadelphia to live with an aunt he barely knew. I remember the first time I laid eyes on him. I'd gone to visit my uncle, after school. He'd promised me a boxing lesson, but at the time he was still drinking and had forgotten that I was coming. I was really mad, and I sat outside on the dumpster, banging my boots against the metal sides. Bobby came out back to see what the racket was, and suddenly I was staring at the most beautiful creature God ever dropped onto the planet. He was 5' 9", (he hadn't had his growth spurt yet) with wavy dark hair and the deepest blue eyes I'd ever seen. They were so dark they looked almost purple. He was wearing the neighborhood special, jeans and a "wife beater" tee shirt, which accentuated his muscular arms. A cigarette dangled from his lips. He seethed with rage, and sadness and adolescent sexuality. That boy was HOT. My face grew red as he gazed steadily up at me. I stared back down at this magnificent Fallen Angel, not knowing what to say. I finally went with "false bravado."

"What're *you* lookin' at?" I sneered, my tone registering a ten on the brat scale.

"What're *you* lookin' at?" He shot back, his eyes never leaving mine. I felt myself being sucked into the deep end of the pool. Suddenly, his face broke into a slow grin, and in one fluid motion he hoisted himself up onto the dumpster lid and sat down beside me. At once the muscles in my lower abdomen contracted, and I felt my entire body flush with a rising heat. The heat settled right between my legs and stayed there.

"My name's Bobby," he said. And I vowed to tell him mine just as soon as I remembered it.

Lucky for me Frankie knew the people who ran the impound lot. The place was closed when we got there, but he managed to contact someone who pulled a few strings, and a couple of hundred dollars later Paul's car was out of hock. Now, if I could just get it home in one piece he'd never have to know about his car's little adventure.

By the time I got home it was after nine. I yanked off my shoes and left them in the front foyer. Then I flopped down on the couch, grabbed the remote and began to channel surf. "Bewitched" was on Nick At Nite, an early episode with the original Darren. Oh, goody. I snuggled deep into the cushions, my legs curled under a blanket. "God, it feels good to relax," I thought, at which point I remembered I had to call John's dad. Groaning, I half dragged myself off the couch and headed for the kitchen. The answering machine was beeping like crazy, demanding attention like a visual whine. I ran back the tape and started to press "play," but then stopped myself. I'd already stalled long enough. John's dad deserved a phone call. I picked up my mother's phone book, off the Formica counter top and flipped to the M's. Taking a deep, cleansing breath I picked up the phone and punched in the numbers. *One, two, three rings.* Okay, not home. I slammed down the receiver as fast as I could, in case John's dad decided he was home after all. I knew it was the chicken's way out, but I was just so happy to have this small reprieve. I had no words of comfort for this man. Sighing, I pressed "play" on the answer machine.

"Hi Sweetheart. It's Daddy. Just checking in with you."

"Ask her does she want me to come home," my mother yelled in the background.

"Who needs to ask her?" My dad shouted back. "They can hear you in Iowa."

"Iowa? What's Iowa got to do with anything? Don't be ridiculous." Sarcasm is not a recognized response in my mother's world. Any attempt at such wordplay just earns the perpetrator the rebuke, "Don't be ridiculous." As sarcasm runs rampant in my veins, she says that to me a lot. "Brandy," my mother spoke directly into the phone, now. "Daddy and I are worried about you. Call us."

"We love you, honey." That, from my dad, who had once again assumed the position of second banana and was relegated to background noises.

"We love you, honey," my mother repeated. Bye bye. Call us."

Call number two was a hang-up, followed by a familiar male voice, a voice on the edge of exhaustion.

"Brandy, it's Bobby." He hesitated, and I could hear the rush of breath leave his lips. "I'd like to talk to you, so could you give me a call? My number's 555-2753. Uh, thanks," he added, uncertainly. I must have played his message ten times over, just to hear the sound of his voice. Guess I have some residual issues, as my friend, Michele would say. With shaking hands I punched in Bobby's number and waited for him to pick up the phone. My heart skipped a beat when his voice came on the line.

"Hey. We're not in right now, so please leave a message." Well, of all the nerve! *We're not in right now.*

Me and the little Mrs. aren't in right now. Mr. and Mrs. FUCKHEAD aren't IN right now! I slammed down the phone without leaving a message.

I returned to the couch and "Bewitched." Apparently, Endora had turned Darren into a donkey. I tried to immerse myself in Darren's troubles, but my mind was definitely elsewhere. Why did I get so mad? It's not like I don't know Bobby's married, but I suppose hearing him refer to himself as part of a "couple" drove home the reality of the situation. He dumped me and now he's part of a happy twosome. I don't even care about getting married right now. Maybe ever. But it would be nice to have the option. I've had six dates in the past four years. Two of those dates included sex but I'd done it with the same guy twice, so there was actually just one lover and I didn't even like him. I only did it to be polite. When I get back to L.A. I am going to look into some serious therapy.

That started me thinking about my life in Los Angeles. I've been happy there, the past four years. Happy enough, anyway. I live six miles from the beach, I have a rent-controlled apartment and I've made some good friends. Why, then, do I feel a perpetual loneliness? Yep, I'm talking serious therapy.

Sleep refused to make an appearance. Instead, fear, angst, frustration and sadness all came to visit, and they kept me up with their incessant chatter. Finally, at about one a.m. I popped an "Excedrin p.m." It's really stupid. I could have just gone with a sleeping pill, which has the same sleep inducers in it, but I'd feel like a drug addict, relying on meds to fall asleep. "Excedrin," on the other hand, is a well-known *pain reliever*. And I'm sure I had a headache. Why that makes it okay in my mind, I have no idea.

Chapter Seven

True to his word, Vince called me early the next morning. He'd gone home last night and stewed about what I'd told him. The more he'd thought about it, the more ticked off he'd become until, at eleven p.m. he picked up the phone and called Detective Charles Strom, the cop in charge of the Konner Novack investigation. According to Vince, Chuck wasn't too happy about being awoken from a dead sleep by an irate district attorney. He was even less happy to hear what Vince had to say.

"He wants to see you this morning."

"When?" I struggled to open my eyes, having just closed them what seemed like ten minutes ago. The clock said seven a.m. Wow, almost five full hours. I started to feel like I'd overslept.

"ASAP."

"What does he want with me?" Vince sighed heavily.

"Seems there's been some sort of snafu."

"What do you mean, snafu?"

"He doesn't know anything about any photographs."

"What?" I bolted upright in bed, banging my head against the walnut backboard. "Ow."

"Are you okay?"

"Yeah." I shifted the phone to my other ear and began massaging the sore spot. "What do you mean he doesn't know anything about the pictures? He was the one who picked them up from John in the first place."

"Ah, that's another thing…"

I scrambled out of bed and dove into the shower, emerging fifteen minutes later, clean, if not refreshed. I had a slight hangover from the sleeping pill and Vince's information made my head swim. Quickly, I dragged a comb through my tangled hair, pulled on a pair of jeans and a black, heavy cotton sweater and brushed my teeth. Then, I set to blow-drying my hair. It was cold outside and I didn't want wet hair hanging down my neck. As I turned on the power full blast, I mulled over the rest of my conversation with Vince.

"Strom said he'd never met with John."

"Then who did?" I fairly screamed.

"I don't know," Vince countered, quietly. My eyes narrowed involuntarily.

"You think John made this whole thing up, don't you?"

"I never said that. It's just weird, is all." I really couldn't blame Vince for his suspicions. For all he knew, the photos never existed, and at the moment I didn't plan to prove to him otherwise. My gut instinct told me to keep quiet about having the extra set of pictures. I trusted Vince, but the first set of prints had already disappeared. Who's to say it wouldn't happen again. Suddenly, I was struck with another thought. "Shit," I said aloud.

"What?" Oh, nothing. Vince, I gotta go. I'll call you later."

I hung up the phone and sat there, staring at it like it was a Simpsons' Magic Eight Ball, and if I stared hard enough, answers would leap out at me. But the only word that kept coming to mind was *Bobby*. The bastard had lied to me. Again. He said he'd spoken to the primary investigator and had looked at John's pictures, and they were worthless to the investigation. Suddenly, I got a sick feeling in the pit of my stomach and I thought for a moment that I was going to heave. I quickly stuck my head between my knees and waited for the feeling to pass. *Bobby can't be a part of some sort of cover-up. He just can't be."* Then why the hell was it looking so much like he was? Oy, this is not good.

Once my hair was dry I trundled downstairs, grabbed a handful of cheerios and shrugged into my jacket. I opened the front door just as Mrs. Gentile opened hers. She had a broom in her hand, and by the look on her face I thought she was planning to whack me with it. "Good morning, Mrs. Gentile," I called cheerfully, as she began to sweep non-existent dirt off her front step. I would charm her with my friendliness.

"These walls are paper thin," she announced by way of greeting. "I hear you clonking around all hours of the night." I opened my mouth to respond, but I thought better of it and just smiled back at her. "You should have some consideration." She turned on her heels and disappeared back into her house.

"I'll keep that in mind, Mrs. Gentile," I called out to her retreating back. Then I remembered I'd left my cell phone on the bedside table. I stomped back inside, slammed the front door as hard as I could and clonked back upstairs to retrieve my phone. "*Consider this*, Mrs. Gentile."

When I got back outside I did a quick inspection of Paul's car, looking for tell tale signs of last night's little joy ride. No, it all looked good. I got in the car and started the engine. It had been years since I'd been down to the police station. As a kid, I used to go there all the time with my mom, to bail out my uncle. I'd gotten to know the cops pretty well, back then. And then when Bobby first joined the force, I'd meet him at the station sometimes, after work. I wondered now if I would run into him this morning. The thought gave me a thrill mixed with an equal dose of dread. What if I start freaking out on him in the middle of the station? I mean, for all I knew he could be the murderer!

Yes, Brandy, in the years since you've been apart, Bobby decided to become a homophobic, homicidal manic. Okay, that scenario was far fetched, even for me. But, realistically, he could end up being a cop on the take. And that thought didn't provide much comfort either.

Although women are a large part of the force now, the station still smelled like armpits and testosterone. I stopped off at the front desk and asked where I might find Detective Strom. A young Latino cop, with a pencil thin moustache and beautiful dark brown eyes looked up at me. He had a large Styrofoam cup of coffee in front of him, which he picked up before answering.

"Is he expecting you?"

"Sort of. My name's Brandy Alexander. I was told he wanted to see me." The cop picked up a phone and punched in some numbers. A moment later he said, "Back through these doors, he's the last cubicle on the right." He buzzed me in.

Detective Strom looked like a cartoon character. He had a large, expansive paunch, which effectively covered his belt buckle as well as the tops of his shoes. His ears could have passed for wings on a jet liner and his jowls swayed when he moved. He looked vaguely familiar and then I realized why. He was the image of Mr. Slate, Fred's boss on The Flintstones. I suppressed a laugh, wishing John were there to share it with me. Strom looked up.

"Thanks for coming in, Ms. Alexander."

Half an hour later, I was out on the street again, more confused than ever. Officer Strom had asked me to repeat what I'd told Vince. He pulled out a pad and pencil from his desk and began taking notes. "So, you're sure your friend John called this precinct?"

"Yes," I said, swallowing my frustration.

"And he didn't tell you the name of the detective who *supposedly* visited him?"

I felt my temper surge, and I clenched my hands together to keep from popping him one. "There was no 'supposedly' about it. Officer Strom, John was not in the habit of lying. He said he called and asked for the detective in charge of the Konner Novack case. Don't you keep a log of incoming calls?"

"Only emergency calls." He sat back in his chair, chewing on the end of his pencil. Part of the eraser broke off and got stuck between his teeth. I turned away briefly to give him time to do something about it, but when I turned back it was still there. "Ms. Alexander, I did not receive a call from your friend. Nor did I go to his house. I was at the scene of another murder during the time that you described."

"Well, then who did visit John, and what did they do with the photos?"

"That's exactly what I'd like to know." Strom pushed himself out of his chair, signaling the end of our conversation. "We'll be in touch, Ms. Alexander."

"Thank you," I responded. For a whole lot of nothin'.

I called Vince from the car and told him what had transpired. "Either Strom's lying about not going to John's or there's some crazy assed person going around impersonating him. This whole thing smells like a cover-up," I exploded.

"Hmm," Vince responded.

"Hmm, what?"

"Nothing. It's just…"

"Damn it, Vince, if you have something to say, say it." I could hear him drumming his fingers on the top of his desk, debating whether to tell me.

"Well?"

"Okay. But I mean it, Brandy, you can't talk about this to anyone." I promised. "About six months ago, some dead guy turns up in a dumpster, not too far from the bar where Novack spent his last evening. By the looks of this guy's outfit, he was heavily involved in the S&M scene. Ya know, dog collar, studs, piercings in places I don't even want to think about. Anyway, He'd had the shit beaten out of him, but what did him in was, he was strangled."

"Just like Novack."

"Yeah, just like Novack."

"So, you're thinking you may have a serial killer on your hands?"

"Could be." I could tell he was holding out on me and I pressed him to continue.

"The similarities don't end there. There was some physical evidence in that case. Some hair samples, I think. But the evidence disappeared before it could be processed."

"Wow." I digested that for a moment. "Vince, who was the primary on that case?"

"Ya know what? I've got a big mouth, and I've told you too much already."

"It's a matter of public record. I can look it up on line. Who was it?" But even as I asked, I knew what the answer would be. There was silence on the other end of the line.

"Tell me!"

"Alright! It was Bobby." I squeezed my eyes shut tight, not trusting myself to say anything. "Look, it doesn't mean anything. It could have happened on anybody's watch." I leaned my head on the steering wheel and inadvertently honked the horn. A uniformed cop approached the car and tapped on the window. I rolled down the window about an inch, and he stuck his head in. "Are you all right, ma'am?"

"I'm fine, thank you." Vince began yelling into the phone.

"Brandy, are you there? What's going on?"

"I'm fine, Vince. I'll call you back." I turned my attention to the cop whose head was now wedged inside, his face practically in my lap. I reached over and rolled the window down another few notches so he could extract himself. Then I started the engine and pulled out of the police parking lot. The place gave me the creeps.

"Bobby, what the hell have you gotten yourself into?" It was a rhetorical question, since he was nowhere in the vicinity when I'd asked. Not that he'd give me a straight answer anyway. It was eight fifty-five a.m. I'd been sitting across the street from the salon where Carla works, waiting for it to open up. After I'd left the police station I'd been temped to go home, yank the covers up over my head and not get up again until Fran's wedding. But I was hungry and in desperate need of caffeine, so I pulled into a Seven-Eleven and tanked up on Tastykakes and some really bad coffee—the kind you refer to as "a cup of Joe." I started picturing myself as a hard-boiled detective, sitting in my nineteen thirty-nine Packard, drinkin' m' Joe and figuring out who stole the Maltese Falcon. Oh my God, I am *so* losing it.

Out of the corner of my eye I spied some movement inside the salon. Shades were pulled up and the door swung open. Out of nowhere a group of elderly women appeared and began to crowd the doorway. Carla stuck her head out and ushered the ladies in. She was a vision to behold in black spandex pants and a hot pink Vee-neck sweater. Her hair looked like an architectural miracle, piled high and held together with big rhinestone butterfly barrettes. She spotted me as I climbed out of the car and waved hello. I crossed the street just as the last of her customers stepped through the door.

"Oh, hon," she started, throwing comforting arms around me. "I would've called you, but Frankie thought you might need a little time to yourself." I nodded, my face smooshed against her chest. A small, gray haired woman, in her seventies approached us. She was wearing the uniform of the day, a pale yellow smock. Carla released me and turned to her. "Gladys, please put Mrs. Russo in the chair next to the window. She says she likes to see what she's missing on the outside, while she's in here, getting 'beyooty-ful.' Oh, and then take Mrs. Waldstein over to get her hair washed. Thanks, hon," Carla added, cheerfully. Gladys didn't look too happy, but she did as she was asked.

"What's the story with Gladys?" I asked when she shuffled away.

"Constipation. She suffers terribly."

"Oh." There didn't seem much else I could add to that conversation so I got right to the point. "Carla, I need your help. But you can't tell Frankie." Alarm spread across Carla's kind face.

"Are you in some kind of trouble?" I shook my head.

"No. Nothing like that. But it's serious, and if you don't want to get involved I'll understand."

"Sweetie, you're scaring me." From the seat by the window Mrs. Russo called out.

"Could you hurry it up there, Carla? I'm meeting my daughter for lunch."

"In a minute, Mrs. Russo." She gave me a palms up gesture and said, "Be right back."

While Carla tended to Mrs. Russo I looked around the salon. An ancient sign in the window advertised that every Monday was Senior Discount Day. There were four chairs, each filled with a little old lady demanding to be coiffed. From the back room emerged two technicians, about nineteen years old apiece, wearing the same pale yellow smocks. One sported a rather large, homemade tattoo on the back of her neck, with the name Carmine, encased in tiny hearts. The other was smoking a cigarette. She cupped her hand and tipped the ashes into her palm, then surreptitiously rubbed them into the leg of her jeans.

"Bonita, put out the cigarette and go help Gladys, please." Bonita sauntered off and Carla turned back to me. "Prison-Work program. She'll get the hang of it. Let's talk in here, hon," she added, pulling me into the privacy of the back room. A fresh pot of coffee sat on the counter. Carla picked up two Styrofoam cups, filled each of them three quarters of the way full, and doused hers with Half and Half. I did the same. She sat down at the table and eyeballed me. "Don't take this wrong, Sweetie, but you look awful." Tell me something I don't know. Any moment now I expected a telegram from the Early Edition News in L.A. saying, "Heard you look awful. You're fired."

"Brandy, you can't fall apart like this. It's the last thing John would want." I nodded in agreement.

"You're right. I'll take a nap when I get home, but Carla, I need you to do something for me."

"Anything. You know that." I took a deep breath and plunged in.

"Okay. You know a lot of edgy people—I mean that as a compliment," I added, hastily. "It shows how well rounded you are. So, I need you to introduce me to someone."

"Who?"

"That's just it. I don't know. Look, some really weird things have come to light lately, and" —I paused dramatically and lowered my voice to barely a whisper. "I have reason to believe that John was murdered."

"*Murdered?* Why on earth would you think he was murdered?"

"It's a long story and I really don't have the energy to get into it now, but trust me, I have my reasons." I must have looked positively deranged, because Carla seemed doubtful. She didn't say anything for a minute. She just walked over to the counter and dragged the entire pot of coffee over to the table. She poured us each a refill. At that moment, Gladys peeked her head in.

"Mrs. Russo says she doesn't want Marie to set her hair. She says the last time she left the rollers in too long and it made her look like a French Poodle."

"Tell Mrs. Russo to kiss my ass. No, don't," she added, quickly. Turning to me she whispered, "Gladys doesn't really get the concept of 'venting'. I'll be right back."

When Carla returned, she had a determined look in her eye. "Listen, Brandy, I'm sure you have your reasons for believing what you do. But if all that you think is true, then you have to go to the police and tell them what you know."

"Carla, I can't. I tried to go to the cops. *John tried to go to the cops.* I think that's what got him killed. There's a major cover-up going on and I have to find out what it's all about."

"I don't understand."

"I know you don't. And I wish I could explain it to you, but right now you're better off not knowing."

"Okay," she said slowly. "You can't go to the cops. Then what about Bobby? I know you have issues with him, but you know you can trust him."

"I can't go to Bobby. He may be in on it too." I was sounding nuttier by the minute. Soon I'd be talking about the Lone Gunman and the Grassy Knoll. "Carla, I do know this sounds like the ravings of a sleep deprived maniac, which, I'll be the first to admit, I am. But please trust me on this. I wouldn't ask you if I wasn't certain that I'm right." Carla gave me a long look.

"Start at the beginning," she said. "And don't leave anything out." Bless you, Carla.

I filled her in as best I could on the Konner Novack murder and how John had stumbled upon some clues.

She listened, mouth agape, as I described Bobby's recent behavior, the blatant lies and the break in at Johnny's. I ended with the missing evidence.

"So, you can see why I can't go to Bobby. I don't know who to trust anymore."

"Honey, this is too much for one person to handle. I know you want to avenge John's death, but you can't do this alone."

"That's why I came to you. Frankie told me once that you have a—a rather *colorful* family." Colorful being a euphemism for "connected," Philly style. "And I thought maybe you'd know someone who could help me gather the information I need. You know, take me places where I wouldn't ordinarily fit in. Someone who really knows the streets." Carla leaned forward on her elbows and studied me for a moment. She scratched her head with the tips of her highly lacquered fingernails. She rolled her eyes heavenward, as if to ask for divine guidance. She sighed. And then, she spoke.

"There's this guy I know."

"Yeah?" I leaned forward as well, eager for her to continue.

"Nope," she decided, shaking her head. "Can't do it. Your uncle would kill me."

"Who? Who is he? Come on, Carla, he sounds great." Carla laughed, a slow, pure rumble of pleasure.

"Oh, he is."

"Then what's the problem?" She leaned forward even closer and looked me directly in the eye. She spoke slowly and distinctly, as if addressing a backwards three year old.

"Nicholas Santiago is trouble. Do you know how to spell TROUBLE?" I sat there, mesmerized by the notion of this mystery man. A man of danger. A man of *trouble.*

"I'll have to think of somebody else."

"No, I want him!"

"That's what all the girls say, hon."

According to Carla, Nicholas Santiago is Robin Hood, Al Capone and Che Guevera all rolled into one explosively sexy package. Part saint, large part sinner and as elusive as an honest politician he is the stuff neighborhood legends are made of.

He owns a martial arts studio on Spring Garden, but rumors regarding other ventures abound. Some say he's got a thriving hit man business. Others believe he runs guns to South America for obscure rebel causes. Nobody knows for sure, and Nick does nothing to dispel these notions. The cops hate him on principal. He has a finger on the pulse of the city, has friends in high places and can crawl along on his belly with the curbside dwellers. He knows things the cops don't and can do things the cops can't. He'd do anything for a friend. Couldn't say what he'd do if someone crossed him. No one's ever been brave enough to find out.

"How do you know this guy, Carla?"

"Through my cousin, Benny. They had some business dealings." She shrugged. "I don't ask and Benny don't tell. It's better that way."

Carla and I came to an agreement. We agreed not to tell Frankie, and she would set up a meeting for me. After swearing on Carla's St. Christopher medal that I would be careful, I left the beauty salon and headed home.

Three cups of coffee had really taken a toll on my internal organs. I flung open the door and raced up the stairs two at a time, barely making it to the bathroom before the dam burst. In my hurry to find the toilet, I'd inadvertently left the front door open. I finished up in the bathroom and was all set to go back downstairs and microwave some popcorn, when I heard a soft knocking at the front door. A moment later someone was calling my name. Holy Crap. It's Bobby. My senses went into panic mode. He'd found out I knew he'd lied. He was on the take, he was the serial killer, he blew up the boat, and now he was here to kill me too. What do I do? What do I do? I was hopping around like a crazy person, pulling up my jeans the rest of the way and grabbing a comb out of the drawer. Even if he *was* here to kill me, I still had some pride. Bobby called my name again. He didn't sound like he was going to kill me. He just sounded tired. Okay, that's probably not his plan anyway, but I just wasn't prepared to talk to him. Not until I had some more answers.

I tiptoed over to the banister and peered over the railing. He had gone into the kitchen. I scurried into the bedroom, unlocked my window, heaved it open and crawled head first, out onto the trellis. I righted myself and shimmied down the rest of the way, hopped into Paul's car and took off like a bat out of hell.

I drove several blocks out of the neighborhood, and then I pulled over to the curb and waited for the return of rational thought. My cell phone began to ring, and I dug around in my pocketbook trying to locate it.

"Hello?"

"Why'd you drive away?" I sighed, feeling more annoyed than scared.

"How'd you get my cell phone number?"

"Paul gave it to me."

"What do you want?"

"Why'd you sneak away from me?"

"Don't be ridiculous. I wasn't sneaking away from you."

"No? I guess you always leave your house by way of the second story window." I didn't really have an answer for that one so I sat there, saying nothing.

"Brandy, I have to talk to you. It's important." Just then my cell phone beeped. I was getting another call.

"Hang on a second. I clicked over to the other line. "Hello?"

It's all arranged," Carla stated without preamble.

"Hang on." I beeped back to Bobby.

"I've got to go."

"Brandy, *please.*" Damn, damn, damn. I was starting to cave.

"I'll talk to you, later," I said, and clicked backed to Carla.

Chapter Eight

Philadelphia is a city teeming with slums. Not just "impoverished neighborhoods," but honest to God war torn disaster areas, complete with condemned, burned out buildings, decayed and crumbling houses and boarded up storefronts. Graffiti covers every micro inch of wall space. People live in these uninhabitable places. Kids play "Double Dutch" in the street, while addicts sit on the stoops of disintegrating structures, bargaining for heroin and shooting up. Gang members roam their turf, protecting their territory and their reputations. Periodically, someone will come in and decide the neighborhood is ripe for gentrification. They will buy up the real estate, refurbish the old buildings and either move in, or resell the properties at quadruple the price. The economic tide slowly sweeps in and washes away the impoverished, relocating them into another less desirable corner of the city. I passed many of these neighborhoods now as I cruised down Delaware Avenue. Although I had grown up accustomed to seeing these neighborhoods it never failed to surprise and sadden me.

At Spring Garden I hung a left, and continued on past Fifth Street. Nick Santiago's studio was nearby. I began looking for the address. The street was deserted. Not a lot of "through" traffic on this end of town. The address Carla had given me was attached to a two story red brick building, sandwiched between a check cashing store and a bail bonds office. The windows were the mirrored kind you see in psych wards and police stations; one way observation jobs, tinted a pearl gray. Graffiti graced the store on the left and the store on the right. It reminded me of a dog lifting its tail to mark its territory. Oddly, the martial arts studio was untouched. I wondered if it was considered a neutral space or if Nick's reputation won out over adolescent posturing.

I cut the engine and scanned the area. Two Latino guys in their early twenties lounged against the side of the building. Both had shaved heads, one had a decorative design tattooed over his ears. The other was talking on his cell phone. He looked up and saw me staring at him. He snapped the phone shut and nudged his friend. They both smiled, showing a lot of gold teeth. I didn't want to seem unfriendly so I gave a little finger wave, but remained firmly rooted to the driver's seat. The shorter of the two sauntered over to the car and leaned against the bumper. He very gently began rocking the back end, slowly at first and then a little harder. I debated my options; put the car in gear and drive off, or politely ask him to stop doing that. I decided not to be such a wuss and went for option number two. "Um, excuse me."

"You talkin' to me?" He had to be kidding. Good. I like a man with a sense of humor.

"Uh, I was wondering if you'd mind getting off the car. You see, it's my brother's and he kill me if anything happened to it." The taller guy, the one with the tattooed head walked over to join his buddy. He was smiling, but it didn't reach his eyes. His eyes looked eerily empty. My stomach dropped, and *not* in a good way. He came closer and I could see a four-inch scar at the base of his neck. It looked fresh. I gave an involuntary shutter. His friend came around to the other side of the car, and I twisted the key in the ignition.

"You want me to stop riding your bumper?" He leered. "No problem." He reached behind his back and pulled out a five-inch blade. It had a chrome handle that glittered in the sunlight. My hand began to shake so hard I couldn't wrap it around the car key. The two could smell my fear and they began to laugh, openly taunting me. The one with the knife bent down, and I realized with sudden clarity that he was going to slash my tires, and then quite possibly, my throat. Without thinking, I threw the car into reverse, effectively putting an end to his fun and games.

"You dumb bitch!" He screamed. "You ran over my hand." He held it up to his chest. It was all bent out of shape and it looked like it really hurt. He grabbed the driver's side door with his good hand and began pounding away, trying to get it to open. His friend stood on the sidelines, convulsing with laughter. I tried desperately to shift into first gear, but I couldn't get my damn hand to stop shaking. So I leaned on the horn and honked the living crap out of it. The door to the martial arts studio opened and out walked a man.

He looked to be around thirty. He wasn't especially tall, maybe five feet ten inches or so, with a lithe, yet muscular body. He wore loose black sweats, and a tight white tee shirt, which only partially covered well-defined Abs. On his left wrist was a silver band. From his right ear, hung a small silver cross. It gleamed against his caramel colored skin. Everything about this man seemed a study in contrasts. There was power and grace in his movements, which were unhurried but purposeful. His hair was a long, wavy mass of brown, swept back from his face by his hand. He had the beginnings of a beard, just a few days old, the beard of someone who had forgotten to shave but would remember, eventually. His full, sensuous mouth was upturned slightly into a wry smile. He was the least self-conscious person I had ever seen, and the most compelling. I could not take my eyes off of him, and I wasn't the only one. The guy at my car door abruptly stopped yanking on it. He took a step back from it as the man nodded his head in greeting. He shook hands with the other guy, and then he walked around to the driver's side of the car. His smile got wider, more genuine, and I breathed a sigh of relief. I rolled my window down a little more and said, "I didn't mean to run over his hand."

"It shouldn't have been there in the first place, right, man?" Wow. For a guy not holding a visible weapon he sure spoke with a lot of confidence. The guy with the broken hand scowled at me and grunted something indistinguishable "I don't think the lady heard you, Raoul."

"I said I was only playin' wi'cha."

"I'm really very sorry," I said, not quite making eye contact. Raoul didn't much look like he cared how sorry I was. His hand was starting to swell.

"You'd better go get that set," the man said, still smiling. "And next time, I'd appreciate it if you didn't scare my guests." The two guys took off around the corner, leaving me to make my own introductions.

"I take it you're Nick."

"I take it you're Brandy."

"I wasn't scared, you know." I unlocked my door and tried to climb out of the car, but unfortunately my legs had turned to Jell-O. Nick caught me by the elbow as I pitched forward. He dropped his voice to barely a whisper.

"You should be scared. The little one is Raoul Sanchez. He just got out of jail, on a technicality. He was in for first-degree murder."

"He a friend of yours?"

"Makes a better friend than enemy."

"Funny, I've heard the same thing about you."

"Yeah? Nick raised an eyebrow. What else have you heard about me?"

"I've heard that you kill people." Oh my God. When was I going to learn to control this mouthpiece? "I didn't mean to say that out loud." Nick eyed me appraisingly, and I blushed under his gaze.

"Carla warned me you've been sleep deprived. It can do funny things to a person." Suddenly, his face broke into a grin. It was magnificent, and I had to bite my lip to keep from gasping. "Come on," he said. "Let's go inside and talk."

There was a class in session, Advanced something or other judging by the black belts tied around everyone's waists. There were nine students in the class, all women. They appeared to be between the ages of seventeen and thirty. It was a racially mixed group of blacks, whites and Asians. The instructor was a stunning Latina woman, about twenty-five years old. She looked up when Santiago and I entered the room. "Hey, Tanya," he called softly to her. He smiled, and she smiled warmly back at him, and I had a sudden, irrational urge to push her down.

We continued on to the next room, a small, tidy office. The furniture was sparse but expensive. There was a leather couch, a TV, a black marble topped desk and a plush red velvet chair. Nick offered me a seat and he took the one behind the desk. I chose the chair. He pulled open a desk drawer and removed a small wooden box. Inside was a pouch. He took out the pouch and opened it. Then he extracted some rolling paper and spread it open on the desk.

"Do you smoke?" He asked.

"Um, no. I never—ah, is that pot?"

"No. It's a special blend of imported tobacco." I watched as he tapped out a small amount of loose leaves onto the paper and began to roll it with expert fingers.

"Neither do I— smoke, that is. I miss it," he added, wistfully.

"Why'd you stop?"

"Didn't you pay attention to those anti smoking films in high school? This stuff'll kill ya." He picked up the cigarette and held it lovingly between his fingers. "I miss the rituals more than the actual smoking," he explained. I nodded. It made sense to me.

"So," he said, sitting back in his chair, "what can I do for you?" And so for what seemed like the millionth time I explained what happened to Johnny. Only this time I left nothing out.

"You have a copy of these pictures?"

"Yes." I was exhausted, and I just wanted to curl up in a little ball in this oh so cozy chair and go to sleep.

"You think your cop friend had anything to do with Johnny's murder?" I shook my head, no. "How about the Novack murder?" Again, an emphatic no. "Could he be involved in some other way, maybe accepting bribes to keep his mouth shut?" I hesitated. "I don't know," I whispered. Sadness washed over me and a lump formed in my throat, making it hard for me to breathe. He waited for me to collect myself, and then he asked, not unkindly,

"What exactly do you need from me?" I shifted in the chair, struggling to stay awake.

"I need information, only I don't know how to get it. Carla says you know people. She says you move in a lot of different circles. I've been away for four years, and even when I lived here I didn't have access to the kinds of people you do. I want to take John's pictures and show them around." I shrugged. "Who knows, maybe I'll get lucky and someone will see something in them that I don't." Before he could ask, I added, "The police are not an option." He seemed to understand that only too well.

"You know that once you let it be known you're looking for this killer, there's no turning back. It could get very dangerous for you." I didn't know. Actually, the thought never crossed my mind.

"Of course I know. I'm not stupid." Nicholas Santiago looked at me for a long minute. He seemed to be trying to make up his mind about me. "I'm a big girl, Mr. Santiago. I can take care of myself. I just need a little professional help, and I intend to pay you for your time." I dug in my pocketbook and extracted my checkbook and a pen. Unfortunately, the only one I had was pink and sparkly, with bright pink feathers on the tip. It looked like it belonged to the Tooth Fairy. Nick shook his head and my hopes fell with a thud.

"Go home, Brandy Alexander. You're in way over your head." He had a look on his face that said there was no room for argument. I stood up and waited for the dizziness to pass. I really needed to get something to eat.

"Thank you for seeing me." My disappointment was overwhelming, but I'd be damned if I was going to let him know it. I smiled and extended my hand. He reached out his hand and placed it in mine. His touch was electric and I felt body parts contracting painfully. I reluctantly disengaged myself and turned to go. Nick came out from behind the desk and walked me back through the studio. It was empty. When I got to the door, I took a quick look around to make sure I didn't have company waiting for me outside. He stopped me before I stepped over the foyer.

"You're going to do this, with or without me, aren't you?" I nodded.

"Wouldn't you, if it were your best friend?" His mouth twisted into a lopsided grin, and for a moment it was all I could do to keep from backing him against the wall and kissing him until his lips turned blue.

"Okay, here's the deal, Nancy Drew." He paused and leaned into me, tucking some stray hair behind my ear. He let his hand linger there a moment, and I felt like I'd just discovered the female equivalent of Viagra. "I'll meet you here tomorrow night at nine. Bring the pictures. There's this club I know. It sounds like the place your friend described to you. You are to stick with me the entire time. No wandering off, got it?"

"No problem." *Oh boy, I get to be with Nick tomorrow night!*

"And I ask the questions. In fact, I don't want you talking to anybody."

"Are you going to make me sit in the car?" I was beginning to get a touch annoyed with all the rules. He smiled and leaned in to me again. His mouth brushed against my ear and I shivered.

"Remember when I said you were in way over your head?" I stared at him, my eyes like saucers. "I wasn't just talking about scary strangers." He placed a hand on the back of my neck and gently guided me to my car. I found my voice and turned to him.

"What made you change your mind, Nick?"

"Hell if I know," he said quietly, and he disappeared back into the studio.

To quote a wise man, "I friggin'love the Wiz." That man is Frank Oliveiri, owner of Pat's Steaks, a Philadelphia institution. The "wiz" he's referring to is Cheese Wiz, the preferred cheese of his famous Philadelphia steak sandwiches. Almost seventy years ago, Frank's uncle Patrick Oliveiri began selling these incredibly tasty sandwiches at a little outdoor stand, located at 9th and Wharton. Originally, Patrick sold hot dogs, but one day he grew tired of the same old taste, so he chopped up some steak scraps and served it on a bun with grilled onions. An employee embellished the recipe by adding some provolone, and the cheese steak was born. The Cheese Wiz came later, and many people feel it's the only true way to experience a cheese steak. But it's got to be the real thing. No cheap imitation Wiz. Eventually, Pat's Steaks moved across the street to its current location, which is where I found myself after I left Nick's studio.

I stood in a long line and when it was my turn I ordered a pizza steak "wit." That's "Philly speak" for cheese steak with onions. I watched as the counter guy expertly wrapped the sandwich. Grease dripped out the back end and I began to salivate. It had been four years since my last Pat's steak and I was going to enjoy every cholesterol-packed bite. But a sudden rush of nutritional conscience washed over me, and I turned to the guy at the next counter who was doling out French fries. "Excuse me." He glanced up, two beefy arms poised over the fryer.

"Yeah, doll?"

"Are your fries cooked in lard?" I inquired. The roar of the kitchen fan swallowed up my words.

"What?" He shouted back at me.

"Are your fries cooked in lard?" I said, much louder this time. He paused for a beat, shaking his head no, and then threw back his head and guffawed, tears welling up and rolling down his corpulent cheeks. "What's so funny?" Gasping for air he said,

"I thought you said, 'Are you friends with the Lord?'" Well, I've always said that eating at Pat's was a religious experience.

I sat outside on the patio with my legs tucked under me, savoring every greasy bite. I washed my lunch down with a Pepsi. A pigeon joined me towards the end, and I tossed it a piece of the roll. A nano-second later he was joined by fifty of his closest friends and relatives, all wanting a piece of the action. Philadelphia pigeons are a lot like native Philadelphians. They are pigeons with "addytude." They circled their food source and began pecking at my feet. "Get away," I called out lamely. I stood up, shaking French Fries off my lap. As they converged on the fries I made my getaway.

On the way home I stopped at an Acme supermarket to pick up a few essentials. A witch greeted me at the door and handed me a shopping cart. She was decked out in a black cape and tall pointy hat. I thanked her and entered the store. The manager sailed past me wearing a George W. Bush mask and devil horns. I maneuvered my way down the aisles, still unaware that anything unusual was going on. It took until I got to the candy aisle for my amazing powers of observation to finally kick in. Stacks and stacks of glorious candy spilled off the shelves into the aisle. Halloween. Unlimited chocolate. Oh boy! I picked up several bags of Milky Ways, Kit Kats and Hershey Bars. Then I threw in some Reece's Peanut Butter Cups for the protein. The night was shaping up better than I'd dreamed. Okay, so I'd have to share a little with those pesky Trick or Treaters, but that's why I bought extra. I loaded up my cart, paid Freddy Krueger and headed home.

Traffic jammed up at around Penn's Landing. I strained my eyes to look ahead and saw a cement mixer sitting in the middle of the street. It was trying to make a u-turn into the construction site, on the left. There was a gigantic hole where the old Brickman building had been, and the sign on the fencing said "Future home of The Theatre Arts Conservatory. Hoffman and Gruber Construction." Boy, I wouldn't mind being either Hoffman or Gruber. They were bound to make a mint on this project.

The cement mixer struggled to turn itself around, but an old orange Volkswagen bug pulled out of line and blocked its path. The guy directing traffic went up to the driver's window and gestured to him to back up. The Volkswagen driver, a little old white haired man, opened the door to his car and stepped out, crossing his arms across his chest. A lot of gesturing took place, first from the traffic director and then from the old man. At one point, the car in front of me decided it would be helpful to start honking. He leaned on his horn and let it rip. That got a number of the other cars doing the same. The old man steadfastly refused to budge. About five minutes later, a cop on a horse appeared. The horse seemed non-plussed over the stupidity of humans. He showed his distain by lifting his tail and taking a huge dump in the middle of the street. I turned on the radio, opened the bag of Milky Ways and waited for everything to be sorted out. After about ten minutes, the old man climbed into his car. He backed it up and edged back into line. The cement mixer completed his u-turn, and the cop on the horse rode off into the sunset. I love this city.

The answering machine blinked hello to me as I walked into the kitchen. I played back the messages as I dumped candy into a big bowl. "Bran, it's Franny. Eddie says he's going to a hockey game this evening, and I don't want to be stuck here answering the door all night, so I thought I'd come by and keep you company. Call me." Damn, I should have bought more candy. The next call was from my boss, wanting to know what I thought about doing a piece on "handsome cabs." She suggested maybe I could drive one around town, wouldn't it make a cute story. Yeah, that's what I want to do. It's just the trick to make people view me as a serious reporter. After that there was a hang up, then another message from Bobby. He sounded frustrated and borderline whiny.

No polite segues, just "I know you're avoiding me, damn it. But this is important. Call me, or I'm coming over." I picked up the phone and called Franny back. We decided to make dinner and rent scary movies. I took a package out of the freezer. It was my mom's homemade lasagna. I had no idea how long it had been there, but it must have been a while, judging by the icicles that had begun to form on the outside of the package.

Next, I called Carla to thank her for introducing me to Nick. Luckily, she wasn't back from the salon yet, so I just left her a message. I didn't have the energy to give her all the details she deserved. So that just left Bobby. What to do? What to do? I drummed my fingers on the kitchen table. Maybe I should call mom and ask her about that lasagna. Twenty minutes later I hung up the phone, knowing more about lasagna than I thought was humanly possible. It was after 4:00 p.m. I'd just missed Oprah, but maybe I could still catch Dr. Phil. I turned on the television, eager to see Dr. Phil fix everyone's lives in fifteen- minute increments. It turned out to be a rerun so I switched channels and watched the local news instead.

"Protesters are crying 'homophobia' in the City of Brotherly Love," announced a perky, young newscaster. "More on this story when we return." The cameras flashed to a live shot of City Hall, surrounded by Gay Rights activists. They were carrying signs with Konner Novack's picture on it. Vince had told me the mayor was taking a lot of heat because of this case. If the police didn't solve it soon, it could cost the mayor some valuable votes in the next election. Little does he know the cops are working overtime to make sure the case stays unsolved. I wondered if I should tell him.

The doorbell startled me out of my thoughts. I ran to the door and peeked out the spy hole. It was Bobby. He was leaning against the post, in his leather jacket and tight faded jeans. His jacket was open, revealing a pale blue work shirt. He looked like he hadn't shaved in about a week, and he had the bedraggled air of someone seriously in need of a shower. Shit. Why'd he have to look so good? I started to back quietly away from the door.

"I know you're in there. I can hear you breathing." I opened the door part way, blocking his way into the house. "Are you gonna let me in or do we have to have this conversation standing on your parents' front steps?" My neighbor, Mrs. Gentile, flung open her door and stared unabashedly at the two of us.

"Go back inside, you old busy body," I growled. Bobby let out a muffled snort. I'd never spoken to anyone over the age of fifty in that tone of voice, but she was really getting on my nerves.

"You should be ashamed," she said, shaking her head. But she went back in and shut her door. I pulled open the storm door and stepped aside to let Bobby in.

"Why have you been avoiding me?" I turned my back to him, trying to buy a little time. Should I lie? Tell the truth? What *was* the truth, anyway? Did I really believe he was a killer, or even a crooked cop? "No," my heart told me. But the evidence, circumstantial though it may be, was hard to overlook.

"Brandy, don't turn your back to me." It was more of a plea than an order, and it almost broke my heart. I slowly turned around. "Can we sit down?"

"Suit yourself," I shrugged. He took one end of the couch and I took the other. I grabbed a pillow and propped it up against my chest and leaned forward on my elbows. "You want to talk, so talk."

"You've changed," he said. I gave him a blank stare, but my heart was racing like a hamster on speed. "You're—I don't know— harder now. Is that what four years in L.A. did to you?"

"No, that's what you did to me, you bastard." Wow, where did that come from? It surprised Bobby too. He jerked his head back as if he'd been physically punched.

"Jesus, Brandy, it's been four years. Johnny's dead. Can't we get past this?"

"Well, I'm sorry, but it's a little difficult for me to 'get past it' when every word that comes out of your mouth is a big fat lie." Bobby exhaled deeply and rubbed his hands against his thighs.

"You found out about the tail."

"You're God damned right I did." What tail?

"Look, I only asked Porter to follow you because after that night I came to see you, you were really upset, and I thought you'd end up doing something stupid. I wanted to keep you out of trouble."

"So you had Porter follow me?" Never mind that I didn't know who or even what Porter was. He'd had me followed!

"Only for a day or so. I thought you knew." Swell investigative reporter I was turning out to be. Some schmuck tails me and I'm absolutely clueless. "I'm sorry." He leaned his head back on the couch and closed his eyes. My head was swimming with this new information. Why did he think I needed protection?

"Bobby." I spoke so quietly I could almost hear the blood pumping through my veins.

"I want the truth and I want it now. So either be honest with me, or get the fuck out." He opened his eyes and repositioned himself a little closer to me. Our knees were almost touching.

"What do you want to know?"

"Everything. Let's start with why you lied about having seen John's pictures, when they never even made it to police headquarters. Yeah, I know about that," I said to his surprised expression. He studied me for a moment.

"You got anything to eat?"

"What are you, kidding me?"

"Look, I've been trying to get in touch with you for days. I'm ready to tell you everything. Swear to God. But I'm starving, here." I guess it was the Jewish grandmother in me, but I couldn't resist the urge to feed a starving man, no matter how pissed I was at him. I popped the lasagna in the microwave. At least I'd find out if it were edible before serving it to Franny.

We sat in silence at the kitchen table, while Bobby chowed down. He'd taken his jacket off and hung it over the back of his chair. He had the sleeves of his shirt rolled up to midway up his arm. I watched as he gripped his fork tightly in his hand, holding it between his index and middle fingers. It was a funny little quirk I'd always found endearing.

It seemed the most natural thing in the world to be sitting there with him. We'd done it thousands of times in the ten years we had been friends. After that first day in back of the boxing gym, we'd been pretty much inseparable. We had an instant emotional connection, but life experience-wise we were decades apart. I'd always lived a safe, sheltered and very loved existence, while Bobby knew pain and abandonment, ever since he was four. He said I was too young for him. But that didn't stop me from loving him. My fourteen-year old heart would break every time he went off with another girl. But I was his best friend, and he'd always come back to me in the end.

When I turned sixteen, the tide turned. I'd always been able to make him laugh, to sort out his problems, to connect with his very soul, but now I had that little something extra. Breasts. And I made damn sure he noticed them. With my full-on urging, Bobby gave me the most memorable Sweet Sixteen present a girl could ask for. After that he never again complained that I was too young for him.

Bobby scraped up the last bit of lasagna off his plate, and then stood and put the plate in the sink. He began to wash it but I stopped him. "Quit stalling, DiCarlo. I'll wash, you talk." He sat back down at the table.

"Okay," he said. "I did lie to you about the pictures. That's why I've been trying to get in touch with you. I felt bad about it."

"Then why did you lie to me?"

"Sweetheart, I'd lie to the Pope if I thought it would keep you safe." I choked back my surprise and let him continue. "When you first came up with this idea that Johnny had been killed because of the pictures he took, I thought the whole idea was whack-o. But I promised you I'd check it out. Which I did."

"And?"

"And the pictures weren't there."

"Did you go to the detective in charge of the investigation?" Bobby hesitated.

"No," he said, finally.

"Why not?"

"Brandy, swear to me this won't go any further than this room."

"I swear."

"I think somebody doesn't want this guy to be caught. And I think he's tied in with the cover-up on another homicide that happened about six months ago. Problem is, I don't who that someone is." I looked at him steadily.

"Some people think that someone is you." He stood up and shrugged back into his jacket.

"I thought we got past that. But if you're so determined to believe I'm a cop on the take, I'll be Goddamned if I'm going to try to convince you otherwise. Thanks for the lasagna." I put my arm on his sleeve and spun him around.

"Oh, quit being such a baby. You didn't earn the right to have hurt feelings." He shot me a look of annoyance, and I let my hand fall from his jacket sleeve. "Listen," I said, more softly, "You really can't blame me for having my doubts. A lot has happened in the past few days. I've been hearing things about you."

"What things?" Gee, where to begin? I sighed. We both sat down again.

"Okay, like you were the primary investigator on the murder from six months ago. The one where hair samples were taken from the lab." He raised his eyebrows in response.

"You've been doing your homework. But for the record, I was never implicated in any of that. And I'm still trying to find the bastard who did take the evidence." While I digested this he continued. "What else ya got?"

"Well, there was that break-in at Johnny's. I assume you were hoping to find another set of pictures, but you sure sounded disappointed when you left." Ooh, he wasn't expecting that one.

"How did you know about that?" I opened my mouth to answer, but he held up his hand in front of my face, stopping me. "Never mind. Ya know if I thought you had entered John's place illegally, I would be bound by law to arrest you."

"Just a lucky guess," I smiled.

"I have to hand it to you, sweetheart, you get around." He seemed impressed, which made me feel ridiculously proud of myself. "So," he continued, "theoretically, if you found something at John's that could help me solve this case, would you turn it over to me?"

"Theoretically? Sure, why not?" He moved closer and dropped his voice an octave, taking on a slightly dangerous tone. This was the Bobby I remembered. The one on the edge.

"We're not talking 'theoretical' here, are we?" I shrugged, noncommittally. "Brandy, don't play games with me. If you're withholding evidence" — I took a reflexive step backwards.

"I'm not." Okay, I was, but this was *my* show and I wasn't about to abdicate power just yet. I avoided eye contact and continued my interrogation. "I also heard that you were assigned to the Konner Novack case, but you left town two days later. I'm sorry, Bobby, but that doesn't sound like a person who's exactly dedicated to his job. It sounds more like someone with something to hide. I'm not saying you were involved," I hastened to add, "but you have to admit your actions seem a little weird."

"There were extenuating circumstances," he muttered.

"Fine." I threw up my hands and looked at the clock. It was five thirty. The trick or treaters would start ringing the bell at any moment, and I hadn't even taken my share of the loot out of the bowl, yet. I tried a little levity on for size. "Listen, Bobby, it's getting late. I don't think your wife would appreciate it if she knew you were eating lasagna at another woman's house." His face clouded over and I instantly regretted my words.

"What's wrong?"

"She left me." He said it so quietly I wasn't quite sure I'd heard him right.

"What?"

"Yeah. She took my kid and left." He slumped back into the kitchen chair, all color drained from his face. I moved to his side, thought better of it and drew up a chair, opposite him.

"When? When did she leave?" All the jokes I'd made about her, all the snide remarks seemed so petty and mean in the wake of this news.

Marie DiCarlo had taken their child and left Bobby two days after Konner Novack was murdered. He had already been assigned to the case, when he came home one day and discovered they were gone. It didn't come as a huge surprise. She had threatened him before. The story poured out of him. They'd met a year and a half after I'd left town. She was from Guatemala. Five years younger than Bobby. It was meant to be a one night stand, but she'd gotten pregnant, and in her family abortion was not an option. "So, you married her."

"I couldn't let my kid grow up without a father. She's the sweetest little thing, Brandy. Huge brown eyes, curly dark hair." His voice faltered and I put a steadying hand on his knee. "She's only just turned two. I miss her," he ended, miserably.

"What about your wife?" I asked, gently. Bobby shook his head, slowly.

"I know it sounds really shitty, but she knew going into this marriage what my feelings were. Things were okay for a while, but about six months ago, she began to— I don't know, want more than I could give. And when she finally accepted that I couldn't return her feelings, she started making noises about moving back to Guatemala with Sophia. He ran his fingers through his hair. "Maybe if I hadn't been so preoccupied with my job, I would've realized how unhappy she was."

"But she stayed with you for another six months," I said. "What made her decide to bolt like this?" He gave me a piercing look; a look so full of longing it took my breath away.

"She heard you were coming back to town. She's always known about you. How I felt about you. How I fucked up the only decent thing I ever had in my life. I guess she felt threatened." What was he saying? That he still loved me? No, he was speaking in the past tense. My ears filled with fluid and I began hearing only muffled sound bites. Absently, I reached out and grabbed a mini Hershey bar. They were small, so I took two.

"Brandy, I'm not trying to make excuses or make you feel uncomfortable. I'm just trying to be honest, here. I guess it's about time." I shook my head to clear away the fog in my brain.

"Do you know where she is now?"

"I tracked her down in Mexicali. She has some relatives there. She said she just needed some time to cool off, and she swore she'd come back. But then she took off again." Suddenly, I remembered the conversation with my mother. But how reliable a source was Lorraine Alexander? She thought the woman came from Puerto Rico.

"Bobby, my mother ran into your wife at the airport in Florida, days ago. At least she thinks it was your wife. I'm so sorry I didn't tell you sooner. I didn't know."

"It's okay. I knew about that. A buddy of mine at the airport has been running checks for me. Plus, she's using my credit cards, so I keep tabs on her that way."

"Does she have any relatives in Philly who could help you bring her back?" He laughed ruefully.

"Her parents despise me, and her brother's as crazy as a loon. I don't want to scare her off. She calls me every few days and we talk." In the recesses of my mind I remembered a late night phone call. A woman's voice, asking for Bobby. I debated telling him about the call but decided he already had enough on his plate. "I figure I'll give her another week to see if she comes back on her own," Bobby continued, "and if not, I'll go after her. I'm not losing my kid." He had that fiercely protective look in his eye, a look that used to be reserved for me, and a flicker of jealousy reared its ugly head. I squashed it down, ashamed of myself for competing with his baby daughter. Bobby stood up and picked a Kit Kat out of the bowl. I did a quick mental calculation and decided to be generous. "Take two, they're small." He flashed me his old grin.

"You sure?" I nodded, and he stuffed a piece into his mouth before I could change my mind. "So, where do we go from here?" He asked, deftly changing the subject.

"What do you mean?"

"I believe you have information about John's death that the police don't have." I stared back at him with equal resolve.

"And what if I do? Would you blame me for not wanting to hand it over to them? How the hell am I supposed to know who to trust?" The hurt in his eyes betrayed the calm in his voice.

"You still don't trust me?" Professionally, I trusted him with my life. Emotionally, *not so much*. I answered with my heart.

"How can we talk about trust when we don't even know each other anymore?" I stood up and busied myself at the sink. Bobby climbed out of the chair and walked towards me, stopping when he was a hair's breath away. I turned and he trapped me at the sink, bracing himself with his arms on either side of me. He willed me to look at him and our eyes locked.

"I know you." His voice was low and seductive. "You can't go to bed without a night light and you talk in your sleep. You love baseball and boxing, but you only watch hockey when the Flyers are in the playoffs. Your idols are Morris Dees, Edward R. Murrow and Sandy Koufax. You won't watch the Godfather movies because you can't stand abuse of power." He leaned in even closer and I squirmed away, breaking eye contact. He held my chin in his hands forcing me to look at him. Tiny rivulets of sweat began forming between my breasts, and I tried my best to ignore it. "You cry when they play the Canadian National Anthem. Your secret fear is being an old lady and having to eat alone in a restaurant. Your favorite fictional character is Junie B. Jones. Favorite movie, Rocky, favorite book, Fried Green Tomatoes at the Whistle Stop Café. Favorite holiday, Christmas. Favorite color, green." I gulped, barely breathing.

"Red. See, you don't know me at all." Bobby pushed himself off of the counter, leaving me shaken and weak-kneed.

"You're a real ball buster, ya know that?" He stuck his hand into the candy bowl and jammed a fistful of chocolates into his pocket. A defiant, "fuck you" gesture. I stopped him before he reached the front door.

"What do you want from me, Bobby?" I looked into his eyes and his pain was palpable.

"I want to be your friend again."

The doorbell rang, effectively ending our conversation. Twin ballerinas stood at the storm door, their tutus peeking out through winter coats. Behind them stood Franny.

"Trick or Treat," they shouted in unison. Bobby brushed by them, giving a slight nod to Franny as he passed.

"Yo, Bobby, where ya running off to?"

"Got people to see, Fran." I shook my head slightly, a sign to let him go. Franny made her way through the front door as I shared my precious stash with the little girls. Three more kids showed up after that, and then things quieted down for a few minutes. I walked back into the kitchen and popped the rest of the lasagna into the microwave. I grabbed a beer out of the refrigerator for me and a soda for Franny.

"Ya want to tell me what DiCarlo was doing here, or should I guess?"

"You couldn't possibly." Franny pulled on the soda and made a face. "I want a beer."

"Nobody told you to have sex, young lady. Now you'll just have to pay the consequences." Franny answered me with her middle finger and took another swig of soda.

We managed to consume the entire pan of lasagna, while I filled her in about Bobby. I may have even mentioned the parts that I swore I wouldn't tell anyone about. But that was to be expected. I tell Franny everything.

"Oh my God, that poor guy. He never mentioned a word. Although I don't think it's much of a shock to anyone. The marriage was a mistake from the start. Well, that explains his mood lately."

"Why didn't he say anything to anyone?" I asked.

"Brandy, It's Bobby we're talking about. Mr. 'Suffer in Silence' Guy. He's not all that much different than when we were kids. If anything, he's gotten worse." She got up to go to the bathroom. "I have to pee every fifteen minutes, these days," she complained. When she returned, she picked up the dishes and began filling the sink with dish washing liquid. "Ya know, Bobby's probably confided more in you in the last hour than he has to any of us in the past four years. And if I know DiCarlo, he's blaming himself for what happened to Johnny."

"But why? He couldn't possibly have known what would happen to John."

"Eddie says it's he's got an overdeveloped sense of responsibility. Probably because he had to grow up so fast." I didn't want to talk about Bobby right now. It was too confusing. I needed some private time to think about it.

"Fran," I asked, changing the subject, "have you ever heard of a guy named Nicholas Santiago?" She thought this over for a minute.

"No, why?" So I told her. Everything. From the way he looked at me, to the way my entire body responded to the touch of his hand on the back of my neck. "Oh my God, Franny, I could like *totally* become his sex slave." Fran snorted.

"Yeah, right. How many times have you had sex since you broke up with Bobby?" I changed the subject again. Some things are just too humiliating to dwell on.

We spent the evening doling out chocolates to the neighborhood munchkins. In between, we watched Nightmare on Elm Street and then something even scarier.

"What's this?" Fran had been rummaging through my parents' videotapes, searching for something to watch. She held up a tape marked "Brandy."

"It's nothing," I said, and tried to grab the tape from her hands.

"Nothing, huh?" She held the tape high above me, taunting me with her height. I would have pushed her down, but since she was pregnant it wasn't an option. She bent over the VCR and popped the tape in.

"I hate you," I said, folding my arms across my chest. Franny grinned.

"Wow, I must've hit the jackpot." A minute later there I was, big as television life, decked out in a poodle skirt and white socks. My hair was done up in a nineteen fifties "flip," and as if that wasn't embarrassing enough, I was wearing pearls.

"This is Brandy Alexander, appearing live on the set of "American Memories," I announced in a generic voice, devoid of all regional accent. "Early Edition News

140

in L.A. will be taking you on an exclusive, 'behind the scenes' tour of this very popular show. So, stay tuned for the hula hoop contest, up next!" I ended with a toss of my hair and a big toothy grin. Franny howled with laughter.

"Hey, what'd you do with your accent? You sound like a frigggin' debutante."

"I swear to God, Franny, if you tell anyone about this, I'll spread it all over town what you did in high school with Jack Passetti, in the bathroom on prom night."

"Oh, fine," Franny relented. "But how come I never saw this? We're best friends. This is the embarrassing shit we're supposed to share with each other."

"I was going to give it to you as a wedding gift, but you've ruined the surprise."

Franny left at nine thirty p.m. We hadn't gotten any more trick or treaters in about half an hour and all the candy was gone. After she left I went in and finished cleaning up the kitchen. I let the lasagna pan soak and scrubbed the microwave, so that it didn't smell like burnt tomatoes anymore. Then, I poked my head into the freezer to see if I'd left any frozen Milky Ways in there. I like to have a bedtime snack. There weren't any, and I was really disappointed. I'd gotten my taste buds all worked up for something sweet. In the corner on the lower shelf, tucked behind some frozen broccoli, I found a plastic bag with something brick hard, inside. I took it out and examined the contents. It was my mother's famous fruitcake. She made it every Christmas, and for the entire next year it sat in the freezer until she made a replacement, at which time the old one would be thrown away. It was tradition, my mother's way of ringing in the New Year. I put the fruitcake back in the plastic bag. I wasn't that desperate… or was I? Just in case I was, I took it upstairs with me.

My plan was to climb into bed and stay there. I was going to get a good night's sleep if it killed me. Just then, the doorbell rang. I glanced at the clock. Ten thirty. "Unhhh." I padded downstairs in my bare feet and looked out the peephole. Someone was standing on the porch, wearing one of those "Scream" costumes that were popular a few years ago. He stood about five feet six, and he held a trick or treat bag in one hand and a plastic hatchet in the other. His voice was muffled behind the mask. "Trick or treat."

"I'm sorry, there's no more candy," I yelled through the door. He rang the bell again. "No more candy," I repeated.

"Trick or treat." Boy, he sure was persistent. Maybe he couldn't hear me. I opened the heavy front door, forgetting that when Franny had left I'd forgotten to lock the storm door.

"No more" —the storm door swung open with a terrifying force. I tried to slam the big wooden door shut, but he shoved it back open with his shoulder. Before I could blink, he was in the house, brandishing the hatchet. In the light of the foyer it didn't look so plastic anymore. I opened my mouth to scream, but nothing came out. At the moment the irony was lost on me, so I turned and began running haphazardly through the house, frantically searching for an escape route. My pursuer came barreling towards me, the sharp edge of the all too real hatchet narrowly missing my arm. Dizziness and nausea swept over me as I zigzagged through the dining room. My elbow banged against a dining room chair, and I grabbed the back of it and flung it at my attacker. He stopped, momentarily dazed, and I raced up the stairs two at a time. If I could just reach the bedroom, I could lock myself in and call the police. Panting, my lungs about to burst, I reached the last step. He was right behind me, so

I tucked and rolled, propelling myself into the bedroom. I kicked the door closed with my foot, grabbed the lock and twisted it. I was shaking violently as I picked up the phone to dial 911. Wham! The hatchet hit the door with unbelievable force. It splintered the wood and got stuck in there. A gloved hand reached out and smashed through the hole, unlocking the door. It swung open, and I stepped backwards towards the bed. He was panting heavily, and he smelled like grain alcohol. Through the eyeholes of his mask, two crazed eyes peered out at me. I swept the room, looking for something, anything to defend myself with. Then I saw it, the frozen fruitcake. My hand automatically reached out and grabbed it. I twisted the bag around my hand, hefting the rock solid brick into the air. I began to swing it over my head, and as it gained momentum I launched the sucker. I hit him squarely in the temple, and he went down like a sack of potatoes. I couldn't tell if he was knocked out or merely stunned, but I wasn't about to stick around to find out. I bolted down the stairs, grabbed my bag off the hallway table and blasted through the storm door.

The adrenaline rush that had gotten me out of the house began to fade. With trembling hands I unlocked Paul's car and crawled in. Locking the door behind me, I punched in 911 on the cell, and then I sat with my head between my knees and waited for the nausea to pass. About ten minutes later, although it seemed like an hour, a patrol car pulled up behind me, its headlights illuminating the inside of the car. I climbed out and walked unsteadily over to the officers. One took my statement while the other cruised the house, weapon drawn. My statement sounded ridiculous, even to me. A guy in a Halloween suit attacks me with a hatchet and I hit him with a fruitcake, rendering him unconscious. From across the street, I could see the other officer searching the grounds, his beam of light making wide circles on the lawn. In a few minutes he came over to give us an update on his findings. It was a brief report. There were no findings. The guy was gone, the hatchet was gone, and did I maybe have a little too much to drink tonight, and get into a domestic squabble with my boyfriend? I wondered if they could arrest me for saying "fuck you" to an officer of the law. I decided to take my chances. They chalked it up to "the vino talking" and encouraged me to sleep it off.

I waited for "Chief Wiggum" and his cop crony to pull away from the curb, and then, very reluctantly, I reentered the house. It was surreal. For the second time today someone had tried to kill me. I mean a person could go an entire lifetime without that happening.

Jeez, what are the odds?

I simply could not bring myself to stay here alone. I ran upstairs and began throwing clothes into an overnight bag. I would call Paul and tell him he was getting a roomie for the night. No, he wasn't up to speed on anything. Why worry him? Franny? Eddie would tell Bobby. Janine. As I debated the best person to call, I heard a soft noise behind me. Before I could turn around, a hand reached out and grabbed my shoulder and I screamed and kept on screaming. The hand clamped me on the mouth as I struggled to get away. I twisted around, freeing myself from his grasp, and then I screamed some more.

"Shut uh-up!" It was the last thing I heard before my head hit the ground.

Chapter Nine

They say that when you are about to die, your life flashes before your eyes. Maybe I was having one of those moments. I could have sworn I saw John's face; heard him tell me to "shut up" before I headed towards that final oblivision. Only I wasn't dead. My head hurt too much to be dead. And apparently, neither was Johnny. He peered down at me with grave concern.

"Brandy, for Christ's sake, get up. I need to talk to you." I forced my eyes open, willing them to focus on the figure hovering above me.

"Oh my God," I whispered. "You're alive." I scrambled to my feet and threw my arms around him, nearly knocking him over. "I can't believe it. The boat— the explosion, how did you" —My body vibrated with shock as I tried to croak out a complete sentence. John carefully disengaged my arms from around his neck and sat down on the edge of my bed. He gently pulled me down next to him. He was dressed in the same outfit he'd worn the last time I'd seen him. It was unfathomable that only two days had passed since then. His clothes were disheveled and stained and smelled like cherry tobacco. I'd never seen John look anything less than immaculate and that, more than anything, disturbed me. "Your father," I started. "Does he know? We have to call him."

"He knows. Sweetie," he soothed, taking my hand in his. "Calm down. I was able to get through to my dad last night."

"Last night? Oh." Suddenly, my concern turned to fury. I yanked my hand away from his. "Why didn't you call me, you little shit? Do you have any idea how devastated I was?" The dam burst and I was crying my heart out. Tears of joy, and anger and mostly relief streamed down my face, onto my shirt. He waited a few minutes while I went into the bathroom for some tissue. I came back with a handful of wadded up toilet paper and sat down again, dabbing at my nose.

"Are you done?" He inquired.

"I think so."

"Ya know it's so typical of you, Brandy. I'm almost blown to smithereens, and you make it all about you!"

"Well," I countered, not to be outdone, "I didn't have the easiest night either, ya know. Somebody tried to kill me too."

"Get out!" I nodded.

"With a hatchet."

"Wow." He lay back on the bed, contemplating this. I lay back too, and gazed up at the ceiling.

"I wonder if it was the same guy who blew up the boat."

"I don't know. Maybe." I shrugged. "I seem to be pissing off a lot of people lately." Bobby wasn't too thrilled with me when he left tonight, but he wasn't high on my list of suspects. An image of Raoul flashed though my mind, and I wondered if he could be my night

146

stalker. They were about the same height, and he did have a penchant for sharp, shiny objects. Then there was whoever was after Johnny. Maybe they decided to make me a target too. John and I continued to lie on the bed, staring into space.

It was a mere stroke of hypochondria that saved John from being blown to bits. After I'd dropped him off at the Marina on Saturday, John and Joel got ready to set sail. But at the last minute John realized he didn't have his Dramamine, plus he had a headache, and he was too cold, he'd forgotten to bring a heavy jacket. Joel was justifiably annoyed, so to placate him John offered to let Joel take the boat out by himself. An avid sailor, Joel jumped at the chance, and they agreed to meet back at the Marina later on. John got off the boat and wandered around the Marina for a while. He tried to call me to have me pick him up, but his cell phone chose that moment to perform the death rattle. He had his camera with him, so he figured he'd just use the opportunity to cruise around on his own a bit, taking pictures of the boats on the water.

"I was adjusting the lens when all of a sudden my boat goes up in flames. I was completely freaked out; I didn't know what to do. And that's when I saw this guy, standing over on the pilings, staring out to sea. He looked familiar, like I should know him, but I didn't. He had this look on his face. It was bizarre. Like he was getting off on the explosion. I kind of shrank back against some fencing and watched him. After a few minutes, he walked off towards the parking lot and got in a black Ford Explorer and drove away. I swear to God, Brandy, it was the same car that's been following me around, and I knew then and there that the explosion was no accident."

"Did you get a picture of the guy?" John shook his head.

"I didn't think of it until it was too late."

"Well, why did you take off? You could've waited for me, or found a phone, or" —

"Brandy, honey, do you really think I was thinking rationally at that point? I didn't know if that guy had friends. I had to get away fast, before anyone recognized me."

"You must have been so scared," I said, quietly. And suddenly, I was crying again.

We held each other for a long time, nursing invisible wounds.

"I called you as soon as I could, you know." I nodded in understanding. John stood up and stretched. "Listen, I'll tell you the rest a little later. Right now, I could really use a shower and some clean clothes." He walked over and examined the splintered bedroom door. "Oh my God, you weren't kidding about the hatchet, were you?"

"Take your shower. I have a feeling this is going to be a long night."

My dad had some old sweat pants in the back of his closet. I pulled them out, along with a thermal undershirt. They were about three sizes too big for John, and definitely not his preferred mode of dress, but it was either that or my mom's flannel nightgown. I guess I could have offered him one of my sweat outfits, but they were all in the laundry. When he came out of the bathroom, he looked more refreshed and didn't smell like cherry tobacco anymore.

We sat in the kitchen and drank peppermint tea while I caught him up on everything that had happened. Then it was John's turn. He'd taken a cab to the boardwalk and bought himself some cheap sunglasses and a baseball cap. Then he holed up in one of the lesser-known casino hotels and waited it out. He figured if enough time elapsed he could sneak back to town and let us know he was safe.

"There were a couple of hang ups on my message machine."

"That was me. I didn't want to talk. I just wanted to make sure you were home so I could come by. I was working on complete paranoia, thinking they'd tapped your phone. That, by the way, is how I figure they knew I'd be taking my boat out on Saturday. Remember I told you I'd been hearing weird clicks on my line? I'm sure it was tapped."

"So, how did you get back here?" John rolled his eyes and let out an exaggerated sigh.

"I think that was the most harrowing part of all," he announced, dramatically. "I took the gray panther special." I choked back a laugh as he continued. "Two hours trapped on a bus with people who talked about their bowel movements as if they were delivering the State of the Union Address." I laughed out loud at that. I couldn't help it.

We stayed up half the night, talking. Images of exploding boats and hatchet wielding maniacs haunted me, rendering me too terrified to close my eyes. And to top it off, the cops didn't believe me. I'd grown up thinking the police were our friends, and rationally I knew we were only talking about a handful of bad apples. But this wasn't a rational world I was living in, these days. All I knew was the people who were supposed to be there to protect and serve me did neither. And there was a good chance they were the very people I needed protecting from.

John had the added burden of guilt. "If I hadn't let Joel take the boat, he'd still be alive."

"And if Daniel had never been born he wouldn't have had a thirtieth birthday party, and this whole stinking mess never would have happened. Don't go there, John. What happened to Joel is not your fault." We focused instead on what we should do next. Did we dare tell any of our friends that he was back from the grave? Of course he'd told his dad. But what about Paul and the rest of our friends? "If you tell one, you might as well tell them all," I reminded him. "You know there's no such thing as a secret in this crowd. Besides, they all love you. They need to know you're okay." John gave me a blank look.

"Does that include Bobby?" I considered this.

"Yeah," I said, finally. "It does." Bobby would be over the moon to know John was alive, and God knows he could use some good news. I believed Bobby when he said he wasn't into any illegal activities, and I know he finally believed me about there being dirty cops on the force. Hell, he'd admitted he had his own suspicions. I just didn't know how ready he was to keep secrets from his superior officers. Was he willing to risk his career, or worse to help me find out the truth? Which brought up another question. How willing would he be to work with me to find Konner Novack's murderer and the people who were after John? For some reason Bobby didn't exactly view me as an equal in the criminal investigation department. "I need to toughen up my image," I mused, aloud. "Maybe I should start carrying a gun."

"I'm sure there's a logical explanation for the most asinine statement you've ever made, but it eludes me right now," John yawned. I made two fists and began shadow boxing all around his head. "Hey, cut it out."

"If I'm going to be working undercover, I've got to get in shape." I threw a right punch over his shoulder. He ducked and rolled off the bed.

"You're really enjoying yourself, aren't you!" I held up my hand, pinching the thumb and index finger together.

"*A little bit.* Look, I started out with the purest of intentions, but now that I know you're okay, I don't have to feel guilty about thinking this is **the most exhilarating thing I've ever done in my life!**" I jumped on the bed and did a little victory dance on the mattress.

"You're a sick woman, Alexander."

At eight a.m. the doorbell rang. We'd just crawled into bed at around five, and I'd barely had time to go through a REM cycle, when the ringing turned to pounding at the door. I nudged John off the bed and he groaned some creative curses at me. "Just get in the bathroom," I hissed, grabbing his arm and pulling him down the hall.

Nervously, I peeked out the spy hole. It was Bobby. Again. I opened the door. "This is getting to be a regular habit with you, DiCarlo." He didn't wait for an invitation. He walked right into the house and headed straight for the kitchen. "Hey. Where do you think you're going?"

"Ya have any coffee?" He began opening and closing cupboards. I reached up and pulled some Folgers from a shelf. I set it down on the counter and began measuring out some scoops.

"I thought you were mad at me."

"I was." He pulled the pot off of the base, and filled it with water.

"So then why are you here?" I began scrounging around the kitchen for something to serve with the coffee. My mother would be appalled if I didn't offer him a snack. My thoughts wandered to the fruitcake.

"I was worried about you." I must've looked at him funny, because he explained. "When I got to work this morning some of the guys were just getting off shift, and they were talking about a call that came in last night. Seems some whacked out sugar junkie had a fight with her boyfriend and started making noises that an ax murderer was trying to kill her."

"So you automatically assumed it was me?"

"It was the part about the fruitcake that gave it away. Always the best part of an Alexander Christmas." I sat down on a chair, elbows on the table, chin in hands and cursed softly.

"Great. So now I'm the talk of the precinct." Bobby pulled out the chair next to me and sat down. He threw a comforting arm around my shoulder.

"You want to tell me what happened?" I did want to. I wanted to tell him every scary thing and have him scoop me up in his arms and hold me and never let me go. Instead, I shook my head, no.

"Believe it or not, there's something more pressing we have to discuss. I got up from the table. "I'll be right back."

Two minutes later I was downstairs again, with Johnny in tow. Bobby did a double take, and then he whooped for joy and lifted John in a huge bear hug. There was much backslapping and a lot of "Jesus Christs" and then for the next hour, we talked. Bobby wanted to know everything, down to the minutest detail. He asked for a description of the guy who had come to see John and had taken the pictures. John did the best he could, but it didn't ring any bells for Bobby. They went over and over the scant information, but they kept coming up empty. I broke down and told Bobby about having copies of the infamous pictures. Predictably, Bobby wanted me to hand over the pictures to him and bow out of the investigation.

"This is not up for discussion, Sweetheart. There are two men dead already, and you and John are on the short list."

"But why would I be a target? It doesn't make sense." Bobby's blue eyes contracted under a deep scowl.

"All the more reason for you to stay out of this. Maybe you asked the wrong questions to the wrong people and somebody got wind of it. I don't know. But you obviously pissed off somebody enough that they came after you with an ax."

"Actually, it was a hatchet." He gave me a look that said he'd like to take a hatchet to me. I really had to stop doing that.

"Whatever. Listen, I can understand you not trusting the police. Until we know who's dirty, no one is beyond suspicion. But that doesn't mean you can start nosing around on your own. You're not a professional, and you could get yourself killed."

"Look," I said, trying to reassure him. "What are you getting so worked up about? I'm just asking a few questions, is all." Bobby's face began to flush under his tan. I knew this look, and it did not bode well for me.

"What do I need to do to get through to you?" He asked in a tightly controlled voice. "This isn't a fucking game." He turned his back to me and addressed John. "Talk some sense into her, will you? She sure as hell won't listen to me."

"And what makes you think she'll listen to me?" John asked. "Once she gets the bit in her teeth, she's like a pit bull hanging on for dear life." I shot John a murderous look. *Traitor.*

"*Hello*, I'm still in the room. You don't have to talk about me as if I'm not here." I sat back, pouting. Bobby pushed his chair away from the table and stood up. A look of impassivity settled on his face. Immediately I was on my feet as well, refusing to allow him the dominant position. John shifted his gaze from Bobby to me, enjoying this test of wills.

"Brandy," Bobby said with infuriating calm, "I'm afraid you're leaving me with no choice. Either you butt out of this investigation and let me handle it, or I'll arrest you for withholding evidence. I swear to God I will."

"You wouldn't dare." I stood, facing him, hands on my hips, defying him to keep his word. In one deft move Bobby grabbed my arms and swung them behind my back. In a flash, he reached into his back pocket with his free hand, pulled out a pair of handcuffs and slapped them onto my wrists.

"You have the right to remain silent." Johnny's jaw dropped in utter amazement.

"Let me go, you jerk! Oh, you are *so* going to pay for this, DiCarlo." I began twisting back and forth, trying to shake myself from his grasp, which only made him tighten his hold on me.

"Do I have to add threatening a peace officer to these charges?" He asked. I wrenched around to get a good look at his face. It was almost a blank slate, but I thought I detected the barest hint of a smile. In a blaze of fury I stretched my leg back and kicked him in the shin. Unfortunately, I was barefoot, so he hardly felt it at all, but it really hurt my big toe.

"You're just racking up the points, sweetheart. Assaulting an officer. Nice one." He began hauling me towards the front door, with me kicking and screaming all the way.

"Won't this give Mrs. Gentile something juicy to talk about over coffee cake?" He said, pleasantly. John chased us through the dining room and stopped short in front of the door.

"Will you two just STOP IT? You're acting like a couple of ten year olds."

"Well, he started it," I said, sulkily, but I stopped struggling. I was tired and I just wanted to go back to sleep.

"Bobby, take those stupid cuffs off of her. You're not going to be safe in your own bed at night if you keep pissing her off like this." Warily, Bobby removed the cuffs, keeping a respectful distance from my feet.

"Look, do you think I want to treat you this way?" He said quietly. I just don't know what the hell else to do to get you to back off." I rubbed my wrists dramatically, as if I were in a great deal of pain. I may have even winced.

"I'll get you the pictures." I turned and walked upstairs. John and Bobby exchanged incredulous looks.

"What's the catch?" Bobby asked, when I returned. I plunked the photos down in front of him.

"No catch." I opened the front door. "Drop me a postcard some time and let me know how your investigation's going." Bobby pulled the door out of my hand and closed it. "Now what?"

"I don't like this," he said.

"You wanted me to butt out—I'm out. Jeez, there's just no pleasing some people." Ignoring me, Bobby did one of those exasperated air blows and turned to John.

"Lay low, John. I'm going to arrange a safe house for you. Not through the cops," he added. "And don't tell anyone you're back." This time John and I exchanged looks. "Oh Christ, who have you told? Never mind, I'm sure I can guess." He gave John one last hug, glared at me and left.

Late afternoon sunlight cast an eerie glow as shriveled pumpkins littered the streets. The day after Halloween is depressing; no candy, no costumes, and only a bunch of sad looking Jack O'Lanterns, their shriveled, moldy faces the only visible remains of the day. I didn't even want to go out. I was scared. Terrified, was more like it, of leaving the relative safety of my home. The only reason I felt safe inside after all that had happened is I blamed my own stupidity. Hatchet Guy didn't break in. I had practically issued him an engraved invitation. But outside, who knew what hidden dangers lurked.

"Oh, Hi, Mrs. Gentile. Sorry about yesterday. I was feeling a little under the weather." Mrs. Gentile had emerged from her den at the same time I opened my front door. She cast me her version of the evil eye, which is really hard to do when you have a unibrow, and began depositing her Halloween pumpkins into a trash bag. I often wondered what compelled her to partake of the traditional pumpkin carving ritual. She seemed to glean no joy from life, and yet her holiday spirit was limitless. By tomorrow, she would have the "First Thanksgiving" displayed on her tiny lawn, replete with little plastic pilgrims and Indians and a horn of plenty that took up half the neighborhood. I think the competition is what really drives her. The people on the other side of her are growing their own corn.

John and I decided that I should deliver the good news to everyone, personally. We didn't trust the phone lines, and I thought a parade of people coming over to the house would raise suspicions, in case it was being watched. Besides, this was bound to be a shock. I wanted to be sure to break the news gently. So I called Paul to tell him I was coming over. He sounded really pleased to hear from me. I know how concerned he'd been about me, and

I think too, he missed his car. I told him we'd be over in about an hour, "we" being me and the Mercedes.

The car seemed none the worse for wear from its little trip to the "car pokey." I pulled up outside Paul's house and parked. Suddenly, Paul appeared at the door. He came out to greet me as I climbed out of the front seat. As he approached, little furrows began to form on his forehead. He walked up to the car and stuck his head under the front end. Paul is growing a goatee, and it's in that awkward, in between stage where it looks like he'd stuck his face in a cup of chocolate pudding, and it left a ring around his mouth. He rubbed his chin and scratched himself, absently. I began to get nervous.

"What did you do to my car?" He asked, his voice an octave higher than usual. He was trying really hard to sound casual, but it put a strain on his vocal chords.

"What do you mean?" He beckoned me with his finger, inviting me to take a look under the front end. Oh Shit. There was a little scrape of paint, about the size of a thumbnail, where the tow truck had attached itself. "I don't see anything."

"Really? It's right there, plain as day."

"John's alive!" I blurted out. Anything to get the heat off me.

Frank was next. I pulled into the gym parking lot and glanced around quickly as I got out of the car. The gym was noisy and hot. Large, sweaty men in boxing trunks danced in front of mirrors, sparring with invisible partners. In the center ring, two young men in their early twenties took turns pummeling each other with equal parts bravado and muscle. One of them reminded me of Bobby when he was that age, all raw energy and untrained talent. Uncle Frankie stood off to the side, watching them. He looked up when he heard his name and smiled at me in greeting. "Remind you of anyone?" He asked, thrusting his chin towards the kid in the black trunks. I kissed him on the cheek and stood watching a moment too. "I've got to talk to you, Frankie. Can we go into your office?" Concern flashed across his handsome face. "Are you all right? You didn't do anything to Paul's car, did you?" I laughed. "The car is fine. I'm fine, but there's something you should know."

I saved Franny and Janine for last. We agreed to meet for an early dinner at a little Mexican restaurant near Fran's office. Janine had been out researching jobs all day and was in the neighborhood. I arrived shortly after they did and sat down next to Janine in the black naughahyde booth. Fran was sipping a coke, while Janine wrestled with a Margarita the size of her head. I eyed the Margarita longingly and then ordered a root beer. After all, I had to have my wits about me when I met up with Nick, later. I guess almost getting hauled off to jail by one's ex boyfriend isn't the deterrent Bobby had been hoping it would be. The way I figured it, "almost" doesn't count.

Janine took a sip of her drink. She had to stand up to get a decent angle on it.

"What's with you two?"

"What do you mean?" We asked, all wide-eyed innocence. The waiter strolled over carrying a basket of hot, greasy chips and salsa. The salsa looked like the kind that comes out of a jar from the supermarket. He plunked it down in front of us and I stuck my nose up close and sniffed. Store brand, at that. Yuck. One thing they do have in L.A. is good Mexican food. I shrugged and dipped my chip.

"Why didn't you order a real drink?"

"This is a real drink." She turned to Franny.

"Now *you* I can understand, what with you being pregnant and all."

"Excuse me?" Said Fran, her eyes nearly popping out of her head. She kicked me under the table, hard.

"Ow!"

"Don't go kicking her, Franny. She didn't tell me. I'm your twin, for God's sake. We have that special twin thing between us. You didn't think I would instinctively know about this?"

"Eddie opened his big mouth, didn't he?"

"Yeah, he did," Janine squealed. She reached across the table to embrace her sister. "Oh my God, Oh my God, I'm going to be an aunt!"

"Okay, Neenie," Fran said, invoking Janine's childhood nickname. Just don't tell mom."

"Yeah, I know," Janine said, rolling her eyes. "She thinks you're a virgin." I reached over and grabbed another grease-laden chip and popped it into my mouth, washing it down with root beer. "Okay, so what's *your* excuse?" And so I told them.

John was asleep in my parents' room, when I got back. I tried to take a nap as well, but I was too keyed up to sleep. Besides, I wasn't that anxious to close my eyes. Vivid scenes of last night kept running through my head like a grade B slasher movie. Only, I was in the starring role. Sometimes I wondered if I'd ever feel safe again. Which led me to ponder why on God's earth I would keep pursuing this. As Bobby pointed out, John was alive, I'm not a professional crime fighter, and if the truth be known, I am just about the most chicken hearted person I know. It is totally in my nature to run away from danger. Let someone else deal with the murderers, rapists, and general miscrants of society. Why then did I embrace this as my personal raison d'etre? And all I could come up with to explain it to myself was a line of dialogue from On the Waterfront, where Marlon Brando says, "I could have been a contender. I could have been somebody." I guess I didn't want to live my life wondering if I could have been more than the girl in the poodle skirt, chasing down the ridiculous entertainment story, hula hooping her way to t.v. stardom. I wanted to know what it's like to feel proud of myself. I wanted to contribute something of value. I wanted to be somebody.

John awoke at a little after seven p.m. I was standing in the kitchen making a grilled cheese sandwich when he stumbled in. He was still in my father's enormous sweat pants, which made him look like he was shrinking. He sat down at the table and eyed the sandwich. "Is that for me?" He asked, hopefully. I sighed. "It is now." I make the world's best grilled cheese sandwiches. I use white cheddar and sour dough bread, lots of butter, and if I really want to get fancy I add roasted red peppers for extra flavor. I moved it off the pan onto a plate and put it down in front of him. "Oh, I couldn't eat your dinner," he protested. But he picked up the sandwich and began munching away. "This is amazing."

"I know," I answered, sadly. There wasn't enough time to make another one. I had to get ready to go meet Nick.

"When did you get back?" John asked, wiping the grease off his chin, and making utterly obscene noises over the sandwich.

"About an hour ago."

"Did you sleep?" I shook my head, no. He opened his mouth to comment and I could see he was revving up for a real "mommy" lecture. I stopped him with my hand to his shoulder. "I can't, John. Not yet. When I'm tired enough it'll happen."

"And what if it doesn't?"

"Then I'll go talk to somebody. I promise." In Los Angeles, anybody who's anybody has a therapist. Well, that and a personal trainer.

While John ate I finished cleaning up the kitchen and filled him in on my afternoon. Everybody wanted to see him, but they understood the importance of keeping a distance.

"I hate to leave you alone, tonight." I said. John looked up.

"Where are you going?"

"I told you, I'm meeting Nick and we're going to the club to show the pictures around."

"But you gave the pictures to Bobby."

"That's right," I smiled. He thought about this for a minute.

"You made another copy." I smiled again. "I suppose it would be pointless to try and talk you out of this."

"I suppose it would. So what do I wear to a joint like this?" I said, changing the subject. "Should I slick my hair back and do the macho-chic look, or do I dress up for the occasion, maybe go with the whole Liza Minelli cabaret thing." John looked like he was about to gag on his last bite of sandwich.

"How about you go with a paper bag over your head and under no circumstances mention that we know each other."

"Now is that nice? And after I fed you and everything." I decided to play it very understated, and just went with a fresh pair of jeans and a sweater. Big surprise.

Chapter Ten

When I pulled up at the curb of Nick's studio, the light was on, but with the mirrored window I couldn't see inside. No way was I getting out of the car unless I was sure he was in there, so I kept the engine running and pawed through my bag until I came up with his phone number. I got out my cell and called him. Nick answered on the second ring. His voice was low and sleepy and thoroughly seductive, and I felt a sudden tingling sensation in my lower regions. Damn, this was starting to become a habit.

"Um, Nick?" I said, brightly. "It's Brandy."

"Hey," came his soft reply, and it sounded like he was smiling. "Where are you?"

"Parked outside." There was a moment of silence as he disconnected, and then the door opened and he beckoned me forward.

He was wearing a black silk shirt, opened at the top, and charcoal colored pants. His hair was tied in a loose ponytail, so that the ends were all wild and sticking out. A long strand flopped over his eye and he brushed it out of the way, loosening the rubberband so that his hair fell softly around his face. As I began to walk toward him, shyness overtook me. He really was beautiful. I don't mean your every day pretty boy model type. I'd seen enough of those in Hollywood to last until the next millennium. No, there was a tangible aura about this man, an almost hypnotic quality that reached out and grabbed at my heart. The more I tried to relax the more I felt myself stiffen, until I was walking like a tin soldier in a tiny pretend parade.

He kept his eyes on me the entire time; gorgeous, almond shaped eyes that crinkled when he smiled. He was clean-shaven, and he smelled faintly of cologne, something exotic and wonderful. He was still wearing the silver band around his wrist and the tiny silver cross, but now he also wore a thin silver chain around his neck. I finally reached the door, and he stepped aside to let me in. He looked like a really well dressed Adonis, while I had the appearance of a fourteen year old, just getting back from a pep rally. It made me wish I had gone with the whole Liza Minelli extravaganza.

I walked into the studio. The entire room was comprised of mirrors, which only accentuated how dorky I felt. Now I could criticize myself from every angle. Nick sensed my discomfort and seemed amused by it.

"So," I said, folding my arms across my chest in a vain attempt at casualness, "Are you ready to roll?" Oh my God, who was writing my dialogue? Starsky and Hutch?

"Just about. I've just got to grab my keys and my wallet. Come on back with me."

I followed him into his office. As he picked up his keys from the desk, his phone rang. He scanned the caller

I.D. "Sorry," he said, gesturing for me to take a seat. "I've got to take this."

"Do you want me to wait outside?" He shook his head no, so I sat back in the comfy red velvet chair and pretended I wasn't listening in. He was talking to someone named Vanessa, asking her how she felt and what her plans were for tomorrow. He sounded all sexy and flirty, and it made me wonder if she was his girlfriend. No, Nick didn't strike me as the type to limit himself to one woman. He probably had dozens lined up at his door, so that when he got tired of one, he could just usher in the next one. She was probably gorgeous though, with long legs and shiny hair. I'll bet Vanessa wouldn't have shown up on his doorstep tonight wearing some infantile outfit. She would have gone with some backless, slinky dress with a slit up the side, to accentuate her long legs. God, I was really beginning to hate her.

I was so busy fantasizing about the faceless woman on the other end of the line that I didn't realize Nick had hung up the phone. He was leaning against his desk, watching me. A smile played at his lips. "You're looking mighty intense there, angel. Wanna share your thoughts?"

"Oh," I said. My face started to flush and I was really grateful for the low lighting. "I was just thinking about eggplant." I really did have to stop going with the first thought that popped into my head. Now I was stuck with it.

"Eggplant."

"Yeah, there are so many ways to prepare it, you know."

"Really. I didn't know eggplant was so versatile." I couldn't think how to follow that up, so I just worked my way out of the chair. Nick extended his hand to help me. It was strong and warm and I held it a little longer than necessary. "Oh, by the way," he said, "I took the liberty of checking out that cop friend of yours. Seems like a good guy by all accounts, but he's been under a lot of stress, lately." I stared at him, open-mouthed.

"You had him investigated?"

"Look, if we're going to do this, then we have to do it right. There are a lot of things you may find distasteful, but it's part of the job. So if you want to bow out, let me know now." His voice was hard and scary, but I knew he was right.

"No, I understand."

"I'm sorry. I should have figured you wouldn't be thrilled with this. I have you pegged as a pretty loyal friend, and I should have known that spying on DiCarlo wouldn't feel right to you. Oh, and FYI, he had you followed."

"I know. He told me." Now it was Nick's turn to be surprised.

"You two have some weird relationship going on?"

"Define 'weird'." Nick threw back his head and laughed. He had a great laugh.

His car was parked around back. It was a nineteen sixty-four hunter green XKE Jaguar, in mint condition. Paulie would absolutely flip out if he saw it. "You actually drive this thing?" He opened the door for me and I slid into the seat. I reached over and pushed open the driver's side door for him.

"Thanks. Yeah, why not?"

"Because it's so rare, and beautiful and expensive!"

"Somebody told me it once belonged to George Harrison."

"And it belonged to a Beatle!" Nick shrugged. I really like the car. I would miss not driving it." Was this man for real?

On the way over to the club I told him about John's triumphant return. "And you still want to track down this murderer?"

"Look, someone tried to kill John. It was just dumb luck that he didn't. Oh, and by the way, someone tried to kill me too." It took me ten minutes to get out the entire story. I tried to stay calm and impassive, but by the end my hands were shaking so hard I had to sit on them. "Maybe someone found out that I'd seen the pictures and now they want me dead too."

"No, this doesn't sound like a professional job. You said the guy smelled like he'd been drinking, right?" I nodded. "A pro wouldn't go off to whack someone, tanked on a bottle of rye. This sounds more personal." Comforting thought.

"What about Raoul?" I asked. I mean I did accidentally run over his hand."

"Makes sense. After all, it wouldn't be the first time. I'll check it out."

Bank Street sits between Market and Vine. It's a narrow, two block stretch that dead ends into a homeless mission. Bank Street is a magnet for winos, junkies and hard-core sexual deviants, all of whom find whatever they're in search of, there, in great abundance.

The Leather Factory is located on the northeast corner of Bank and Rose. Its large, neon sign features a rather graphic rendition of the good time to be had inside, if one were drunk, gay and prone to bondage. For people like Johnny and his friends, mainstream, middle class gays, The Leather Factory is a harmless walk on the wild side. But for others, it is a way of life, and occasionally, death.

On the ride over to the club I started to get nervous. I mean here I was sitting in a car with a virtual stranger, on our way to some sleazy S&M porn festival to catch a killer. No one knew where I was except for John, who, until recently, had been dead. I glanced over at Nick. He drove with his head back against the headrest, one hand lightly holding the gearshift. He seemed very relaxed; not at all concerned about the adventure we were about to embark on. Maybe he was too comfortable. Maybe this was, God forbid, his *element.* Who *is* this guy, anyway? What do we really know about him? Okay, Carla met him through her cousin Benny, and Benny said he was cool. But Benny's last known job was pounding out license plates for the state of Pennsylvania, so I don't know how much stock to put into his opinion. Plus, I really couldn't figure out why he'd agreed to help me. I mean what I could offer him in monetary compensation, he could make in a minute in illegal gun sales to El Salvador, or whatever rebel country he was supposedly in cahoots with. We weren't blood related, so he wasn't bound by family guilt to help me, so that just left sexual favors. Now, the general consensus would probably be that I'm passably cute, but I'm not exactly the stuff wet dreams are made of. So I doubted he was going to all this trouble just to get me into bed. It just didn't make sense to me, and when I don't understand something, it makes me really, really nervous. And for the first time since I started this whole idea of "Brandy Alexander, Crime Fighter at Large" I began to think that maybe I was in a little over my head. I bit my lip hard to keep from crying.

Nick reached across the console and I flinched involuntarily. He gave me a quizzical look and popped open the glove compartment. "Sorry," I whispered. "I guess I'm a little nervous. It's not every day I get to drive in a car that used to belong to a Beatle."

"Are you sure that's all it is?" He leaned in and extracted a CD and closed the glove compartment again. I shook my head. I was so damn tired, and all I'd eaten was a bunch of chips and some third rate salsa. Hunger and exhaustion tend to make me embarrassingly honest.

"I'm scared." He brought his arm up and gently ruffled my hair.

"Good. Like I told you before, you should be. It'll keep you on your toes."

What I didn't tell him was what I was most afraid of was him. I figured he knew that already.

Nick approached the entrance of the club, while I trailed behind like a shy kindergartener hiding behind its mother on the first day of school. The bouncer, an enormous, well-muscled guy in a black tank top, eyed Nick with a mixture of curiosity and lust. Nick nodded his head in greeting. The bouncer moved slightly out of the way to allow Nick to brush past him, and then he turned his attention to me.

"I'll need to see an I.D., little girl." I started to protest, but Nick put an arm around my shoulder and bent down to speak into my ear.

"Show the nice man your I.D., honey." I elbowed his arm off me and rooted around in my bag until I found my wallet, muttering the whole time about discrimination and whatever other social injustice I could come up with. "Kids." Nick shrugged congenially to the bouncer, and they shared a conspiratorial smirk. Seething, I whipped out my California driver's license. It was taken four years ago, when I truly did look sixteen. The bouncer made a big show of studying my picture, and then he asked me what year I was born. This amused Nick no end. When the bouncer had exhausted all possible ways to humiliate me, he stepped aside and bowed, letting me pass.

"I'm glad you thought it was funny," I fumed, stuffing my wallet back into my bag.

"He was just doing his job, angel, protecting the innocent."

"I'm not all that innocent," I grumbled. "I've been around, you know." Nick looked at me fondly, the way a father would look at his daughter. Oh crap. He couldn't be more than thirty- two, only four years older than I am, and paternal feelings were definitely not the kind I wanted to inspire in him. A stab of disappointment stuck me in the gut, and I just wanted to go home. Instead, I pushed forward, swinging my hips in what I hoped was a saucy and seductive fashion. Of course, I ended up tripping over the carpet and knocking into a six foot two transvestite wearing a hot pink leotard. Nick grabbed me around the waist and steered me towards the bar. "Wait here," he said.

"Where are you going?"

"To the men's room. Wanna come?"

"No thanks," I smiled weakly. While Nick was gone, I looked around. It was dark, lit primarily with weird strobe lighting. The music was blaring; some obscure group that must have had its hey day in the disco era. I found it very disorienting. The bartender approached and asked me what I wanted to drink. I ordered a bottled water, not trusting the sanitary condition of the glasses. Nick came back and took the seat next to me. My cell phone began to ring and I found it at the bottom of my pocketbook. I stuck the phone to one ear and put my finger in the other to block out the noise.

"Hello?"

"It's Bobby. Where are you?"

"Out." I was still royally pissed at him for cuffing me.

"I can hear that. Out, where?"

"Why? Last time I checked, I wasn't under house arrest. Are you planning to come by and handcuff me?" Nick raised an eyebrow at that. I turned away from him and spoke into the phone. "Why are you calling?"

"I found a place for our friend to stay," he said cryptically.

"Oh." That was good news for John, but I would miss his company. "That's great."

"So, are you out with Fran and Janine?"

"No."

"Do you really think it was such a great idea for you to go out alone tonight, what with all that's been going on?" How dare he lecture me? I was this short of yelling, "You're not the boss of me" into the phone. *And* he assumed I was alone!

"Listen, I've got to go. My *date's* waiting for me." I sneaked a surreptitious look at Nick, but he seemed to be absorbed in his own thoughts.

"Did you say you were on a date?" He didn't sound pleased. Good.

"I'll call you when I get home. Gotta go." And I hung up.

"So, we're on a date, are we?" Nick flashed me that lopsided grin, as I turned bright red.

"It's a long story."

"I've got time." I shook my head to dismiss the conversation and leaned over the bar to catch the bartender's attention. "Bloody Mary, please." Nick held up his hand and gestured to make that two. In retrospect, I probably should not have ordered a drink. I did it because I thought it would relax me, and because I was mad at Bobby, and because I felt so young around Nick and I thought I'd feel more grown up with a grown up drink in my hand. All very mature reasons. However, I failed to take into consideration the fact that I hadn't slept in days, I was drinking on an empty stomach and alcohol makes me uninhibited in ways only my best friends should ever be a witness to. Ah, hindsight. What a wonderful thing. I pulled out the pictures that John had taken and handed them to Nick.

"So, where do we start?"

Half an hour later we struck pay dirt. We had been circling the bar, chatting with the more ostentatious patrons, the ones with the whips and chains and other obvious signs of interest in domination-submission activities. Most of the people were understandably reluctant to talk to two strangers. But then Nick ran across an acquaintance and he paved the way for us by vouching for Nick. He took out the pictures and showed them to a group of men. They passed the photos around, looking intently at each one and clucking sympathy for the fate of Konner Novack. After a moment one of the men zeroed in on one particular picture. "I know this guy. He's a real sick bastard, if you ask me." My heart started racing. Finally, we were getting somewhere.

"Who is he?" I asked, pointing to the man in the photo, sitting next to Novack.

"Not him," said the guy. "Him." He pointed to a fuzzy shot of a thin, sandy haired man seated at one of the tables in the background. He had a drink to his lips, and he was turned to another man, whose face was obscured by the sandy haired man's head. "He picked up a friend of mine one night, at a club out in Jersey. Beat him senseless. Almost killed him."

"Do you have a name?" Nick asked.

"No, but if you hang on a minute, I may be able to get one for you." Nick and I nursed our drinks while the guy punched in some numbers on his cell phone. Actually, Nick was nursing. I was guzzling. The salsa had made me really thirsty. I finished my Bloody Mary just as the guy disconnected on his phone call.

"That was my friend. He says the guy's name is Curtis Maitlin. Or at least that's what he told him it was."

"Why didn't your friend report the beating to the police?" I wondered. He looked at me with an indulgent smile.

"Our lifestyle doesn't exactly lend itself to um, shall we say, complete disclosure? My friend and I are both teachers, and if word got out about our extra curricular activities, well, you can see it might present a problem." As in "you'll never teach in *this* town, again." Wow, this guy in a spiked choke chain and leather chaps is a teacher? It was hard to picture him discussing the effects of the Industrial Revolution with a class full of ninth graders. Nick reached into his wallet and extracted a business card. It was black with silver printing, and it had "Nicholas Santiago Enterprises" etched on it. I wondered what the enterprises might be.

"You've been really helpful. If you or your friend can think of anything else..." He passed the business card to the guy, and then he bought him and his friends a round of drinks. I was still thirsty and everybody at the bar seemed a lot less intimidating since I'd finished my Bloody Mary, so I ordered another drink too.

Nick and I found a relatively quiet booth and slid into the seats, opposite each other.

I leaned back and closed my eyes, letting the warmth of the vodka spread throughout my body.

"I can't believe it," I said. "We finally got an honest to God lead."

"You done good, Brandy Alexander." Nick leaned back in his seat, his hands fondling the straw from his drink.

"I didn't do anything." My voice sounded small and far away. The second drink had worked its way around my brain, and I hoped I didn't start saying things I'd regret later, like when I had nitrous oxide at the dentist's and told Dr. Calahan that I loved him.

"You showed up. That was really brave of you." I couldn't tell if he meant it or if he was making fun of me, and that feeling that I was going to start bawling my head off came over me again.

"You're making fun of me," I decided. His look turned serious. He leaned over the table and took the drink from my hand and held my eyes with his.

"No, I'm not. Loyalty counts with me and obviously it counts with you too. It's a rare commodity where I come from." I forced myself not to look away, my curiosity about this man growing by the minute.

"Where *do* you come from, Nick?"

"Hell's Kitchen."

"Are we speaking metaphorically here, or the neighborhood in New York?"

Nick's laugh was bittersweet.

"Both. Actually, I was born in New Orleans. My mother was French and Cherokee. My father was Columbian. They met in Louisiana. I lived there until I was twelve." He stopped abruptly, shaking his head. "Ya know what? I feel like dancing."

"Now?"

173

"Sure, why not? We scored big tonight. Let's celebrate."

I looked around the club, with its weird inhabitants and bad disco music. Now, I was all for broadening my horizons, but I wasn't quite drunk enough to broaden them with the S&M crowd. Nick sensed my reluctance.

"Not here," he said, pulling me out of the booth. "I know this place. Come on." I let him lead me through the club, past the bouncer and out the door to the car. The clock on the dashboard said eleven thirty.

"I should be home, switching channels between Leno and Letterman to see who has the better guests on," I thought, fleetingly. But the second Bloody Mary had reached my bloodstream by now and was nestled in the spot where good sense usually resided. In my defense, I did make a halfhearted attempt to protest.

"I don't know, Nick. It's kind of late."

"Where's your sense of adventure?" He challenged. "After all, we *are* on a date."

I whipped my head up, giving him the classic "deer caught in the headlights" look.

"Well, isn't that what you told DiCarlo?"

"How did you know I was talking to him?" I blushed.

"Deductive reasoning. You want to make the guy jealous, tell him you're out with another guy. I'm not about to make a liar out of you. You owe me a date."

We drove to a little Latin club down on Wingahocking. I had fallen asleep in the car on the way over and when I woke up, I found myself curled up against Nick's shoulder. He had draped an arm around me to keep me from toppling over.

"Oh, sorry." I said, acutely embarrassed. "I guess I'm a little more tired than I thought." Quickly, I pulled myself up and began running my fingers through my hair in an attempt to look more presentable. Nick pulled into the parking lot and handed the keys to the valet. The effects of the drinks were starting to wear off and gross insecurity began to set in.

"Nick, this place looks really fancy. I'm not dressed for it." I waved my hand around at the other patrons, to prove my point. Many of the women were decked out in flouncy, colorful dresses, some wore short, tight numbers with stiletto heels, all exuded sex appeal. I felt miserably out of place.

"You look fine." He picked a rose out of a vase of flowers, broke the stem in two and carefully placed the flower behind my ear. "There, now you're perfect."

People knew him at the club. The hostess came by with a bottle of very good cognac and set two glasses down in front of us. The smiles they exchanged were so intimate I almost told them to "get a room."

"Thanks, Anita," He said warmly.

"Yes, thank you, Anita," I shot her a scorching look, hoping she'd take the hint and disappear.

I didn't want to drink any more, but the booze definitely helped to drown the butterflies that kept flapping against my stomach.

"Are you hungry?" He asked me.

"No." I was starving, but I didn't think I could eat in front of him. I mean what if I got food stuck in my teeth or something? "But you go ahead and order if you're hungry."

He sipped at the cognac and settled back in his chair. I took a sip too, and a couple more after that for good measure.

"Tell me about you and the cop," he said, lazily. I felt my cheeks go red.

"There's nothing to tell."

"I think there is, and I don't want to step on anyone's toes, especially a cop's."

"Bobby's married," I blurted out.

"There are all kinds of married." Nick shrugged and took another sip of his drink. Wow. He wants to know about Bobby and me. Could Nick be interested in me? A big fat NO sprung to mind. After all, he had the long legged Vanessa to keep him warm at night. He probably just didn't want to do anything to piss off the law. I guess in his line of business that was prudent. Whatever his business *was* anyway, which I had no idea.

The music pulsated in the background, permeating the air we breathed. Nick stared at me, and I flushed under his gaze. Damn, isn't there some kind of pill you can take for congenital blushing? I shifted uncomfortably in my seat. Wordlessly, he stood and stretched his arm out to me.

"I'm not a very good dancer," I apologized.

"Neither am I," he said, as he took me in his arms. Liar.

I was melting in a sea of exquisiteness. Nick had one arm wrapped around my waist, the other one pinned to my side, our hands intertwined. I loosely hung my other arm around his shoulder, and he tightened his grip on me so that our bodies mashed against each other. My head reached the top of his chest, and I turned and buried my face in the open space of his collar. Oh my God. He smelled so good. That was no cologne, I realized. It was his natural scent. I groaned softly into the hollow of his neck. I couldn't help myself. It was like I'd been living in a sensory deprivation tank my entire life, waiting for this one moment in time. Never had I felt this turned on, this electric, this completely and overwhelmingly hormonal. I thought I was going to faint, and I would have, had Nick not had such a tight grip on me.

As the beat slowed, he slipped a leg between mine, pressing his thigh against me. Oh my God. We moved slowly around the dance floor, Nick subtly applying more pressure in between my legs, rubbing his thigh gently back and forth. He was driving me crazy and he knew it. I squeezed my legs together; a completely involuntary reaction, and let out a small moan as a shock wave rippled through my body. Oh *please* don't let him know what just happened. I will absolutely die if he knows. He tensed his thigh muscle and it happened again. I tried to pull back from him but he wouldn't let me. Turning his head he whispered in my ear. "You're a sensual woman, angel. Why hide it?" OH MY GOD! My nipples did a little salute against my sweater, as I wrenched myself from his grasp. He followed me off the dance floor and back to our seat. I grabbed my jacket and put it on, hoping to draw attention away from my boobs, which were now, thanks to him, sticking out in front like mini tent poles.

"Ya know, it's getting late and I have to get home. Thanks for the dance. It was fun."

"Fun." He cocked his head and slowly drained his cognac, never taking his eyes off of me.

"What are you staring at?" I snapped, taking a self-conscious sweep of my breasts to make sure they were behaving themselves.

"You are refreshing company," he said simply. There wasn't a hint of teasing in his voice. He took my elbow and guided me out the door.

Johnny wasn't there when I got home. He'd left a note on the kitchen table.

"Thanks for the hospitality. I owe you a hostess gift." There was a message from Bobby, as well.

"Call me." Underneath that, John had scribbled another message.

"He beat it out of me, Sunshine. Don't be mad." And underneath that, in Bobby's handwriting, "What the *hell* were you thinking?" *Oh boy.*

Nick had followed me home. I'd told him it wasn't necessary, but he said he always walks his dates to the door. I drove faster than I should have, considering I was three sheets to the wind and had forgotten my glasses, (my night vision is terrible) but he made me nervous in ways I couldn't describe, so I thought I'd better create some physical distance between us. I mean this guy was so far out of my league we weren't even playing in the same ballpark.

I parked right in front of the house and hopped out of the car. Nick pulled in behind me, so I gave a little finger wave, signaling he was free to go. Ignoring me, he climbed out of the jaguar and leaned up against the door, folding his arms across his chest. I couldn't very well leave him standing there, so I walked over to him to say goodnight. The air had turned cold, and I jammed my hands inside my pockets for warmth.

"You trying to get rid of me?" There was a hint of amusement in his voice.

"Um, sort of." He laughed out loud at that and pulled me in close to him, and for a brief, panicky moment I thought he was going to kiss me. Instead, he turned the jacket collar up around my neck and tucked my scarf inside the collar. The hairs on the back of my neck stood on end as his knuckles grazed my skin. Wow. This was getting ridiculous. I was going to have to give my libido a serious talking to in the morning. I took a step back, and as I pulled my hands out of my pockets a slip of paper fluttered to the ground. I picked it up and studied it for a moment. It was the license plate number of the black SUV I'd seen the day John picked me up from the airport. I handed it to Nick.

"I don't know if I copied this correctly, and I'm not even sure this is the same guy John saw down the shore, but it may be something."

"I'll check it out," Nick said. "And I should have some information on Maitlin within the next few days."

"Thanks. Listen, Nick, we never discussed payment, and I just want you to know that I fully intend to reimburse you for your time."

"I fully expect you will." He flashed me a smile that could melt rocks and I felt a slow spread of heat emanate from my belly down to my crotch. "In the mean time, don't answer the door to any more midnight callers. In fact, why don't you just lay low until I can get back to you?"

"Um, I don't think I can do that."

"I figured as much, but I thought it was worth a shot. Just watch your back." Nick pushed himself off the car and opened the door.

"Uh, Nick?" I was never one for leaving well enough alone, and curiosity was eating away at me, so I plunged right in. "What did you mean when you said you fully expected I'd reimburse you? I just want to make sure we're on the same page here."

"I meant just what I said, angel."

"Um, well, that doesn't really clarify it for me. I mean you seem like a really good guy and all, but" —

Nick raised a hand to my cheek and rubbed it softly with his thumb.

"Don't ever mistake me for a good guy, angel. You'll only end up surprised and disappointed." He leaned in and kissed me lightly on the mouth, and while my heart got busy remembering how to beat again, he climbed into his car and drove off.

Am I becoming a major slut or what? I mean I haven't felt this much hormonal action in four solid years, and suddenly my poor, sex starved body is lusting over every male within spitting distance. Soon I'll be hitting up Sam Giancola for a rousing game of hide the salami. Now I know what Sleeping Beauty must've felt like when she awoke from her hundred-year nap. She must've been horny as hell.

My boss called me at midnight, Los Angeles time, which made it three in the morning in Philly. Funny, how sleep deprivation seems to get in the way of a good mood.

"Gail, " I croaked. "Do you have any idea what time it is?"

"Well of course I do. I'm not an idiot. There's a three-hour time difference, so that makes it nine p.m. in Philly. Don't tell me you're in bed already." I didn't see the point in highlighting the fact that she *was* in fact an idiot, so I just asked her what she wanted.

It turned out that "Huggable Hounds," the annual canine beauty contest was being held at noon at the Philadelphia Convention Center. Our general manager thought that since it was being covered by our sister station, I could go down there and do a "cute piece" on dogs and their owners, maybe interview the Philadelphia mayor, who was the honorary Master of Ceremonies for the event.

"Gail, didn't you tell him I'm on vacation?"

"Well, yeah," she wheedled, "but you know, with budget cuts and all, it's hard to turn him down. Besides, you *are* right there, so he thought you wouldn't mind."

"I do mind. I can't believe you didn't stick up for me. I— did you say I'd be interviewing the mayor?" Okay, so I can be bought with the promise of a little prestige. So sue me.

Chapter Eleven

The Huggable Hounds show was scheduled to start at ten a.m., but I got there early to meet the crew and talk to the line producer. The way Gail had described it I was supposed to hug a few hounds, interview owners about life on the canine beauty contest fast track, and then do some dorky bit with His Honor while he bonded with Pomeranians. I couldn't believe the mayor had even agreed to this, but apparently his P.R. department felt his image needed a little sprucing up, and what better way to appear loveable than to be surrounded by man's best friend. Not everyone was buying the "warm fuzzies" routine, however.

When I pulled into the parking lot of the convention center I noticed a group of protesters from the watchdog (no pun intended) organization, Equality for Gays, milling around just outside the gate. They were carrying signs that read, "We're Gay and We Vote" and "The Conservative Right is Wrong!" A few were holding banners with pictures of Konner Novack and the John

Doe from the other unsolved case, with the slogan "Their **family values** them and so do we."

I parked the car and walked over to a young woman in her twenties, who was holding up a sign that said, "Justice for Konner Novack." I sucked in my breath. The family resemblance was uncanny.

"He was my twin brother," she told me. Her name was Lynne and she had been here since six, hoping to catch the mayor on his way in. "This administration has made no bones about their hatred of the gay community," she explained. "They couldn't care less what happens to them. I just want him to be held accountable." Her grief and frustration were heartbreaking. This was the story I should be bringing to the public, not some puff piece designed to garner the 'Poodle Lovers' vote for an ineffective mayor. Lynne Novak deserved to be heard. Maybe I could be her voice and light a fire under the mayor's office. "Lynne," I said, linking arms with her, "Ditch the sign and come with me."

They say, or at least Andy Warhol did, and I'm paraphrasing here, that everyone gets their fifteen minutes of fame. Well, make that *infamy* for Brandy Alexander, Visiting Anarchist. I swear, people are so touchy about their elected officials. I mean it's not like I *meant* to cause a riot. It all started out very cordially. I asked the mayor if he was a dog owner, (yes) which breed he preferred (They're all special in their own way—very diplomatic), and what he thought of the current pooper-scooper laws. (He'll have a committee examine the issue and get back to me on that.) He preened his way through the taped segment and kissed enough puppies to ensure his reelection clear to the next century. When tape stopped rolling, I thanked him and then introduced him to Lynne.

Okay, so maybe I should have thought this through a little before dropping a bomb on him like that, but I figured there was no time like the present, and, typically, I plunged right in. As soon as Novack's name was uttered, a swarm of reporters converged on the mayor like wolves to raw meat. Apparently, it was a major faux pas to mention a murder victim while the mayor was busy ass kissing his way into the hearts of dog lovin' Philadelphians, and they couldn't wait to see what this gauche, L.A. upstart would say next. I looked around. "Well, aren't you people at all curious as to why evidence has disappeared *twice* now in murder cases that seem to be connected?" Shit, I wasn't supposed to say that. The press reared itself up en masse and began firing questions at Richardson, who looked like he was trying really hard not to swallow his tongue. They asked him if my allegations were true. This is where it got really tricky for the mayor. If he said yes, he would appear like he was running an incompetent, and/or corrupt police department. If he said no, and it turned out to be true, he could kiss his reelection and dreams of the governorship bye-bye. He turned to me with the waxen look of someone who had spent the day being embalmed. "These are very serious charges, young lady." No duh.

"I agree, Mayor. All the more reason to take immediate action. Unless what the gay community is saying is true; that you're dragging your feet because you don't want to alienate the Extreme Right, those who think it's a waste of taxpayers' money to investigate a gay man's murder." At this point Marty, the line producer jumped in. "Well, that's about all the time we have, folks." He wrapped a companionable arm around me and whisked me down the hall, away from the mayor and his apoplectic entourage. "You couldn't just stick to the script, could ya?" No, I guess I couldn't.

I made the six o'clock news. I'd stopped off at DiBruno Brothers down at the Italian Market, to pick up some cheese and artichoke hearts. I figured that once my boss got wind of what I'd done I'd be out of a job, so I may as well eat while I could still afford the luxury. I tore off a hunk of fresh Italian bread and slapped a piece of cheese on it. Then I walked into the living room and flopped down on the couch. I'd forgotten a fork, so I picked some artichokes out of the container with my hand and then licked the brine off my fingers. No wonder I live alone. The phone rang just as I flipped on the t.v. to watch The Simpsons. "Turn on Channel 10."

"Yo, Carla, what's up?"

"You're on t.v. Hurry." Well, there I was, big as life, announcing to the entire Lehigh Valley that the mayor's a doofus who doesn't know what's going on in his own back yard, and that I have managed to obtain secret information that could discredit the entire Philadelphia Police Force. Way to go, Brandy.

"I guess I got a little carried away."

"You're telling me," Carla agreed.

"Maybe nobody saw it. I mean who watches the news when The Simpsons are on?"

Turns out, a lot of people. Vince called after I hung up from Carla. Seems I'm the new hot topic over at City Hall. Paul called too, and Frankie. Janine wanted to know why I wore black when everybody knows my color is red, and Bobby left a message on the answer machine that was so full of expletives it sounded like he was speaking a foreign language. I think my big mouth ensured me a place on the "cop shit list" so if any bad guys visited me tonight, I'd be pretty much on my own.

Just when I figured I'd finally run out of people I knew in the Greater Philadelphia area (even Mindy Rebowitz called to offer beauty tips. She said the camera lights made me look pasty and I should consider using foundation) the phone rang again. It was Nick.

"Are you calling to congratulate me on my east coast television debut?"

"Ah, I think I missed something here. Want to fill me in?"

When I was through, he gave out a long whistle. "Trouble just follows you around, doesn't it?"

"It's not my fault," I sighed. "I have excitable genes."

"Come again?"

"My mother's side of the family, the Italian side. Very emotional people."

"I'll take your word for it." I could almost hear him smiling through the phone. " I've got a line on the SUV."

"Already? Wow. How'd you do that?"

"Trade secret."

"And what trade would that be?"

"That's another secret. The car belongs to a guy named Thurman Williams. It seems that our man Thurman has been one busy dude. He's served time for armed robbery, and was arrested for attempted murder a few years back, but it never went to trial because the key witness disappeared."

"You're kidding."

"Afraid not. There's more. Williams was dishonorably discharged from the army, something drug related, it looks like. But guess what field he'd been trained in before he got discharged."

"Demolition?"

"Bingo." I squeezed my eyes shut and tried to visualize the bastard who'd almost succeeded in turning my best friend into burger bits. "I have one more thing," Nick continued. "He's working construction now for a local company."

"Who in their right mind would actually employ this guy?" I shrieked.

"It says here he works for Hoffman and Gruber Construction."

"Why do I know that name?"

"They've built half the city. They've got projects in various stages of development all around town."

"Hey, aren't they building the new sports arena?"

"Yeah. Plus, they were just awarded a massive renovation project that's due to start the beginning of the year."

"Well, you'd think these people would do a better job screening potential employees." I could just picture this guy's resume. *"Extensive experience in murder and mayhem. Good with people and making them dead."*

Nick put me on hold while he answered his other line. While he was gone I tried to establish a link between Maitlin and this Williams guy, but I kept coming up empty. Nick came back on the line.

"I have to take this call."

"Okay. Nick, thanks for all your help. I just have to figure out how it all goes together. It doesn't make sense to me."

"Maybe not yet, but give it some time." Boy, how little he knows me.

Gail phoned. Predictably, the general manager was less than thrilled with my impromptu performance and threatened to pull my contract if only they could find someone else who was willing to humiliate herself on a daily basis, for a ridiculously small paycheck. My network is notoriously cheap.

I felt lonely and depressed. Not even the Hershey bar I'd hidden in case of emergency was able to cheer me up. I called Franny, but Eddie said she was at Carla's getting her moustache waxed. He must really love her to be privy to that kind of information and still be willing to go through with the wedding. Paul was at the club. I thought about driving over there, but I wasn't in the mood for a lecture. Frankie offered to take me with him to a hockey game, only he was going with three other guys, and I'd have to sit on someone's lap on the car ride over. And Janine was off getting her aura cleansed. I briefly wondered what Mindy Rebowitz was doing.

When the doorbell rang at eight thirty, my stomach muscles contracted and I began to break out in a sweat. Everyone I knew was busy, so that left Hatchet Man. Maybe he'd come back to finish the job. I peered cautiously out the spy hole. Bobby peered back at me, his face a road map to hell. Mad didn't even begin to describe it.

"Brandy, open the door."

"No."

"I mean it, Alexander. Open the Goddamn door."

"No. You're scaring me." He changed tactics, his voice growing quietly controlled.

"I'm sorry. I didn't mean to scare you. I just want to talk, okay?"

"You're not going to yell at me?" He thought about it.

"I can't guarantee that."

"Then go away." I'd had enough trauma for one day and I didn't need any more, no matter how attractively packaged it was. Bobby sighed loudly. He shifted his stance and I caught a glimpse of his gun, hidden under his jacket. God, I hope he's coming off shift. I'd hate to think he wore it just for me.

"I won't yell." I unlatched the chain and twisted the deadbolt open. He sauntered in, looking like an Irish Italian God, all heat and muscle and long lean body. He tossed his jacket onto the couch and unhooked his holster, placing it on top of the television set. Then he sat down heavily on the couch, and stuck his legs up on the coffee table.

"Comfy?" He closed his eyes and leaned his head back on the cushions.

"Gimme a minute. I'm getting there." While he took his minute I began thinking about what it would be like to be married to Bobby. He'd come home after a hard day of shooting criminals, and I'd be waiting at the door in a shirtwaist dress, the kind June Cleaver used to wear, and a Martini in my hand. He'd kiss me chastely on the cheek and listen intently while I told him all about the trouble I'd had with the vacuum cleaner, and by the way, "The Beaver" was suspended again for sticking marbles up his nose.

"That's my boy," he'd grin, proudly.

"What?" I asked, aloud. Bobby opened his eyes.

"I said do you stay up nights thinking of ways to make me crazy?"

"Yes, Bobby. It's all about you." As if I gave him any thought at all. Sheesh. What an egomaniac. I nudged his feet off the coffee table "You're gonna leave scuff marks." He gave me a slow grin.

"You're getting to sound more like your mother every day."

"Take that back or die, DiCarlo." He eyed the gun resting on top of the television and took it back.

"How's John?" I asked, joining him on the couch.

"Fine. Bored. He's stashed at a house in the country. He says it smells like feet and he swears dinner tonight was baked road kill. By the way, when did John become a vegetarian?"

Bobby kept his promise not to yell at me—for about fifteen minutes. But then a "teaser" came on television advertising "News at Ten," and guess who was the lead story? Just my luck, no 7.0 earthquake in Japan that wiped out an entire village, to take the heat off me.

"What the fuck is wrong with you, Brandy?" Bobby was sitting up now, hands clenched on his thighs, his jaw muscles working overtime.

"You said you wouldn't yell at me."

"Yeah, well that was before, when I'd just heard what you'd done. Now that I've seen it for myself —what the hell were you thinking? Advertising the fact that you know there's something squirrelly going on in the department, and accusing the mayor of God only knows what. Did ya think this was a *good* thing? 'Cause I gotta tell ya, from my point of view, it's *not* helpful!" I decided to ignore the insults and take a reasonable approach.

"Bobby, can't we just agree to disagree on this?"

"What are you, insane? You accused the mayor, on national television of being some kind of monster who goes around covering up crimes against gay citizens. Then you make the entire police force out to be this corrupt, evil organization" —

"Not the entire police force," I said, quietly. "And for what it's worth, I'm sorry. I didn't mean it to come out that way. I just got really upset when I met Konner Novack's sister. Somebody had to speak up for her." The phone rang and I ran to get it, grateful for the diversion. It was a man's voice; at least I think it was a man's. He sounded like he was speaking through a distortion device.

"If you want to know what happens to people who can't keep their noses out of other people's lives, just look out your front door." He hung up quickly, and I stood there, stunned, the phone dangling from my hand. Bobby followed me into the kitchen. He took one look at my ashen face and grabbed the receiver from my hand. He listened a beat and then put it back on its cradle.

"Who was on the phone?"

"I don't know."

"Well, what did he say?" I started for the front door.

"He said to look out my front door."

"Don't," Bobby swatted my hand away as I reached for the doorknob. He grabbed his gun off the television set and motioned me out of the way. Cautiously, he opened the door a tad, and then a bit more. "Christ," he muttered and slammed the door shut again.

"What is it?" I pushed passed him and tried to open the door, but he grabbed me around the waist and swung me around. "Get out of my way, Bobby," I screamed angrily.

"Brandy" —

"Move." He stepped aside and I opened the door. On the steps was the head of a goat, its neck tendons severed and dripping blood. Its eyes were wide open, exuding pain. And buried between the eyes, splitting its face in half was a hatchet. Bile shot up my throat and I forced it back down. I shut the door again but could not seem to let go of the doorknob. Bobby gently pried my hand loose and guided me over to the couch. He shoved my head between my legs until he was sure I wasn't going to pass out, and then he said, "Tell me exactly what he said." So I did.

"Bobby, do you think you could, um, clean it up for me?"

"I'm sorry, sweetheart, but we've got to call the cops in on this."

"Why? They're probably the ones who left it there in the first place." He opened his mouth to argue the point, but I guess he didn't have the heart to follow through.

"Go upstairs," he said, instead. I stood on shaky legs and climbed the stairs to my bedroom.

Twenty minutes later Bobby joined me there. I was sitting on my bed, hugging my knees to my chest. I couldn't seem to get warm, even though the blankets were piled around me. I looked up when he came in and smiled weakly. "All gone?" He nodded. "Thanks." Bobby sat down on the bed, next to me. "Boy, somebody really doesn't like me," I said, and then I began to cry, big fat tears that traveled down my cheeks and pooled at the base of my collar. Bobby put a tentative arm around my shoulder and hugged me to him. I looked up at him; his face was tense, and his eyes burned in the semi darkness.

"Why are you doing this?" He asked, his voice husky. "Why are you putting yourself at risk?" I spread my hands across my face, wiping away the tears. Then I pushed the covers off me and scooted down to the edge of the bed and slid off. I walked over to the window and gazed out into the night.

"Remember the time I got suspended because a teacher was bullying one of the ninth graders and I stood up for her?"

"As I recall you called him a dickhead." He smiled at the memory.

"Well, maybe I went a little too far, but—it's who I am, Bobby. I can't stand by and watch the bullies win. And maybe I don't always think things through, and maybe I don't always get it right, but I'm never going to just sit by and do nothing while there are people in the world who can't fight for themselves. You used to be able to accept that about me."

"It used to drive me nuts, but I knew there was no stopping you. But this is different. This is life threatening." He climbed off the bed and joined me at the window. "Brandy," he said, forcing me to look at him, "I know I gave up the right to tell you what to do a long time ago. But I care about what happens to you." I reached my hand to his cheek and held it there.

"I know you do. Look, you'd said you wanted to be my friend, again. Can you accept me as I am? Because I'm not going to change, for you or anybody." He took my hand off his cheek and turned it palm upwards, placing a light kiss on the fleshy part of it, before letting it drop to my side.

"Can I reserve the right to worry about you?"

We went downstairs and I made a pot of herbal tea. What I really wanted was hot cocoa, but I knew sleep was going to be an up hill battle, without adding caffeine to the mix. As a gesture of trust, I filled Bobby in on what I'd learned at the club. He said he'd look up Maitlin, check for priors. I didn't tell him that Nick was already doing that. Why rock the tenuous truce we'd struck. But Bobby wasted no time in asking me about Nick. Who was he? What did I really know about him? Why did I feel I could go to a virtual stranger for help rather than him?

"He's not a virtual stranger. He's a friend of Carla's cousin, Benny."

"Benny the gun runner? Oh, that makes me feel tons better."

"Okay, let's not dwell on the negative, here." I took a TastyKake out of the cupboard to balance out the tea. "Want one?" I tossed the package to Bobby. "Oh, and another thing." Then I told him about Thurman Williams.

"Jesus, Brandy." Bobby began.

"Yes?" Let's just see how far he was willing to go to accept our friendship by my terms.

"Nothin'. I was just going to say," he swallowed hard, "good work."

I grinned. "Thanks."

We talked until one a.m., going over the clues. I tried to sum up what we knew or suspected. "Curtis Maitlin was a violent guy who had a history of beating up his lovers. He was at the bar the night Konner was killed, and is a viable suspect for the murder. The M.O. was the same as another murder that took place six months ago, and both times, evidence disappeared. Thurman Williams, an employee of a successful construction company was hired by someone to kill John, because John had seen the pictures and could potentially identify Curtis Maitlin. And all this started happening the minute John went to the police and told them he had pictures of Novack, the night he was killed. So someone in the police department is protecting this guy, Maitlin. Who's protecting him, and why?"

"We have to look for common links." Bobby said.

"Like?"

"Like, I don't know. It's late. I've got to get some sleep. Why don't we table this until tomorrow?"

"But we're just getting started. I'm so pumped I could go all night," I argued, suppressing a huge yawn. Bobby smiled and pulled me to my feet.

"You're exhausted and you're afraid to go to sleep. I'll stay with you until you drift off."

"I'm not afraid," I countered, letting him lead me up the stairs. "But if it makes you feel better, you can stay."

"Thanks."

I didn't even bother to change out of my clothes. I just shoved all my stuffed animals to one side and climbed into bed. Bobby tucked the covers all around me. "Could you turn on the night light, please?" I yawned. "In case you need some light when you leave," I added.

"That's very considerate of you." He walked down the hall into the bathroom and flicked on the switch. When he returned he stood in the doorway, watching me. "What's wrong?" I asked, panicking. He shook his head.

"Nothing. There's just no place to sit."

"Oh. Well, um, you could sit on the bed if you'd like." In the semi darkness Bobby walked towards the bed. He kicked off his boots and shoved my stuffed animals onto the floor. Then he sat down and swung his legs up onto the bed and stretched them out in front of him. Sitting upright, he leaned his head against the headboard.

"Goodnight," he whispered.

"Goodnight."

I awoke to something hard pressing into my back. I tried to move, but I was pinned to the bed by an immoveable object. Cautiously opening one eye, I saw that Bobby's arm was slung across my chest, my body snuggled up against his, spoon-like. I peeked under the blankets. We were both fully dressed, but there was still the matter of the hard thing at my back. It wasn't a gun in his pocket—he'd left that on the dresser. So I guess he was just glad to see me. Trying not to disturb him, I glanced over at the clock. It was after nine a.m. I had to check twice to be sure I was reading it correctly. I'd slept for eight solid hours, which was nothing short of a miracle. It was the first real night's sleep I'd had in a week. I wanted to stay snuggled next to him forever, but I had to get up to pee. It also occurred to me that waking up in a married man's arms may not be the smartest thing if you're not the one he's married to. Well, this was awkward. I shifted slightly and he groaned, so I quickly shut my eyes again, feigning sleep. Let *him* deal with it. I felt him remove his arm and sit up. Slowly, I opened my eyes as if for the first time. Bobby's hair was all tousled, and his five o'clock shadow had deepened overnight. He rubbed his hand over his face and yawned. "Hey," he said, softly.

"Hey." I sat up too, conscious that I hadn't brushed my teeth. "I thought you were going to leave when I fell asleep."

"Nah. I got too tired. I hope you don't mind."

"I don't mind." A sudden shyness swept over me, and I looked away. "I'll be right back." I scrambled out of bed and ran to the bathroom. Some hideous girl had taken up residence in my bathroom mirror and she was there to greet me when I walked in. "Ahhhh! How could I let him see me like this? My face was creased with sleep, and my hair looked like birds had nested in it. I peed and brushed my teeth, and then I grabbed a brush and yanked the tangles out of my hair, which now hung limply to my shoulders. When I returned to the bedroom Bobby was out of bed. He'd straightened the sheets and fluffed up the pillows.

"I didn't know it was so late, " he said, grabbing his gun off the dresser. "I've got to get to work." I followed him down the stairs and tripped over the last step, catching myself before I landed on my nose.

"I could make you some breakfast," I offered.

"Don't have time," he replied, shrugging into his jacket. "Besides," he grinned. "You don't know how to cook."

"Shows how much you know. I happen to be very good at it now." If you count Slice and Bake cookies and the occasional grilled cheese sandwich as knowing how to cook. Bobby stopped on his way to the front door.

"I'm not trying to tell you what to do," he started, "but please be careful today. I don't like the idea of you being alone."

"I don't much like it either," I admitted. "I'm going to call Janine to see if she'll meet me for lunch."

"Why don't I drop you off at her place?"

"No, you're late. I'll be fine." Bobby turned back to the living room and plopped down on the couch.

"Humor me. Please?"

"Well, since you asked so nicely." I called Janine.

"How'd the aura cleansing go?" I was sitting in Janine's studio apartment, tossing peanuts out the window to the pigeons down below. Janine lives in a four-story walk-up, near St. Dom's. She's always threatening to move to a larger apartment, but the place really suits her personality. It's quirky and comfortable.

"Apparently, my aura was friggin' filthy. She wants me to come back next week and finish cleaning it."

"Are you going back?"

"Fuck, no. What a racket." Janine finished applying her third layer of mascara and wiggled into the shortest skirt I'd ever seen. I looked down at my blue jeans and sighed.

"I'm boring."

"True." She studied me for a moment. "But it doesn't seem to make a difference."

"What do you mean?" Janine rifled through her closet alcove, pulled out a beige, off-the-shoulder cashmere sweater and yanked it over her head.

"I swear to God, sometimes you can be so dense." I opened my mouth to protest, but she beat me to it. "That boy is so in love with you, he wouldn't care if you were wearing a potato sack with arm holes. He'd still think you were the most beautiful thing that ever walked the earth." This time my mouth flew open and stayed that way. "Oh, come on. Don't pretend you didn't know."

"I didn't," I whispered, getting all emotional. Was it possible that Bobby still loved me?" It was too much to think about. "Janine, I told you, the only reason he stayed with me last night is because he knew how scared I was, and NOTHING HAPPENED. He was just being a friend, that's all." Janine added some bangle bracelets to her outfit and was good to go.

"Okay, Toots, if you say so."

"Well, don't say it like that," I replied, irritably. "Say it like you mean it."

"But I don't mean it," she grumbled under her breath. Sometimes Janine can be a royal pain in the ass.

Chapter Twelve

We decided to go to Sargenti's for lunch. Sargeniti's is a family owned restaurant, located at tenth and Locust Streets that offers up home style cooking at affordable prices. As my mother says, "The food isn't very good, but they give you a lot," which was fine by Janine and me because we were both really hungry.

We walked into the restaurant and were greeted by Angie, one of fourteen Sargenti children ranging in age from sixteen to twenty-nine. Janine veered off to the bathroom while I perused the newspaper rack for throwaway papers. I love free stuff. My eye fixated on the "Philadelphia Freedom News," an independent press whose slogan is "Underground and Above Board since 1967." My dad was one of the original founders of the paper, and although he's long since given up his spot to a new generation of conspiracy hunters, I still get a kick out of reading it from time to time. I flipped it open to the editorial page.

Silence of the Lamb?
By
Ken Robbins

Democratic mayoral candidate Ira Lamb is an outspoken critic of ultra conservative mayor Bradley Richardson. Lamb has challenged Richardson on everything from his views on gay marriages to his tax cuts for the wealthy. Why then is he being uncharacteristically silent when it comes to demanding full disclosure of Richardson's campaign finances? Could it be that Lamb had been warned off by the ghost of investigations past?

The last time an incumbent was investigated for alleged irregularities in campaign financing the FBI ended up embarrassingly empty-handed, while public outrage over what was perceived as major harassment tripled the former mayor's re-electability quotient. He won in a landslide.

Perhaps Lamb is smart to overlook certain glaring questions regarding Mayor Richardson's campaign finances—such as: how did he manage to raise so much cash without any visible fundraising efforts, and who has benefited most from his time in office? I'm an inquiring mind and I'd really like to know. And if you're reading this newspaper, chances are you'll want to know too.

I tucked the newspaper into my bag as Janine came out of the bathroom. Angie seated us at a booth and said that Monica would be with us shortly. Janine and I went to school with Monica. That is, until she became pregnant and dropped out in the eleventh grade. I hadn't seen her since high school, but she looked exactly the same as the last time I laid eyes on her—short, freckle-faced and eight months pregnant. Monica looked over at us and lit up as recognition dawned.

"Brandy, is that you?" She waddled over and slid into the booth next to me. It was a tight fit.

"Oh my God! It's been so long." She threw two beefy arms around me and squeezed me hard.

"Hey, Mon, how've ya been?"

"Busy." She rubbed her stomach and laughed. Hank and I are on our third." Hank, being Henry Winiki of Winiki Brothers Construction Company. They got married about a minute before Henry Jr. was born.

"Listen, you guys," Monica whispered, in what I came to realize was a gesture of respect, "I just wanted to say I'm sorry about Johnny."

"What *about* Johnny?" Asked Janine, tearing at a piece of Italian bread like she'd never seen food before. I was really thirsty and I wanted a glass of water, but it just didn't seem right to ask Monica to get up again, seeing as she looked like she was about to plop the next kid out at any given moment. Monica shot Janine a puzzled glance.

"You know, the accident."

"Yeah, bummer," Janine said absently, stuffing the bread into her mouth. I kicked her under the table and she looked up, confused. "Oh, I mean it was a tragic loss." Monica nodded and crossed herself. I did too, just for the hell of it. My cell phone rang and I scrambled to get it.

"Hey, angel." My body temperature shot up about twenty degrees at the sound Nick's voice. It was soft and low and sounded like really good sex.

"Oh, hi." I turned away from Monica and Janine, but not before they caught me turning beet red. Two sets of elbows leaned forward as they strained to listen in.

"Are you alone?"

"Not exactly. I'm at a restaurant having lunch with some friends." I pictured Nick sitting behind his desk, rolling one of his exotic cigarettes that he would never smoke, gently in his hands. Then I pictured him touching

Shelly Fredman

me the same way. I shifted uncomfortably in the booth. "What's up?"

"I thought you told me you and the cop are just friends." Well, I certainly wasn't expecting that.

"We are. Why?"

"He's been asking around about me."

"He has?"

"As we speak." I thought about this for a minute.

"Will he find out anything interesting?" Nick laughed, softly.

"Let's hope not. By the way, word on the street is Williams disappeared a few days ago. Maybe he heard someone was able to I.D. him and it made him nervous."

Nick and I hung up and I turned my attention back to Janine and Monica, who were, by now, flat-out ogling me.

"What?"

"Somebody's got a boyfriend," Monica sing-songed. Janine snorted with laughter. Now I remembered why Monica and I didn't hang out together in high school. She has the emotional maturity of an eight year old. I looked to Janine for help, but she was busy finishing off the bread.

"I don't have a boyfriend, Monica. That was a business associate. So, how's Hank?" I asked, not really caring but needing a change of subject. Hank always struck me as really boring.

"Eh, not great," she said, settling in. I think she'd forgotten all about being our waitress and was now planning to catch me up on the past decade since high school. Janine looked over at me and sighed. I gave her a "What can I do?" shrug in return. We both gazed longingly at the now empty breadbasket. "Business has been really slow, and with the new kid on the way, Hank gets nervous."

"Has he considered freelancing for another company?" I asked. "Just until business picks up? I see signs for Hoffman and Gruber Construction everywhere. Maybe he could work for them for awhile."

"Hank would never do that," she sighed. "First of all, it would be a major slap in the face to his brothers, and secondly, he says Hoffman and Gruber are notorious for shoddy craftsmanship and cheap materials. A couple of people on Hank's crew used to work for them, and they said it was a wonder buildings weren't falling down all over town. It just really ticks me off that they were awarded those huge contracts, when my Hank is struggling to make ends meet." I couldn't help but wonder if it was just sour grapes on Hank's part—which I would have gladly eaten if they'd been offered to me, because I was starving by now and it didn't look like I'd be getting much of anything else to eat. Then I remembered the article in the Freedom News.

"Who awards these contracts?"

"Essentially, the mayor's office." I opened my bag and took out the article and began to scan it. *Who has benefited most from his time in office?* I'd always assumed the mayor's rich right-wing friends were financing his campaign, but now I wasn't so sure. Could Hoffman and Gruber be bankrolling the mayor's campaign in exchange for the building contracts? Janine's cell phone began to ring before I had a chance to think this through. "That was Franny," she announced, snapping her phone shut. "She just arranged an interview for me with her boss. They need some temp help and I've got to get there right away. I'm sorry, Bran. I'll drop you off at your place, on the way." I glanced sadly at the menu as I gathered up my jacket and pocketbook. Monica walked us to the door. I hesitated at the cash register. There was a bowl of those round, red and white mints sitting on the counter, so I reached in and grabbed a few. Monica turned to hug Janine and I tipped the entire bowl into my pocketbook. I felt guilty but that didn't last long. Being a master of rationalization I figured that if Monica had been a better waitress, I'd have been fed by now, and I wouldn't have to resort to stealing her crappy mints. So, clearly, it was Monica's fault.

I was reluctant to go home to an empty house. Petrified was more like it. Maybe Mrs. Gentile would be home, and I could invite her in for a "Girls' Night." We could do each other's hair and take turns reading from fan magazines. I could go over to Paul's club, but I'd been sort of avoiding him and Frankie for a while now. I love them both and I know they'd move Heaven and Earth for me, but I just couldn't handle the inevitable questions. I wasn't up for justifying myself to anyone. I'd done enough of that with Bobby. Franny was still at work, and so was DiCarlo. John was God knows where, eating raccoon and living the good life. I opened my bag and took out my cell phone.

Janine pulled up at the curb. "Are you sure you want me to leave you here?"

"I'll be fine. Thanks for the ride, Janine. Good luck on your interview." I ran the five steps to Nick's studio and tapped on the door. Nick opened it a minute later, and I turned to wave goodbye to Janine. She caught a glimpse of Nick and her mouth dropped open.

"He's gorgeous," she mouthed to me.

"I know." I mouthed back.

I was lying flat on my back on the floor of the studio. Nick hovered above me, grinning like an idiot. I had told him that I wanted to come by because I thought I needed to learn some basic self-defense moves. The trouble was he was doing all the moving, which is how I landed in my current position. He extended an arm and pulled me to my feet. It was one p.m. and I'd just missed the eleven o'clock advanced class, taught by Tanya. Darn it. I'd really wanted to make a complete fool of myself in front of her. There wasn't another class until three, so Nick and I were alone until then.

Nick was dressed in faded black jeans and a soft, gray crewneck sweater. He had the sleeves rolled partway up, revealing strong forearms. Wrapped around his wrist was his signature silver band. His hair was pulled back in a loose ponytail, which he now untied, freeing an unruly mass of beautiful brown waves. I stood in front of him, my chest heaving, and tiny beads of sweat dotting my forehead. "Whew, what a workout."

I wiped my face with the back of my sleeve. Nick checked his watch, a very expensive vintage Rolex. "Four minutes. You must be exhausted."

"Only four minutes? Are you sure?" I shrugged. "Oh well, it's the quality that counts. Not the quantity." Nick shook his head in amusement. He slung an arm around my shoulder, drawing me to him and began guiding me towards his office.

"Come on, darlin', let's go in back where you can get comfortable, and then you can tell me why you're really here." I started to protest, but he raised his eyebrows at me, stopping me in mid lie. "Do you want to go another round?" Boy, did he ever fight dirty.

I curled up in my favorite spot on the big red velvet chair, tucking my legs beneath me. Nick reached under his desk and brought out two Perriers. He popped one open and offered it to me. "Thanks," I said, taking it.

"So, what's up?"

"I kind of don't want to be alone, and everyone else I know in town is busy." A flicker of annoyance crossed his face, and it occurred to me I might actually have insulted him.

"Well, what about your boyfriend, Bobby?"

"I told you, I'm NOT BOBBY'S GIRL!" Did I really say that? Unhhh! "Look, I'm sorry I took up your valuable time." I struggled to my feet. He really didn't want me there, and I felt like I was throwing myself at the man.

"Sit down." It was said like an invitation, but we both knew it was an order.

"No, thank you. I think I'll stand." He did the eyebrow thing again and I sat down. And then I told him the whole story. About the phone call, and the goat's head, and how I was tired of people trying to chop me up with hatchets and that I just wanted a little peace, and for some reason that I really couldn't figure out, I felt safe sitting in his red velvet chair, in the office that smelled faintly of exotic tobacco that was savored but never smoked. And by the time I was finished, I was so mortally embarrassed I couldn't even raise my head when he called my name.

"Brandy, look at me." I peeked up at him from under my bangs. "It's only natural that you'd be scared. You're dealing with some scary shit. You're welcome to stay here as long as you like."

I stayed all afternoon. After filling Nick in on my theory about Hoffman and Gruber financing the mayor's campaign, he set me up on his computer so that I could do a little research into their company. Nick's phone rang. He checked the caller I.D. and frowned. When he picked up the receiver, he spoke in rapid fire Spanish, punctuating his words with gestures of frustration that couldn't be seen on the other end of the line. I felt equally frustrated. I don't understand Spanish, and it was frustrating as *hell* not knowing what he was saying. The only two words I recognized were "guns" and "Ecuador." *That couldn't be good.* Finally, he left the room and I concentrated on the task at hand.

I found various articles and began to piece together a history. Hoffman and Gruber Construction company was started in the early nineteen eighties by two college buddies, Michael Hoffman and Philip Gruber. They started out doing large residential projects but eventually turned to the more lucrative commercial property developments. They managed to make it through various recessions, at times drawing on family money to keep the business afloat. Gruber came from old money, his grandfather having something to do with linoleum. In nineteen ninety-nine their business really took off when they bid successfully for their first city contract. I checked the dates and noted that the contracts were offered three months after the election of Mayor Richardson. There were more articles, but one in particular caught my eye. It was written a few months after they received their contract. It was an obituary for Michael Hoffman. I scanned it quickly, soaking up the pertinent facts. According to the news report, Hoffman, forty-seven, was on medication for depression. He died of an accidental overdose when he mixed his meds with alcohol. His partner, Philip Gruber was quoted as saying that his untimely death was a great loss to everyone who knew him. There was a picture of the two of them together at a charity golf tournament, on the Main Line. Gruber, wearing traditionally goofy golfing attire, mugged into the camera, while Hoffman, the more reserved of the two, remained in the background. Gruber appeared to be about five feet nine, slightly built and a little on the nerdy side. A multi- million-dollar nerd, that is. The article also stated that he had been married briefly to a woman named Marlo, but there were no details on the marriage. After that I tried to look up the mayor's campaign financing records, but I didn't know how to or even if things like that were a matter of public record. So then I looked up SoapOpera.Com to see what was happening on Days of Our Lives. When I was finished catching up, Nick still hadn't come back into the room, so I curled back up in the chair and fell asleep.

It was almost dark when I awoke. I glanced at the clock. Four forty-five. Wow. I'd been asleep for almost two hours. For close to a week I don't sleep at all and now at the drop of a hat I'm dead to the world. Maybe I have narcolepsy. *Oh goody, something new to worry about.* Where was Nick? A thin stream of light emanated from underneath the office door and I peeked out to see what was going on. A class was in session, but this was no housewives group here. I'm talking major muscle. A testosterone festival. Big, make that *enormous* men, of various ethnicities were standing in a line as Nick demonstrated self-defense techniques. Nick was at least three inches shorter than the smallest of the lot and was outweighed by a good fifty pounds, and yet he was the focal point of the action. One by one he outmaneuvered them and they dropped at his feet with incredible ferocity, sometimes accompanied by a great deal of pain. Although his face remained blank there was a look of deep satisfaction in his eyes. Quickly, I shut the door. If I wasn't convinced before that Nick was dangerous, that little demonstration changed my mind in a hurry.

While I waited for the class to be over, I turned on the TV hoping for some comedic diversion. I guess the networks don't think people need to laugh during the dinner hour, because breaking news permeated the airways. Two young boys were playing in a ravine when they came across a car that appeared to have been firebombed. Inside were the charred remains of its driver. They cut to a tape of earlier today and suddenly Bobby's face flashed across the screen. I'd always known Bobby's job was stressful. At times it could be incredibly gruesome. This was one of those times. I stared into his haggard face and felt very sad for him. He imparted the following information as succinctly as possible.

"The victim appears to be a white male in his mid to late twenties. The coroner has estimated that the victim has been dead for at least two days. His identity has not yet been confirmed. If anyone has any information regarding this crime, please call the number located at the bottom of the screen." A shudder ran through me. What a world.

Nick drove me home. I hadn't eaten anything the entire day, so we stopped off at Hop Li, the Chinese restaurant around the corner from my parents' house. I ordered a whole bunch of food, hoping I could entice him to stay for dinner. I really didn't want to be alone in case another goat's head showed up at my door. Then again, there's nothing like a severed head to kill an appetite.

As we pulled up to the house I noticed Bobby's car parked out front. He was slumped in the driver's seat, eying Nick and me as we emerged from the Jaguar. He didn't look happy. I began pulling bags of Chinese food out of the back seat. Bobby appeared at my side and relieved me of some of the packages. Nick came around the other side and took the rest of the bags from me. I closed the car door and began rooting around my pocketbook for my keys. Nick sensed my discomfort and smiled brightly. Evidently, this was great entertainment for him. "Aren't you going to introduce us?"

"Oh, sorry," I said, not looking up. "Bobby, Nick. Nick, Bobby." Nick stuck his hand out and Bobby reluctantly did the same. "I feel like we know each other," Nick told him.

"Yeah? How's that?"

"Well, from what I hear, you did a little research on me. Was it captivating reading?"

"Not really."

"Found them!" I said a little too loudly. I held up my keys for inspection. The guys eyed each other like roosters in a cockfight and followed me to the door.

"Um, does anyone want to stay for Chinese?" They both took me up on my offer. Lucky me. As if things weren't complicated enough already.

I set out plates and grabbed some beers from the refrigerator. Bobby sidled over to me and bent down, whispering in my ear. "I've got to talk to you. Privately," he added, pointedly. I looked at Nick who was busy digging into his Moo Shu vegetable.

"Oh, that reminds me. I saw you on tv today. That poor guy in the car."

"That's what I wanted to talk to you about. They've identified the victim." Nick glanced up from his plate.

"Pass the soy sauce, please." He looked very sweet sitting at my dining room table, happily munching his Moo Shu. I had to remind myself that he could chop a man in half with the flick of his wrist. I passed him the soy sauce and turned my attention back to Bobby.

"Bobby, maybe we should wait until after dinner." If we were going to discuss burned up bodies I'd rather do it on a full stomach. He shot a look at Nick.

"When is he leaving?" He whispered hoarsely. Nick raised his head and flashed a beatific smile.

"Oh, I'm sorry. Am I keeping you two kids from something?"

"No!" I'd had enough male posturing at this point to last a lifetime. "Bobby, if you have something to tell me, just say it."

"Fine. The guy in the car was Curtis Maitlin."

"Get out!" I dropped my plate and chow mein noodles went flying. Ironically, they landed on my mom's Oriental rug. "Are you sure?" I shouted scooping noodles back onto my plate. I had to move fast. That grease can really stain a carpet. Nick stopped eating. "Well, this puts a new spin on things." NO DUH!

There was just enough of Maitlin left to be able to identify him. Turns out he'd had a bunch of priors, some of which included some pretty violent sex crimes. He'd managed to beat the rap on them, but due to the similarities the cops are looking at him as the prime suspect in Konner Novack's death. But that still didn't answer the question of who was protecting Maitlin in the first place and why. And it sure didn't give any clues as to why suddenly he was expendable. The method of death, on the other hand, was a dead (no pun intended) giveaway.

"Thurman Williams," I surmised, aloud. "I mean it had to be. Fire bombing. The guy's a demolitions expert. He blew up John's boat."

"And now he's gone missing." Bobby whipped his head in Nick's direction. "How do you know that?"

"I've had some people keeping an eye on him. He vanished about two days ago." Bobby gave him a begrudging nod.

"Just about the time Maitlin was whacked," Bobby concluded.

Nick finished his meal and passed on the almond cookies. "I've got to run," he said.

"So soon?" It was the first time Bobby cracked a smile all night.

I walked Nick to the door and stood out on the porch with him, away from Bobby's prying eyes.

"Nick," I put my arm out to him and he turned, facing me. His expression was unreadable, and not for the first time I felt infinitely younger than he was in every way that counted. "I just wanted to thank you for letting me crash at your place today. And for helping me, and—and for being my friend." Nick looked beyond me towards the house.

"Some people may think that's not such a good idea."

"Yeah, well, some people had better just get used to it." That earned me another smile. He leaned forward and kissed me on the forehead and left.

Bobby was cleaning up the dishes when I got back inside.

"Thanks." I took a towel and began drying and putting them away. I knew he was dying to ask me about Nick. In fact he looked about ready to burst. To his credit, he asked instead how my day was, if I'd had a nice time with Janine, and oh, by the way, how'd I end up getting driven home by what's his name again—Mic?"

"You know damn well it's Nick," I smiled sweetly. You spent enough time investigating him."

"Sez him." I arched my eyebrows.

"Do you really want to do this?" Bobby sighed deeply. He rinsed off the last dish and turned off the water. Then he pulled out a chair and sat down. I followed, grabbing the almond cookies. Since Nick hadn't wanted his, I took two and offered Bobby the other one. We sat there eating cookies and processing the new information.

Williams was hired by somebody to suppress evidence about Curtis Maitlin. We came up with two possible reasons why someone would want to help Maitlin get away with murder. Bribery or blackmail.

"Okay, let's look at bribery," Bobby began. "If Maitlin was paying someone to destroy information that could link him to a murder, then why would that person then have Williams kill him? That doesn't make any sense. On the other hand, if Maitlin was blackmailing that person into helping him, there'd be a reason to want him dead."

"Makes sense to me."

"We also know that Williams wasn't the only one helping Maitlin out. Someone from the precinct was involved in pulling the evidence and passing along information."

"Not to mention whoever's been stalking me. Ya know, hiring crooked cops and hired assassins can't be cheap. This guy must have some bucks to be able to afford an operation like this." I polished off the cookies and wiped the crumbs off my hands, onto the kitchen table. Bobby grabbed the sponge off the sink and wiped down the table. When did he become so domesticated? He picked up my elbows to wipe under them.

"You seem to be enjoying this a little too much."

"What?"

"This whole investigation business." He tossed the sponge back into the sink.

"That's just what Johnny said," I replied, sulkily. The phone rang, interrupting my sulk. It was my mother. "Oh, hi, Mom. How's Daddy?" Little crunching noises emanated from the other end of the line. It sounded like celery.

"Your father's fine, honey. Crunch, crunch." It was really getting on my nerves.

"Mom, you're crunching." She stopped, mid crunch.

"I can't help it. I started a new diet, today. I'm starving. But I can have all the celery I want."

"Well, do you think you can hold off until we hang up?" She agreed, reluctantly, and then she threw me for a loop.

"I got the oddest phone call from Doris Gentile, today."

"Mrs. Gentile called you? Whatever for?" I thought she'd stopped all communication after the Santa Shooting of '87. My mother hesitated. I could hear her muffled crunching before she spoke again.

"She said that Bobby DiCarlo has been coming over quite a bit and that last night," she dropped her voice, dramatically, "he spent the night." *That little snitch!*
"Of course I told her to mind her own damn business. What my daughter does is none of her concern, and she can just keep her big nose out of it."

"Good for you, Mom!" I shouted, proudly.

"Brandy," she wailed, "Tell me it isn't so!"

It took me fifteen minutes to calm her down. I made up some wild story about how I'd won tickets to the policeman's ball and he'd come over to tell me the good news, but he'd forgotten to bring me the tickets, so although it *looked* like he'd spent the night, in actuality he'd left and come back early the next morning. I am going straight to Hell.

When I hung up with my mother, I found Bobby bent over the kitchen table, scribbling on a napkin. I leaned over his shoulder to get a better look. "What's that?" He'd drawn a diagram with the name "Williams" encircled in the middle and arrows pointing away from it, with other names encircled as well. On the top of the napkin he'd written "CONNECTIONS."

"This is just conjecture, but let's assume for now that it's all true. We've got Williams, who blew up John's boat in order to keep evidence about Maitlin from surfacing. We know that Williams is on the Hoffman and Gruber payroll as a demolitions expert." He then pointed to the next arrow, with the words Mayor Richardson encircled. We suspect that Hoffman and Gruber Construction are financing the mayor's campaign in exchange for highly lucrative contracts. We've got a cop" —

"Or cops" —

"Or cops who are stealing evidence that could incriminate Maitlin. Now again, assuming all this is true, and we're going with the blackmail theory, here, who has the most to lose if secrets about him suddenly became public? Who has a direct connection to the police force, and unlimited funding, thanks to a silent partnership with a very rich construction company?"

"The mayor!" I yelled excitedly, as if I'd just discovered the number one answer on "Family Feud." Bobby sat back, a satisfied grin on his face.

"Now, all we've got to do is prove it. We can start by figuring out what Maitlin had on the mayor."

"Isn't that obvious?" I asked. "Maitlin somehow figured out that the mayor was being secretly funded by the construction company, so the mayor had to pay him off to keep his secret. But Maitlin didn't want money.

He was in big trouble and took his payment in stolen evidence. But then something changed."

"What?" There was a spark in Bobby's eye, and I could tell he enjoyed watching me try to figure it all out.

"Well," I said, slowly. "Maybe the mayor got cold feet over protecting a killer, so he decided to put an end to the blackmail, once and for all." Unfortunately, the one person who held the answers was AWOL. Thurman Williams. "I think I should pay Philip Gruber a little visit." Bobby blanched at my suggestion.

"What are you, nuts?"

"I thought we were past the name calling stage. Besides, what's wrong with my asking a few questions?"

"Not a thing. Write me a list and I'll be glad to ask them for you."

"You're not leaving me out of this, DiCarlo. I mean it."

"Brandy, use your head. I'm a police officer. I can go there on official business. What are you going to do, say you're with Early Edition News in Los Angeles, and you want to get the fashion scoop on what "hardhats" are wearing this holiday season?" Sometimes even mule-headed Irish-Italian cops come up with good ideas.

Bobby had to get back to work. Before he left he inspected every door and window in the house to make sure they were locked up tight. He even offered to come back at midnight when his shift was over, but I steadfastly refused. "Mrs. Gentile has already ratted us out to my mother. That's all you need is to have it somehow get back to your wife that you're having sleepovers with your ex girlfriend." He knew I was right so he didn't press the matter, but I was touched that he cared. Maybe it *was* possible that we could be friends again.

The night stretched before me. I wished I could see John but Bobby thought it best that he stay hidden, at least until Thurman Williams was caught. Janine had a date with a guy she met over the Internet. I was supposed to call her at nine to see how it was going. If it turned out that he was dyslexic and when he wrote in his online profile that he was 6' 3" he really meant 3'6" she might need an excuse to end the date early. So maybe that was shallow, but as Janine says, being a five foot nine inch fourth grader was no picnic, either. Frankie and Carla dropped by at eight to see if I wanted to join them at the movies. The Earlen Theater was playing Nightmare on Elm Street. They didn't even know how funny that was. After they left for the movies I did two loads of laundry and scrubbed out the refrigerator. As a reward for all my hard work I ate a chocolate TastyKake. Well, not the whole thing. I ripped off the cakey bottom and just ate the icing. At nine o'clock I called Janine.

"Can you talk?"

"Yeah, he's in the bathroom."

"Well," I said, impatiently, "does he look like Johnny Depp, like he said in his profile?"

"Oh, he looks like Johnny Depp, all right. In 'Ed Wood.' He's wearing a *dress*!"

"Are you sure it's a dress? Maybe it's a kilt. He could be Scottish."

"I don't think so. Plus, he ordered a 'Pink Lady' and he threw a hissy fit when they forgot the umbrella." I offered my condolences and hung up. At ten Franny called to remind me that tomorrow the bridesmaids were going for a final fitting on their dresses. Damn, that meant I'd have to shave my legs. I hadn't worn a dress in ages and I hadn't had sex in longer than that, so there'd been no big rush to attend to that bit of female vanity. I pulled up my pant leg. Ahhh! I was going to need a power mower to get the job done. Well, that should kill the rest of the evening.

Chapter Thirteen

On Saturday morning six women of various shapes and sizes stuffed themselves into identical gowns in the communal dressing room at Mia's Bridal Shop. "Mama Mia" as she insisted everyone call her, bustled back and forth, pinning, poking and prodding us into submission as Franny beamed with pride. I don't know what it is about weddings that transform "Brides to be" into Fashion Nazis, but Franny proved to be no exception.

"Franny," Janine said with surprising restraint. "I thought we'd agreed to lose the ass bows. Remember we all voted against them at the last fitting."

"Yeah, well I voted them back in," Franny said. "I think it gives the dress more pizzazz."

"Pizza?" Chirped Eddie's cousin, Gina. She'd just flown in from Milan and spoke about five words of English, all food related.

"Well, I'm not walking down the aisle with a gigantic bow stuck to my butt, " Janine insisted. "I look like a float in the Rose Parade."

Franny gazed around the room. Her eyes settled on Celine, her buddy from work.

"Celine?" She asked, hopefully. Celine actually looked a little afraid. She refused to make eye contact.

"I could live without pizzazz," she gulped.

"Brandy?"

"I love ya, babe, but I'm with Janine on this one. I vote no on the ass bows."

That just left Carla.

"Well, I think they look great!" Carla enthused, unasked. Franny sighed. If Carla thought they looked great there, was only one thing to do. She turned to Mama Mia.

"Lose the ass bows."

After the bridal shop we stopped by Victoria's Secret, because Carla insisted it wouldn't be a proper honeymoon unless it involved crotchless panties. Personally, I was never one to go in for kinky underwear. I get embarrassed just *looking* at thongs. Eeew! I could never bring myself to wear one. I was more of a "military surplus underwear" kind of gal. Wholesome and modest and thoroughly boring. I sighed, fingering some pale pink silk bikinis, and my thoughts began to drift to Nick. Decidedly unwholesome, immodest thoughts. And suddenly my old utilitarian underwear just wouldn't do for a moment longer. While the rest of the crew was busy picking out slut wear for Franny's big night, I sidled up to the counter surreptitiously holding three pair of very lacy French-cut bikinis, in black, mauve and beige. For the black ones I even threw in a matching bra. *No need to make a big announcement. Just buying some underwear. No big deal.* "Do you have any plain paper bags?" I whispered to the saleswoman, in hushed tones. She looked at me as if I were crazy, which I was. On impulse I'd just bought seventy-five dollars worth of panties because when I fantasized about having wild, unbridled sex with Nicholas Santiago, I wanted to look nice. *Like he'd ever see me naked. Chance!*

Our last stop was Levi's, on Broad Street, for lunch. Levi's is the best Jewish deli this side of the Mississippi. It's got foot-high sandwiches and killer matza ball soup. And they serve double fudge espresso cake that has been described as orgasmic, and not just by me. Each slice is the size of a football field.

No sooner had we settled into the big booth in the back when in walked Bobby, followed by another cop. A small, well muscled man who looked like a compact version of "The Hulk." Bobby spotted us and sauntered over with Bruce Banner in tow.

"Yo," Bobby grinned, leaving everyone at the booth a little damper in the panties. He bent down to kiss Franny, Janine, and Carla on their cheeks, and then nodded to the rest of us. I would've pushed him down if he'd tried to include me in his little kiss-fest, but being lumped in with the second-string nodders felt even worse. Gina smiled up at him, all goo goo eyed and "Milanish." I didn't even know what that meant, but in my head it wasn't a compliment. Bobby squeezed in next to Franny and gestured to his friend to pull up a chair. "Lou, this is everybody. Everybody, Lou." Lou grunted hello.

"Hey, Lou," we all greeted him. It turned out to be Lou's birthday, so we ordered the chocolate cake first, because what's a party without cake, I always say.

As Franny moved her pocketbook to make more room for Bobby, she inadvertently dumped it onto the floor. Out popped the Victoria's Secret bag. Bobby scooped it up and began to examine its contents, one by one. "So what'cha got here, Franny? A little present for Eddie?"

"Will ya give that back to me?" Franny reached over and tried to grab her newly purchased thong out of his hands, but he was too quick for her. He held it up to his face, giving it a thorough inspection. "What is this? An eye patch?"

"You're gonna need an eye patch when I'm through with you," she hissed back at him. Lou reacted with a hearty guffaw and, God help me, I laughed too.

"I'm sorry, Fran," Bobby said. Only he didn't look one bit sorry. On the contrary, he was enjoying himself immensely, and I realized this was the first time since I'd been back that I'd seen Bobby playful and relaxed. Franny stuffed her underwear back into the bag and turned to me.

"And what were *you* laughing at? Don't think I didn't see you sneaking that sexy-assed underwear up to the counter." I stiffened.

"I don't know what you're talking about." *Deny, deny, deny.*

"Oh no?" In a flash she had my pocketbook upside down and out fell the panties. Bobby's eyes dilated at the sight of the skimpy lingerie.

"For your information I bought these for my mother." Everyone busted up, even Gina of the limited vocab. *"I did!* It happens to be *her* birthday too." Haughtily, I gathered up the panties and deposited them back into the bag. "I think this concludes our discussion."

Bobby and Lou had to get back to work so they ordered "to go". When it was ready Bobby stood and made his goodbyes. Then he leaned into me and whispered, "Walk me to the counter." I excused myself to go to the bathroom and followed him up to the cashier. While Lou paid for his order Bobby said, "I've got something to discuss with you. Can we meet later?"

"Can't you tell me now?"

"No." Bobby laughed at my impatience and nodded in Lou's direction.

I thought quickly and shook my head.

"I'm supposed to meet Frankie at the gym later on. I haven't seen him in days and he thinks I'm trying to avoid him because I've gotten myself into some kind of trouble."

"Imagine that."

"Shut up." Lou turned around, his arms laden with "to go" food. Bobby held the door open for him and told him he'd meet him at the car. To me he said, "I'll see you at the gym at six. I haven't been there in a couple of weeks, what with all the shit with my wife." He let his voice trail off and shrugged. "I could use a workout." I hated that he looked so bummed, but there wasn't much I could do. *I* didn't tell him to marry the bitch. Okay, God, strike that last thought. I really am trying to be a more compassionate person. *Honest.*

He left me with an admonition to be careful, which was totally superfluous, because I was so damn paranoid I'd arranged every nano second of my day so that I'd be surrounded by friends and loved ones. No room for disembodied goat heads in my posse.

At ten till six I hung a left on South Street and pulled into the gym parking lot. South Street Boxing Gym is not exactly your upscale yuppie sports center. It's pretty bare bones, no "spin" classes or Hatha yoga. But the club has turned out more than its fair share of heavyweight contenders, and if a person is serious about boxing, this is the place to be.

It was becoming second nature to me to look over my shoulder before I got out of the car. I took a good look around now. The parking lot was dark. Two street lamps were busted, the glass still littering the streets. When we were kids we used to pop them with bee bee guns. Good clean fun. I silently cursed the little brats who put these lights out of commission. It made it that much harder to locate the boogiemen. Taking a deep breath I swung open the car door and ran like hell through the lot and into the gym.

Uncle Frankie was busy until six thirty, but this would give Bobby and me a chance to talk.

"Brandy, is that you, honey?" I looked up at the familiar smiling brown face of Danny Jenkins, one of the club's night managers.

"Danny," I cried, delighted. We extended arms in a complicated handshake we'd made up when I was a kid, and ended in a huge squishy hug. Danny must be in his seventies by now, but he has the body of a much younger man, and according to Frankie he's still one of the best trainers around. He held me away from him, giving me a long appraising look.

"You been sick?"

"No."

"Too skinny," he concluded, shaking his head in disapproval.

"I'll work on that," I laughed. "Have you seen Frankie around?"

"He's in the back office. Somebody else here you might want to see," he added with a glint in his eye. "Bobby DiCarlo's goin' at it with the new kid, Chuckie T, but I don't think you should distract him now. He's got his hands full keepin' up with Chuckie. And you *know* what a distraction you can be to that boy." I blushed from head to foot, remembering the time Danny had caught Bobby and me behind the dumpster doing the unmentionable.

"That was a long time ago, Dan. Is it hot in here?" I took off my jacket and edged my way past a group of men working out with weights, their toned bodies glistening with sweat. Although more and more women are entering the boxing arena it is still primarily a male dominated sport. I took a quick look around. At the moment I was the only female in the joint.

It was cold outside so I'd dressed warmly, but the heat inside the gym was stifling. I pulled off the next layer, a black turtleneck sweater, leaving just a tight fitting thermal undershirt in its place. The sweater was loaded with static electricity, which made my shirt rise up when I peeled off the sweater. That earned me a wolf whistle from one of the guys working out on a punching bag. I kept on walking, eager to find Bobby.

He was down at the end of the room, sparring with a guy about his height but who looked like he had about twenty-five pounds on him. Bobby is six foot one and weighs in at about one seventy-five. They were both wearing sweat pants and were naked from the waist up, which gave me a great view of Bobby's abs. They were hard and tight, not an ounce of fat anywhere. I felt my own stomach muscles contract in response. He looked up at me and nodded an acknowledgement. Danny was right. Chuckie T was giving him a rough time. Bobby's eye was slightly swollen and he was dripping water while Chuckie looked like he hadn't even broken a sweat. He punched Bobby a good one and Bobby reeled back along the ropes. I winced and Chuckie T glanced my way.

"Hey Baby, you're looking mighty fine. You want some a Chuckie T?" He pulled one gloved hand down to his crotch, thrusting his hips forward in a rotating motion.

"No, thank you." Bobby tensed, taking it all in.

"What'sa matter, bitch? Ya think you're too good for Chuckie T?" I didn't get a chance to tell him that yes, I did, in fact, think that very thing, for at that moment Bobby came charging towards him, swinging for all he was worth. He caught Chuckie square in the mouth and blood spurted everywhere. Chuckie responded with a right upper cut but Bobby deflected this and renewed his attack on the larger man. He pinned Chuckie against the ropes and pummeled the crap out of him. This was not skill at work. This was pure rage. While I stood there open-mouthed, a small circle of on-lookers had begun to form, among them my Uncle Frankie. He jumped into the ring and pulled Bobby off of Chuckie. "Okay boys, that's enough." Still holding on to Bobby he suggested that Chuckie's workout was over for the day. Chuckie raised one gloved hand to his mouth, wiping away the blood that was now trickling down his chin. "You're crazy, man," he spat at Bobby. Bobby tried to charge him again but Frankie held him tight. "If you ever even look in her general direction again I will make sure you regret it," Bobby growled low in his throat. Chuckie grabbed his towel and stormed off. Frankie signaled me over. "Do me a favor and watch him for me."

"I don't need a babysitter, Frankie," Bobby fumed.

"Ya coulda fooled me." Frankie let go of Bobby and climbed out of the ring. I wasn't sure how I felt about what I'd just witnessed, but I think it fell somewhere between flattered and pissed off.

"Was that really necessary?" I asked him.

"Probably not." Bobby shook his head, and tiny beads of sweat flew off his hair.

"Then why" —He cut me off.

"He had it coming."

I waited in Frankie's office while Bobby changed into his street clothes. Frankie closed the door behind me. "He's a walking time bomb," he said, shaking his head. "This thing with his kid is really getting to him." I nodded in agreement, but I knew there was more to it than that, only it was nothing I wanted to articulate.

Bobby emerged from the locker room a few minutes later, a sheepish grin plastered on his face.

"Feeling better?"

"Yeah. Sorry about before. I know you could have handled it." I wasn't quite so confident but I'm glad he thought so.

Frankie still had some paperwork to take care of and he didn't think Bobby should be left alone, so he gave me a raincheck on dinner. That left Bobby and me on our own for the evening. I wasn't sure how good an idea that was, but curiosity got the better of me and I suggested we go somewhere so we could talk.

Half an hour later we found ourselves sitting across from each other in a booth, chugging long-necked Buds at DiVinci's Pizza. DiVinci's is your basic dump. Scarred brown wooden booths, paintings of cigar smoking dogs playing poker on velvet backgrounds, lights low so that you don't notice the cockroaches as they shuffle their way across the floor. It's very popular with the college crowd. We were lucky to find seating.

"So, do you want to tell me your big news? I think I've been patient long enough," I said, pulling on my beer.

"I went to see Philip Gruber today."

"You what?" I choked, doing a classic spritz all over the table. "You friggin' went to see him without me?" I slammed my beer down and regretted it immediately,

227

when it began to foam all over the table and onto my lap. "Unhh!" I began mopping up the mess.

"Let's get this straight here, Sweetheart. I'm a cop. I don't need to report to Suzie Citizen before doing my job. Now if you want to know what happened, I suggest you shut up before I change my mind about telling you." I opened my mouth for a snappy and very rude comeback and then thought better of it. "Tell me," I said, instead.

Bobby visited Gruber's house in the early morning, wanting to catch him off guard. Gruber lives alone in a two-story house on the Main Line, which is a very posh section of Philadelphia. Gruber was very cooperative with Bobby. Gracious, even. He invited him in, offered him a cold drink and took him for a tour of his home.

"The guy is a total egomaniac, if you ask me. He's got an entire wall of his office devoted to pictures of himself with famous people at charity events and stuff like that. And there are a bunch of shots of him and the mayor at groundbreaking ceremonies. Oh, and get this, he's got a 'trophy room'."

"Ya mean like bowling and tennis trophies?" Bobby shook his head and took a healthy swig of beer. When he put it down on the table, I picked it up and took a hit too. My beer was in my lap, soaking into my jeans.

"Not exactly. Turns out the guy is a big game hunter. He had deer heads and bears; you name it, all staring down at me from the walls. It was bizarre."

"Any chance he had the back end of a goat there?"

"Huh. I hadn't thought of that." Bobby shook his head, dismissing the notion. "Nah, too easy. Not worth his while." Wow. I thought back to the picture of Gruber in the goofy golf attire. He looked like your standard issue nerd. The guy was really starting to creep me out.

"So what did he say about Williams?" Our pizza arrived and we took a minute to each grab a slice. Bobby dug into his right away, while I patted the grease off mine with a paper napkin. Some of the napkin ended up sticking to the cheese but I was too hungry to care.

"Well, I told him the police were looking for one of his employees, Thurman Williams, in connection with an ongoing investigation. He acted all shocked and said that Williams hadn't been to work in several days, and he hoped he wasn't in any serious trouble."

"Did you believe him?" Bobby shrugged and helped himself to another slice of pizza.

"I don't know. If he's lying he's damn good at it." He drained his beer and signaled to the waitress for two more. She almost broke her neck trying to get to our table and gave him a look that said she didn't move that fast for just anyone.

"Can I get you anything else? She addressed this to Bobby even though I was the only on looking directly at her.

"No thanks," he said, barely looking up.

"Are you sure?" The poor thing was positively wistful. I took in this little scene with amusement tinged with something I couldn't quite put my finger on. The waitress left reluctantly.

"She's cute," I announced, testing the waters.

"Who?"

"Oh, come on. The waitress! She was practically sitting in you lap. Don't tell me you didn't notice," Bobby cracked a smile.

"Jealous?"

"What! Pfft. Get over yourself, DiCarlo. *I did* a long time ago!"

"Is that so?" He asked softly. He leaned across the table, on his elbows, until he was so close our foreheads practically touched. I tried to scoot back, but he took my wrist gently in his, forcing me to stay where I was. My mouth got really dry and I licked my lips in nervous anticipation. He gazed longingly into my eyes and reached his other hand out to me. "You gonna eat that?" He asked seductively. I looked down to where he was pointing. A slice of pizza sat untouched on my plate. I had zero appetite. Slowly I picked up the pizza, my eyes never leaving his, and shoved the entire slice into my mouth. Bobby sat back. "I'll take that as a yes."

We talked for hours. At first we restricted our conversation to the purely professional, going over what he'd learned or more specifically didn't learn at Gruber's house. Trying to figure out where to go from here. But three beers later, and I don't know about him, but I was ready to move on to subjects of a more personal nature.

"Bobby, why did you threaten that guy, Chuckie tonight?" Bobby slumped down in his seat, stretching his legs out under the table. They came to rest against mine. I let myself enjoy the sensation for a moment before moving away.

"The guy's an asshole." He didn't seem inclined to elaborate so I pushed.

"Is that the only reason? He stared at me, not answering, the muscles in his jaw clenching and unclenching reflexively.

"Ask me another question," he said finally.

"Why did you leave me?" Shit! I *know* I said that out loud, but for the life of me I couldn't figure out why. "I'm sorry." Quickly I jumped to my feet. Too quickly. The beer had relaxed me to the point where I had trouble standing up. I stumbled as a wave of dizziness swept over me. Bobby leaped up and caught me before I reeled backwards. He eased me down into my seat.

"Are you okay?"

"No," I groaned inwardly. But to Bobby I just gave a humiliated nod. When he didn't say anything I added, "I don't know why I said that."

"Yes you do." The noise inside DiVinci's was deafening and for a brief moment I thought he'd said, "Yes, you Jew."

"What?" Bobby stood up and threw some money on the table. Then he reached his arm out and pulled me up from the booth. We were standing very close. Mere inches apart. He leaned into me and the air around us stopped moving.

"I said, 'yes, you do.' Come on."

We walked along Penn's Landing. The fog coming in off the river had a haunting effect as it rolled across the water. My jacket was buttoned up to my neck, but still I shivered in the damp air. I've always been overly sensitive to the cold, and I guess Bobby remembered this about me, because he stopped and took off his scarf and wrapped it around my neck. I stood there like a three year old and let him take care of me.

We hadn't spoken a word since we'd left DiVinci's. How could I have shot off my mouth like that? Four years ago I'd sworn on the old *and* the New Testament that he would never know how much he'd hurt me. Four years of denial right down the friggin' drain.

Bobby stopped walking and leaned against the guardrail. I stopped too and looked out over the water. There was something very soothing about the water lapping against the big ships in the shipyard. He turned to face me but I couldn't look at him. I just kept staring out over the river.

"Brandy, four years ago you wouldn't have this conversation with me. We've gotta have it now. It's long overdue."

"I'm listening."

"Well, do you think you could *look* at me? I'm not *that* hard on the eyes, am I?" I knew he was attempting a joke, trying to relax me, so I responded by lifting my eyes to him. Encouraged, he heaved a big sigh and continued. "I guess you know I never had much of a childhood. When I met you I was so screwed up. My mother had just died and I was living with a stranger. A stranger who didn't even like me. My aunt was bound by family obligation to raise me, but she didn't have a clue what I was going through."

"I know. I was there. Remember? Your aunt was a total bitch, by the way. He cracked a smile at that; a brief respite before it turned serious again.

"Listen, I know I'm not telling you anything you don't already know. And I swear I'm not looking for excuses."

"What *are* you looking for, Bobby? Absolution? You got it." I hated that I couldn't control the sarcastic bitterness in my voice. I hated even more that he knew with such clarity how I still felt, after all these years. I turned away again, but not before my eyes welled with tears. He spun me around, forcing me back into the guardrail, demanding that I meet his gaze. I had nowhere to go except into the river, so I opted for dry land.

"You trusted me and I fucked up, and if I could take it back I would in a heartbeat."

His words reverberated in my head, until suddenly, I was struck with the mother of all epiphanies, and the reason for all the anger and hurt of the past four years became crystal clear to me. *It was never a question of love. It was a question of trust.* I knew Bobby loved me and he always would. I would always love him too. I also knew that when he said he would "take it back if he could," he didn't mean the part about breaking up with me. We were so young when we'd started out, breaking up was inevitable. I could have forgiven him for wanting to be with other people. I would have forgiven him anything, if only he'd had the guts to tell me the truth in the first place. Because for me the real loss wasn't the sex. It was the loss of our friendship. A friendship built on complete trust. Okay, so I missed the sex part too, but why quibble in the middle of an epiphany. The anger I'd been carrying around with me for so long seemed to drift away in the harbor fog. Suddenly, I smiled. It was the first completely genuine, pain free smile he'd seen on my face in four years. It took him by surprise.

"Want to let me in on it?" I put my hand up to his cheek. It felt cold to my touch. He reached up and placed his hand over mine. "Bobby," I said, "I think this is the beginning of a beautiful friendship."

I got home at around eleven. Bobby insisted on following me to my house. I could have tried to talk him out of it, but the truth is that since Halloween Night I've been living in a perpetual state of fear. The thought is never far from my mind that at any given moment some hatchet-wielding maniac could jump out of the bushes and chop me into tiny bite sized pieces. So when Bobby told me what he planned to do, I made the obligatory "that's not necessary" noises before I gave in and let him follow me home.

He checked all the doors and windows and even took a cursory walk around the outside of the house, and when he was satisfied that all was secure he left, after issuing the standard warning to be careful.

It was too quiet in the house so I flipped on the t.v. "Rocky" was on. Yeah. While Rocky beat up a side of beef I ran into the kitchen to get a snack. Just then the phone rang. My stomach lurched as I reached for the receiver and said a tentative hello. It was only Franny.

"Hey Fran, what's up?" I grabbed some Fruit Loops from the cupboard and ate them dry out of the box.

"Eddie and I just had a fight about whether we should let his crazy uncle Nuncio make a speech at the wedding, and I told Eddie he wasn't even invited to the wedding, so now Eddie's mad and he's in the bedroom watching "Rocky.""

"Me, too," I said, hoping she'd take the hint. It's not that I didn't want to hear all about Uncle Nuncio. I just really wanted to see "Rocky." I've seen the movie a hundred times, but I still get really worried that he's not going to be able to "go the distance" without me there to cheer him on.

"Hey, speaking of boxing, is it true that Bobby took out Chuckie T tonight? Eddie's friend "Jimmy the Tuna" was at the gym and said Frankie had to break them up. Something to do with some girl."

"That would be me," I sighed.

"I *knew* it! Franny yelled. "Tell me and don't leave out a thing!"

"So you forgave him and now you're friends again."

"Basically, yeah."

"And that's all you want. Friendship." I paused for a minute, thinking about this.

"Yeah. That's all. He's married Fran, and I don't do married men."

"Unhappily married."

"I don't do unhappily married men, either. And before you ask me how I'd feel if he weren't married, I think I'd feel the same. At least for now." Ask me if I was still attracted to Bobby. Fuck, yes. But we're different than when we started out all those years ago. Things change. Bobby used to complete me. Now I complete myself.

I woke up early and had an inexplicable urge to go to Sunday mass. I hadn't been in years, but I figured with all that's been going on lately it couldn't hurt. Afterwards, I stopped by Paul's and brought him bagels and cream cheese. He'd heard about the incident at the gym from Frankie and wanted all the details.

"Jesus Christ!" I yelled, forgetting I'd just spent an hour and a half in church exacting penance on myself for, among other things, taking the Lord's name in vain. "Should I take out an ad?" Paul settled for the abbreviated version and an onion bagel.

I was back home by eleven after making a pit stop at Starbucks for a "redeye. I'd been on an emotional roller coaster starting with my talk with Bobby, and I hadn't had time to think about the whole Maitlin-Williams-Mayor connection. I was going to devote today to working on it, but I needed a jumpstart. I settled in with my coffee and drummed my fingers on the table. I came up with nothing. "Okay, then."

I wandered into the living room and put on some music, the soundtrack from "Cats." My parents are seriously in need of an update on their CD collection. When the phone rang I grabbed it absently and said hello.

"Is this Brandy Alexander?" The unfamiliar male voice was low and rough and panic surged through me. "Who wants to know?" I growled, trying to sound tough, although it was hard to pull off with "Jenny Anydots" blaring in the background. He brushed off the question.

"Not important. Look, I know you've been investigating the mayor, and I have some information you may be interested in."

"Why would you think that?" I was stalling for time, trying to get my thoughts straight, and he knew it.

"I don't have time to play games." Something in his voice told me he was more scared than threatening. "I want you to meet you somewhere." Between the caffeine and the adrenalin my heart was pumping so hard I thought it would pop right out of my chest.

"Where?"

"Thirtieth Street Station."

"What's in it for you?" He went quiet for a minute and I thought he'd hung up. When he spoke again what he said surprised the crap out of me.

"Hopefully, my life." He gave a sardonic laugh and a chill ran through me. I should have hung up, but I never seem to be able to do the things I should. I was too fascinated.

"When do you want to meet?" He answered right away, as if he'd been anticipating that I'd agree to this.

"Tonight at eight. I'll meet you on the southwest corner of the station, in front of the newsstand." Good. Lots of people. Lots of witnesses in case he turned out to be Hatchet Man. If he hacked me up and stuffed me in one of those little station lockers, someone would be bound to notice. This isn't New York, after all.

"Okay," I said. I could always change my mind. *Was changing my mind as we spoke, as a matter of fact.* "How will I recognize you?"

"I'll recognize you." Well, that was creepy. "Oh, and I know you're friends with that cop, DiCarlo. No cops or the deals off." What else did this guy know about me?

There was no way I was going to meet him alone. What if my mystery date turned out to be Thurman Williams? I already knew how things turned out whenever he was around. I couldn't call Bobby. He fell into the cop category. Frankie? Paul? No, I would not involve them in something that could get them killed. Why was it again that I agreed to meet this guy? "I have one more question," I said. "Why me?"

"I trust you." Shit.

The phone rang four times and I was just about to hang up when a woman's voice answered. She sounded sleepy and annoyed. I panicked and hung up, not sure if I'd dialed correctly, praying that I hadn't. I tried again. Same woman, only this time she just sounded annoyed. "Um, may I speak with Nick, please?"

"He's in the shower. Who's calling?" My throat got all lumpy and I couldn't answer her if I tried, so I hung up again. I sat at my kitchen table, shredding a paper napkin and trying to figure out why I was feeling so mad I wanted to rip the heads off of live chickens. Ten minutes later the phone rang.

"Hello?"

"Good morning, Brandy Alexander." *Nick.* His voice was teasing, and very "just woke up after a night of hot sex" husky. I don't know who I hated more, him for sounding that way or her for making him sound that way.

"Oh, hi Nick. What's up?" *Very cool.* I could hear him whisper something to her in the background and it pissed the hell out of me. So I repeated in my best "bitch" voice, "What's up?" He came back on the line.

"I don't know. You called me."

"I did not." *He has no proof.*

"Oh. Your name turned up on Caller I.D. My mistake." Unhhh! Now I look like a bitch and a liar. I decided to ignore the whole thing.

"Well, since I've got you on the line…"

I told him about the mysterious phone call and my plan to rendezvous at the train station at eight o'clock.

"And you want me to come with you."

"Well…" More whispering in the background, this time female. He said something back to her and they both laughed.

"Ya know, Nick, it sounds like you're busy. I'll catch you when you're not so preoccupied." And for the third time that morning I hung up.

He must've hit redial because the phone rang right away. I contemplated not answering, but he already knew I was home.

"What?"

"We weren't finished with our conversation. What time do you want me there tonight?" He asked, pleasantly. *Oh he thinks he's so cool.*

"It's nice of you to offer, but I think I'll field this one myself." *God I could be childish.*

"Okay." *Okay?*

"I can take care of myself, you know," I added belligerently, as if he'd given me an argument.

"You're very capable," he agreed.

"So, I'll be going then—alone—to meet some stranger. *Could* be a rapist. *Could* be a murderer…"

"What time do you want me to pick you up?"

"Seven thirty."

I had absolutely no right to feel this way, but I hoped they'd had a big fight after we hung up the phone. She'd beg him to stay and make passionate love with her all night, but Nick would say, "No, bitch. Brandy needs me. I'm outta here." Where was I getting this stuff? Nick doesn't talk anything like that. I decided I had way too much time on my hands and went off to do something productive.

I typed in Schoolmates.com on Janine's computer, and Philip Gruber's name and the name of the college and year in which he graduated. Janine was off to her mother's for her weekly "Laundry and Lecture," but she told me to take as much time as I needed. There was something weird about Philip Gruber but I couldn't quite put my finger on it. Judging from the list of charities he donated to, he certainly played the role of nerdy philanthropist to the hilt. But I got the feeling there was another Philip Gruber lurking behind the bespeckled nice guy image. Call me crazy but anybody who collected animal heads to glue on his wall can't be as mild mannered as this guy was making himself out to be. I hoped that his old college buddies might be able to shed some light on him.

Two hours later I had a much clearer picture of Philip "The Jackal" Gruber than before. I introduced myself as Brandy Alexander, features editor for the Philadelphia based Magazine "Newsworthy!" and I told them I was doing an article on one of their college friends, Philip Gruber. According to his classmates, the guy *had* no friends, with the possible exception of the man who eventually was to become his partner, Michael Hoffman. The general consensus was that Gruber would sell his grandmother's dentures if he thought he could turn a buck. He was nicknamed "The Jackal" after a particularly nasty incident, in which he was suspected of taking money to trip up another runner in a high stakes relay race so that the favored runner could win. The guy who fell broke his leg in three places and had to forfeit his athletic scholarship. Well, no one accused Gruber of not being enterprising.

On a whim I then looked up his ex wife, Marlo, in the phone book. According to the article I'd read on Gruber, Marlo owned an art gallery in Center City. She answered the phone herself and I made my fake introductions. I have always found that the key to successful lying was in believing the lie myself. I was really starting to like my pretend job with Newsworthy!

Marlo Gruber's cheery "phone answering" voice died as soon as I mentioned her ex husband's name. I could feel a physical shift in her demeanor as she told me in no uncertain terms that she was not willing to discuss the man. I would have chalked it up to the usual post divorce bitterness, except that she didn't sound bitter. She sounded scared shitless. What was with this guy, anyway?

When I was finished at Janine's I headed home to get dressed for my rendezvous with the mystery man. What does one wear to a clandestine meeting with a stranger? Nick would be there too, which definitely upped the ante. Okay, we were meeting outside a train station. How out of place would I look dressed in a slinky black gown and four-inch stiletto heels if I even owned that kind of wardrobe, which I don't. But I wanted to look nice for Nick. I settled on a fresh pair of jeans and my new black underwear. At least *I'd* know I looked nice.

By seven twenty-five I was ready to go. My freshly washed hair smelled like vanilla and fell tangle-free to my shoulders. The new bra was slightly push-up, which gave the illusion that I actually had breasts to speak of. My jeans were tight and my top was low. I debated about shoes, but in the end I opted for my old shit-kicker boots, just in case things turned nasty and I had to kick the shit out of somebody. This was totally uncharted territory and I wanted to be prepared for any eventuality. I knew it was kinda sick to turn this into a "date with Nick" of sorts, when some poor schlub was counting on me to save his life. But who knew when I'd have another opportunity to spend time with Santiago, and I'm a big believer in multi tasking.

At exactly seven thirty the doorbell rang. Suddenly the seriousness of what I was about to embark on hit me. "Oh my God, this isn't a game. This is a real life murder investigation, with informants and dead people and everything." I opened the door and I freaked. "Nick," I screamed, my neurotic impulses bearing down on me, "I can't do this. Who do I think I am, Woodward and Bernstein? I investigate Flower Shows and Doggie Beauty pageants for a living. I'm strictly small potatoes. What made me think I could pull off meeting some stranger who says his life is in my hands? He's wrong. I can't be trusted. I'm so sorry I dragged you out here tonight. I can't go. You look very nice, by the way." He was wearing a pair of faded Levi's and an old herringbone jacket, the sleeves pushed up to reveal his ever- present silver wristband. I could tell he was trying hard to keep from laughing. He stuffed his hands in his jacket pocket and the front of the jacket fell away, revealing what appeared to be the business end of a .38. "Is that a gun under there?" I asked.

"It's illegal to carry concealed." I waited for him to go on, but that was it as far as he was concerned. I stepped aside and let him into the house. It felt weird to have dangerous, scary, beautiful Nick standing in my mommy's living room. He smiled at me, encouragingly. When he spoke his words were non judgmental and soothing.

"If you don't want to do this, I'm not going to push you. I just want you to think about how you'll feel if you don't go." He had me there.

We found parking out on the street several blocks from the station. Since we were a few minutes early we went over the plan again. I would walk up to the corner alone, Nick following behind at a discreet distance. It would be crowded at the front of the building, so Nick would blend in nicely with the commuters. He wouldn't be more than a few feet away; even if I couldn't see him I had to trust that he was there. If I felt any discomfort at all, I was to raise my hand like I was hailing a cab and Nick would appear at my side. It was a simple plan and, as it turned out, quite unnecessary.

My heart lodged firmly in my mouth, I walked stiff legged to the appointed corner. Casually I looked about, noting the people around me. Most of them appeared to be business folk, coming home after an exhausting day at work. Some carried luggage. A few had shopping bags. After a few minutes I noticed a man about Nick's height walking towards me. He did a cursory glance around before his eyes settled on me. The man wore a gray sweatshirt and jogging pants. A Phillies' baseball cap obscured his face. Someone jostled him and he jumped back slightly. When he realized it was an accident, he nodded and quickened his pace. He was within handshaking distance when a crackling sound stung the air, and in that instant his head exploded like a Halloween pumpkin that had been dropped from a second story window. Hysterical screaming echoed all around me, and in a blink I was sent sprawling as a heavy weight tackled me from behind. My head hit the concrete and I had just enough time to register Nick's face hovering above me before I blacked out. I remember thinking he looked terribly handsome.

People were running, screaming, crying. Sirens wailed in the distance. And pieces of a man's broken and bloodied head lay inches from my own. I tried to get up but felt Nick's strong hand gently push me back down. His dark eyes roved over me and for the second time in a little over a week I was checked for signs of concussion. Finally, he allowed me to sit up. "Are you okay?" He asked. *Okay? A man's head just exploded in my face. I have bits of someone else's cerebellum stuck in my hair. Of course I'm not okay!*

"I'm fine." I crawled to my knees and threw my guts up. The police were beginning to arrive on the scene. Nick scooped me up and forced his way through the crowd. There were too many people and not enough cops, so Nick and I managed to slip through the cracks. I drifted in and out of consciousness as he carried me beyond the police barriers and back to his car.

A familiar voice penetrated the fog in my brain. Bobby?

"Put her down, Santiago." A gun, waved directly in Nick's face, accompanied the command.

"She can't stand up on her own," Nick explained calmly. "She's in shock."

"What are you doing here?" Bobby's voice was controlled, but barely.

"That guy who was shot, he was meeting Brandy tonight. He said he had information for her about the mayor." Nick paused. "She didn't tell you about this, did she?" Oh God, why bring that up now? I struggled to climb out of Nick's arms, but he wouldn't put me down.

"Let me explain," I said weakly.

"We don't have time. Look, DiCarlo, the police are going to want to question her. You can do that on your own, after we get her out of here. Do you really want her exposed to God only knows what danger now? That bullet could have been meant for her, for all we know, and every second that we stand here chatting only puts her in more danger. I can protect her. You know I can."

"You did a hell of a job protecting her tonight." I felt Nick's arms tighten automatically around me.

"My head hurts."

"Get her out of here," Bobby hissed through gritted teeth. "But I swear to God if she's harmed in any way"— Nick reached into his pocket and took out his wallet. He balanced me on his knee and handed Bobby a business card.

"Here's my private phone number and home address. Call or come by as soon as you're finished here." Bobby took the card and stuffed it in his pocket. Then he leaned over me and pushed my bangs aside, and placed a kiss on my forehead. There was hurt in his eyes and I knew I'd put it there. Why hadn't I told him about tonight? Well, I'd have plenty of time to think about it, because after this evening I wasn't planning on being able to sleep again for the rest of my life.

Chapter Fourteen

Nick pulled up in front of a beautiful, ivy-covered, brick apartment building overlooking Rittenhouse Square. It was four stories tall, with large beveled glass windows and a marble entryway. The place was quietly elegant and smelled of old money. Somehow it suited Nick. He parked right out front in the loading zone and ran around the side of the car to let me out. I'd spent the entire ride back to his place curled up in a fetal position in the passenger's seat. He had a blanket in the trunk, which he'd wrapped around me, but I just couldn't seem to get warm. Nick kept up a steady stream of comforting words, occasionally reaching out to touch me. A concussion was not out of the realm of possibility and he fought to keep me awake. It was quite a struggle. My head was throbbing and my body ached. But mostly I just wanted some relief from the agonizing image that kept floating across my mind. When a man's head shatters right before your eyes, it tends to stay with you.

I tried to walk on my own, but my knees kept giving way. Nick picked me up and carried me to the elevator.

"I'm sorry I'm so much trouble," I mumbled into his shoulder. It was uncharacteristic of me to act like such a wimp, and I really hated myself for it. Nick pressed the elevator button for the fourth floor. The doors opened and he stepped in, and I felt the floor drop beneath us as it began to ascend. The elevator doors opened again, and he carried me down a long hallway, stopping at the door at the end.

"Are you able to stand up?" He asked. I nodded and he let me down slowly, propping me against the wall while he dug in his pocket for his key. The door opened onto a small foyer, which led into the living room. It was a large room with hardwood floors and cathedral ceilings. It was furnished with an overstuffed beige leather couch, and two matching chairs. There were wall-to-wall bookshelves, filled to overflowing with books, but the most impressive piece of furniture, by far, was the magnificent old baby grand piano that stood in the corner by the window.

I wandered into the middle of the room, not knowing what to do with myself. Nick threw his keys on the table in the foyer and guided me over to the couch, and I sat down, grateful not to have to support my weight.

"Can I get you something?" He stared at me, concern creasing his face.

"A toothbrush, if you have an extra one. And a bottle of scotch." He smiled and disappeared down the hallway. A minute later he returned, carrying a new toothbrush, still in its wrapper. He directed me to the bathroom and turned on the light. The bathroom had mint green and black tile and an old- fashioned stand-alone sink. Very art deco. I closed the door and sank down onto the toilet seat lid. On cue, the tears began to fall, slowly at first and then with increasing force. As my mind replayed the events of the evening, my body trembled so violently I

almost fell off the seat. I sat there for several minutes, my
arms wrapped around my knees, rocking back and forth
trying to soothe myself. When I was sure I could stand up
without collapsing, I bent over the sink and brushed my
teeth, scrubbing away the sour taste of bile in my mouth.
I washed my face and blew my nose and turned off the
light. With any luck at all, Nick wouldn't know that I'd
been crying. I swung open the bathroom door. He was
waiting for me on the other side.

"Oh, hi." I said, feeling suddenly shy. Once again I
was struck by the fact that in spite of our recent history, I
barely knew this man. We had shared a terrifying ordeal
tonight, and some fairly hot (at least by my meager
standards) moments on the dance floor, but other than
the fact that I was unbelievably attracted to him, what
did I actually know about Nick? *And what was wrong
with me that I should see a stranger's head smashed to
smithereens and still have the hormonal energy to be
turned on by a pretty face?* Oh, I am sooo going to Hell
over this one.

"Feeling better?"

"Uh huh. Thanks for the toothbrush."

"Want to talk about it?" I shook my head, no.
Gathering up my pseudo courage I asked him if he would
mind taking me home, or if I should call a cab.

"You're not going anywhere, tonight, angel."

"I'm not?" Thank God he wasn't throwing me out! I
simply couldn't bear to be alone. I would have to move
in with Mrs. Gentile.

"I don't know what would piss off DiCarlo more,
having you stay here or sending you home. But I get the
feeling he'd rather you be safe, even if it means spending
the night with me." The words rolled off his tongue with
the barest hint of a southern slur. Funny, I'd never noticed

it before. It took me another beat to register what he'd said, and when it did, my stomach lurched joyfully. *I'm spending the night with Nick. Oh boy!*

"Listen, darlin', eventually we're going to have to talk about what happened tonight."

"I know," I sighed. Just— not yet, okay?" I was curled up on one of the leather chairs, my legs tucked up under me, listening to the soft strains of an exotic CD. It was Gypsy music, very haunting. Very Nick. Earlier, he had suggested that I take a hot bath. My muscles were beginning to seize up on me, and it was becoming increasingly more difficult to move. I felt really funny about performing such an intimate— make that *naked* task in his house. He seemed to sense my discomfort and was amused by it. "I could help you," he offered. "You know, scrub those hard to reach places."

"Ya know what? I probably don't need a bath. I read somewhere that too much bathing is bad for your internal organs. It shrinks them and then they don't function properly."

"Brandy, trust me, you need a bath." I looked down at where he was staring, and for the first time I realized that parts of me and my clothes were splattered with the dead man's blood. He disappeared into his bedroom and returned a few minutes later, holding a pair of gray sweatpants and a long sleeved, crewneck, black cotton shirt. He put them on the bathroom sink, ran the water for me, and left, quietly closing the door behind him. I thought about locking it but that just seemed rude.

I stayed in the bathroom for a good half an hour, first soaking in the tub, then rummaging through his medicine cabinet. You can tell a lot about a person by his medicine cabinet. For instance, Nick was very neat. He had the standard pain relievers lined up on the first shelf, and there were no old bottles of cough syrup with crust forming on the cap lurking in the back. A box of Band-aids took up the next shelf, and an open box of condoms. Hmm. My thoughts wandered back to the woman who had answered the phone this morning and I felt a sudden surge of hatred for this nameless creature. And I wasn't too happy with Nick, either. I slammed the cabinet door shut with such force it popped back open, causing one of the glass shelves to dislodge and crash into the sink. Oops.

"Are you okay?" Nick called from somewhere in the other room.

"Um, yeah, I just needed a Band-aid." Maybe he won't notice the missing shelf.

After I cleaned up the mess and vowed in my head never to go snooping in other people's stuff again, I resisted the urge to peek in Nick's bedroom and strode back into the living room. I had hitched up the sweatpants as far as they could go, and then rolled the waistband down until they settled comfortably on my hips. After much internal debate, I had decided to forgo underwear so that I could wash it out and have something clean to wear in the morning. As they lay dripping wet on the edge of the tub I decided it felt too weird going without panties, but it was too late to do anything about it.

It was after twelve and I was utterly exhausted, yet too full of anxiety to sleep. Bobby hadn't called and I was beginning to get worried. I expressed this to Nick. Just then the phone rang. Nick picked it up and listened for a moment. "Speak of the devil." Bobby was calling to check up on me. I took the phone and assured him that I was all right. All hell was breaking loose at the station and he couldn't get away. It turned out that the man who tried to meet me tonight was a cop named Tom Belski, a twenty-four year veteran who was up for retirement next year. On a hunch Bobby faxed over a picture of him to Johnny at the safe house, and Johnny positive I.D.'d him as the detective who had shown up at his doorstep, masquerading as Detective Strom. I relayed all this back to Nick.

"I'm leaving here in about an hour," Bobby said. "I could come and get you and take you back to my place."

"I don't think that's a very good idea, Bobby."

"I know." He sounded absolutely miserable. If the neighborhood grapevine got wind that I'd spent the night at his house, he'd never get his kid back.

"I'm fine," I told him with all the false conviction I could muster. "I'll see you tomorrow."

Nick showed me to the spare room. I felt equal parts disappointment and relief that he didn't try to sweet talk me into bedding down with him. I really hoped it wasn't due to lack of interest but out of consideration of my feelings. The room doubled as an office. It had a computer, and file cabinets and a comfortable sofa bed. I climbed in and pulled the covers up to my chin, propping myself up against the pillows. Nick stood in the doorway, watching me. I didn't know how to ask him about a nightlight, without sounding like a complete baby, so instead I said the only other thing that was on my mind. "I'm sorry, Nick. I am so sorry." He pushed off the doorjamb and settled down at the end of the bed. Even in the dark I could see him smile.

"For what?"

"How much time ya got?" He laughed softly, shaking his head. "You turned me down at first," I reminded him. "I guess you should have stuck with your first instincts."

"And miss all the fun?" He leaned in and tucked the blankets around me. "Goodnight, Brandy Alexander." A lone tear slid down my cheek and for once I was grateful for the dark.

I woke up about an hour later, sweat pouring off me, drenching my clothes. The dream was disjointed and terrifying. I lay in bed and tried to get my heart to beat normally, but I couldn't stop the icy fear that gripped me. A sliver of light emanated from under the door, so I climbed out of bed and crept down the hall. Nick was sitting at the piano, softly playing a beautiful, heartbreakingly melancholy tune. He was wearing loose black sweatpants and a white, sleeveless undershirt, which revealed a tattoo right below his shoulder. It looked like some kind of ancient tribal symbol etched into his caramel colored skin. He was smoking one of his thin brown exotic cigarettes, the ones he had sworn off, and he looked indescribably sad. He stopped playing and glanced up at me. "Bad dream?"

I nodded, unable to speak. He blew out a breath of smoke and extinguished the cigarette. Then he walked over to me and led me by the hand to the big leather chair. He sat down, pulling me onto his lap, and wrapped his arms around me. "I know it's not the red velvet chair, but maybe this will do for now." I lay my head against his chest and felt my body relax in his protective embrace.

"Nick," I said very quietly, "What does it feel like to kill someone?" He let out a small sigh.

"It depends."

"On what?"

"On who it is. Sometimes it's sad. Sometimes, it's— satisfying." Slowly, conscious thought began to drift away and I fell into a dreamless sleep.

I woke up alone in Nick's bed. He must've moved me in the middle of the night. Did he sleep in here with me? I really wish I knew so I could be retroactively thrilled. He had a king sized bed with navy blue sheets and a blue and green tartan plaid comforter. The dresser was dark wood, and devoid of personal knick-knacks, except for two small framed pictures. One was an old, faded photograph of a beautiful young woman with her arm draped around a little boy. He looked to be about five years old. The other photo was recent and showed Nick surrounded by a group of men in Israeli army fatigues. The bed stand was an antique and books were piled high on top of it, an eclectic mix of philosophy, self-defense, military strategies and Erotica. I felt myself blush and hopped out of bed. It was a little after nine. I headed off for the bathroom, but the sound of an angry, raised voice coming from the kitchen stopped me. The voice belonged to Bobby.

"How could you let her go, man? She could have been killed." Then, Nick's voice, softer, more controlled.

"Any suggestions on how to stop her? She was going to do this, with me or without me. I thought it would be better if I went along."

"Jesus Christ." Bobby banged his hand down on something hard. "She's just so—so fucking stubborn sometimes."

"Yeah, I picked up on that." Oh fabulous. Now they were bonding over my personality flaws.

"What are you getting out of this, Santiago? You don't strike me as someone who would do something for nothing." I strained against the door to hear his response.

"What's it to you, DiCarlo?" Nick answered smoothly. So much for male bonding. I decided to make an appearance before Bobby challenged him to a duel.

"Hey."

"Hey." Nick stood at the sink, filling the coffee pot with water. Bobby sat at the kitchen counter on a barstool. He'd been up all night at the station and was just going home to grab a shower and change clothes. All available cops were on duty. When one of their own is killed, it's a very big deal. Bobby didn't tell anyone that I was at the train station to meet Belski. He wasn't convinced that Belski was the only cop who had been hired by the mayor, and it seemed prudent to keep his mouth shut until he had more information.

"Has anyone at the precinct mentioned that Belski may have been on the take? I mean we have proof now that he impersonated another officer and got the pictures but didn't turn in the evidence. And it would only stand to reason that he was the one who stole the evidence in the last Maitlin murder too."

"Brandy," Bobby said, "You're forgetting that we're the only ones who know that. Everyone else thinks John is dead. It's a little tough for a dead man to I.D. someone."

"Well, maybe it's time to resurrect John. And while we're at it, I think we should have a talk with the mayor too." Bobby and Nick exchanged long-suffering looks.

"I saw that, " I snapped. "Look, I know that a lot of this is just conjecture on my part, but we know certain things to be true. Fact," I said, ticking them off on my fingers as I went along, "Thurman Williams worked for Hoffman and Gruber. Fact, Williams blew up John's boat. Fact, or common knowledge, same difference, Hoffman and Gruber Construction Company paid a lot of money to have Mayor Bradley Richardson elected so that he could turn over city contracts to them. Now, suppose Curtis Maitlin somehow found out about this little financial arrangement and threatened to expose the mayor, unless he pulled the evidence on the first killing. I'm not saying that Richardson was happy about doing it, but what if Maitlin told him it was an accident, he didn't mean to kill the guy, and Bobby, you said yourself that the guy who died had no family, nobody who seemed to notice he was gone. Maybe in Richardson's eyes, it was one less pervert to clutter up his city. But then the second guy was killed and suddenly people are taking notice. That cop Belski was scared. Everyone associated with this case is ending up burnt toast. I think he knew he was next, and that's why he wanted to spill his guts to me." I stopped, exhausted. I'd been up for close to fifteen minutes and I hadn't had any coffee or chocolate. I wanted both. Nick poured me a cup and I sat down on the other barstool. I turned to Bobby. "It made sense before and now that we have this new information it seems even more clear. Thurman Williams may have pulled the trigger, but someone else is pulling the strings. The mayor's our man. Or possibly Gruber."

"Why rule out Williams?" Bobby yelled. "Maybe he had some vendetta against Maitlin and he was acting alone. You can't go around accusing people with a bunch of speculation, because what it amounts to is you don't know jack shit." Boy, he sure was irritable.

"Bobby, they must realize I'm close to putting it all together or else they wouldn't be trying so hard to scare me off." Bobby closed his eyes and I could almost hear his mental "count to ten." When he opened his eyes he said, "Why don't you lay off this thing before they shut you up permanently?" He pushed himself off the barstool and headed for the front door. "Call your brother. He's worried about you." He gave a brief nod to Nick and was gone. I turned to Nick. "I think I should contact the mayor." Nick fought back a laugh.

"You really *don't* listen to a thing that guy says, do you?" I thought about it. No, I guess I don't. "Look, I hate to be a party pooper, but I have to go along with DiCarlo on this one."

Nick finished his coffee and went off to take a shower. I waited until I heard the bathroom door close and then I picked up the phone and dialed four one one.

"Philadelphia. City Hall, please."

I stated my name to the receptionist and, when asked, told him my business was of a personal nature. I was put on hold for a minute and then the mayor's voice came on the line. He sounded formal and strained, and frankly not very happy to hear from me. "Thank you for coming to the phone, Mayor. I wasn't sure you would."

"Ms. Alexander, I'm a busy man, and after the stunt you pulled, I'm a whole lot busier. What is it that you want?" Okay, not in the mood for chit chat. I totally understood how he felt, because now that I had him on the line common sense reared its ugly head, and I was sort of wishing I hadn't called him.

"Mayor, recently, certain facts about you have come to my attention, and I believe it would be mutually beneficial to get together to discuss them." I was formulating my plan as we went along, and I just hoped an idea popped up in my brain before it was my turn to speak again.

"I'm afraid I don't know what you're talking about." That made two of us.

"I think you do."

"No," he insisted, annoyance creeping into his voice. "I don't." I sighed. Blackmailing a public official is probably a federal offence so I was trying to be subtle. But this guy just wasn't getting it. I decided to go for broke.

"So, any breakthroughs in the Curtis Maitlin murder case? I've heard he was into all kinds of disreputable things, involving the most surprising people." *Hint, hint, you moron.* For all I knew I was being taped and Federal agents were bearing down on my door at this very moment. I held my breath and waited for what seemed like a really long time. When he spoke again, it was with the tightly composed voice of a seasoned politician.

"Ms. Alexander, I have a very full schedule today, but if you would be so kind as to join me for a drink at my home, later this evening, I would be happy to discuss whatever it is you have on your mind. My family is away visiting relatives for a few days, so we can be assured no interruptions." I copied down his address and told him I'd be there at eight, and then I hung up before I said anything else that could get me ten to twenty.

"I assume you have a plan." I jumped a mile at the sound of Nick's voice. He was standing in the doorway of his bedroom, his arms raised, lightly touching the top of the doorframe. His wet hair was slicked back from his face, and a towel was wrapped around his waist, showcasing his incredibly toned body. He had a slighter build than Bobby, but equally powerful. His chest was smooth and his stomach muscles, tight. I sucked in my breath at the sight of him. Quickly, I turned away and poured myself another cup of coffee.

"When did you get out of the shower?"

"Don't you mean, 'How long have I been standing here?' Long enough to know I can't leave you alone for a minute." I glanced back at him. He seemed more amused than angry.

"Okay, so I don't always follow other people's advice. My gut was telling me to call the mayor." Barely suppressing a smile he inched towards me, a wild cat stalking his prey. His towel hung precariously low on his hips.

"And what's your gut telling you right now?" Nick said, his voice deepening.

"Run." I squeaked. He laughed, throwing his head back, and I got a rush at the sight of him.

"I make you nervous." It wasn't a question.

"Sometime," I gulped. "A little bit."

"Why?" He backed me up against the kitchen counter, spreading his muscular arms on either side of me, bracing himself on the counter top. He stared down at me, his eyes a dark pool of melted chocolate. He began to slowly press himself against me, smiling as I tried to wiggle free.

"Well, there's that, for starters," I breathed, staring down at his towel, which had grown noticeably larger and was rubbing against my stomach. Nick reached out and framed my face with his hands. He stared intently at me, and then slowly pressed his soft, full lips over mine. *Oh my God!* I didn't move a muscle, which is more than I could say for Nick. I let myself enjoy the feeling for a moment, but panic set in and I tried to move away again. This time he let me.

"You've got to stop doing that," I said, hoarsely.

"Why?" That smile again. I wasn't sure why, and I would be really disappointed if he did stop. But I felt like he was teasing me, and after a four-year dry spell I was in no mood to be teased. "You really don't know how sexy you are, do you, Brandy Alexander."

"Shut uh-up!"

My plan was simple. Make that imbecilic. I was going to meet the mayor and convince him that I had evidence that Curtis Maitlin was blackmailing him, because Maitlin knew about the deal with the contracting firm, which would effectively end the mayor's political career and probably earn him some hefty jail time. So he had Maitlin and everyone connected to him wasted. Then I would offer to keep quiet, for a price. The mayor would cave in to my demands, and I'd get it all on tape. He'd be arrested and carted off to prison before he could make me his next victim, and I would win the Pulitzer Prize for my phenomenal investigative reporting. Whoo hoo!

Nick agreed that I'd already stuck my foot in too deep to step out gracefully now.

"So, is this a one-woman operation, or did you have someone in mind to back you up this evening?" God, I hated to ask, but he was going to make me.

"Actually," I replied casually, "I thought I'd ask Carla if she wanted to ride shotgun, tonight. She's always up for a little action."

"Carla," he repeated, a smile playing on his lips. "I've got to admit, I'm a little disappointed. I've got all this neat new surveillance equipment that I've been anxious to try out. But if you've already promised Carla..." He shrugged. I breathed a sigh of relief and tried to look like I'd just made up my mind.

"Look, you've done a lot for me, so I'm sure Carla will understand if I let you come with me, instead."

"Thanks," Nick said, solemnly. I won't forget this."

My eyes filled unexpectedly with tears.

"Neither will I."

Nick had appointments all day, something to do with training rebel soldiers from Algeria, in his highly specialized form of self-defense. I'm not exactly sure, since I obtained this information through my usual method of listening at the door, and Nick has very thick doors. He arranged for an associate to stick with me so that I could go home, change my clothes and do some errands. I didn't like the idea of spending my day in the company of a stranger, but it seemed to work out well for Whitney Houston in "The Bodyguard." She ended up with Kevin Costner, and the more I thought about Kevin Costner in The Bodyguard, the more the idea began to appeal to me.

A half an hour later the doorbell rang, and in walked the largest woman I'd ever laid eyes on. She must have been about six foot eight in both directions, with muscles bulging out of her blue denim work shirt, and tree-trunk legs encased in super stretch blue jeans. Next to her I looked positively two-dimensional. Her name was Nell and she was from Sweden. Apparently Nick had never seen "The Bodyguard."

"Nell doesn't speak much English, but she's very good at her job. Just don't make any sudden moves around her."

There were three messages on the answering machine when I got home. Message number one was from my mother. She hadn't heard from me in a few days and she hoped that I wasn't too bored being stuck in Philadelphia, after the exciting life that I lead in Los Angeles. Call number two was from my producer, Gail. She had the "cutest" idea for a segment for when I returned from my vacation. "You know how Los Angeles is the plastic surgery capital of the world. What do you think of "On Air" Rhinoplasty? The station will get a top L.A. plastic surgeon to give you a nose job in front of morning viewers. And it won't cost you a thing!" *What's wrong with my nose?* According to Gail the general manager loved the idea. I hate my life.

Philip Gruber was call number three.

They say that "three's the charm" and Philip Gruber was nothing less than charming. He identified himself in a voice that was strangely pitched and a little on the whiny side, but the man was smooth. He said he hoped that he'd gotten the correct phone number and to forgive his boldness at calling, but he had heard that I was interested in doing a story on him and wondered if he could be of assistance. Wow. What a lovely way to let me know he was "on" to me.

He left his phone number and asked me to call him at my earliest convenience. I jotted it down and peeked into the living room. Nell had taken up residence on the couch and was flipping through the channels on the TV. I went back into the kitchen and sat down and tried to figure out what to do.

I really didn't want to meet with Gruber. The truth is I am a fearless reporter over the phone and far away from the bad guys. But face-to-face I don't do so well. My heart gets all racy, and I start to sweat and my stomach feels all bunchy, and I'm just a big fat bundle of chicken nerves. But there's also that part of me, that optimistic, "look on the sunny side" of me that says, "What are the odds of anything bad happening?" And I figured that after what happened last night, the odds would have to be tipped in my favor. Besides, it was the middle of a workday. People would be in and out of the office, Nell would be close by and the glock she was carrying concealed in the waistband of her super stretch denims gave me that little added air of confidence.

I picked up the phone and called him.

Like my old friend Bruce says, "It's easier to ask for forgiveness than to ask for permission." It's also faster. Not that I *needed* Bobby's permission to go see Gruber. I just didn't have time for the inevitable lecture that would follow. I'd tell him when I got back.

I slipped into a pair of black linen slacks and a beige top and ran a comb through my hair. I grabbed my bag, my L.A. press badge, a clipboard and some pens advertising Sam's Delicatessen. Then I handed Nell my new digital camera—it was still in the box, I don't know how to use it, and anointed her my camera crew. A quick look in the mirror and we were good to go.

I had planned on driving the Mercedes, but Nell couldn't fit into the bucket seats, so we took her Hummer instead. Forty-five minutes later we pulled into the parking structure of the old Jefferson Building on Walnut Street. Hoffman and Gruber Construction occupy a suite of offices on the penthouse floor. I climbed into the elevator and waited for Nell to follow. She stood outside the doors shaking her spiky blond head, no.

"What's wrong?" I asked.

"Too small." She said.

"No, see, there's plenty of room." I squashed into the corner, allowing her a wide berth.

She didn't budge. She was thinking hard, her face screwed up in concentration.

"Closetphobia," she said, finally.

"Closet—Oh! You're claustrophobic!" Nell nodded her big head vigorously.

"We take steps."

"No, *you'll* take steps. I'll take the elevator." I reached out to push the "close" button, but Nell was faster. She grabbed a hold of my arm and yanked me out of the elevator.

"We don't separate. We both take steps."

"But it's twenty-six floors," I whined. She nodded again, smiling, the glock resting comfortably against her hip. I sighed. "Oh, fine," I said, taking the steps two at a time in order to keep up with her. Fifteen minutes later we reached the top. My lungs were burning, and I was panting like a dog in heat while Nell barely broke a sweat. It's not my fault I wasn't born in Sweden where they emphasize all that physical fitness crap. I ran my fingers through my hair and walked out onto the floor of Hoffman and Gruber Construction.

The receptionist picked up the phone and a moment later Philip Gruber emerged from his office to greet me. He was not what one would describe as physically imposing, yet there was something about him that held an audience. He settled his eyes on me and a smile fell into place on his lips, and I got the sudden and very creepy feeling that I was in the Hollywood Wax Museum. The man did not seem human.

"Ms. Alexander," he said, extending a well-dressed sleeve towards me. His hand felt cool and soft, almost doughy. Mine was still sweaty from the hike up the stairs and the beginnings of a panic attack. The second we'd made skin contact I wanted to run screaming from the room.

"Mr. Gruber." He glanced over to Nell who grunted in greeting. "This is Nell," I stopped, realizing I didn't know her last name. "She's my camera person," I finished lamely. This was too dumb. He knew who I was and why I was there. But I couldn't let go of the charade.

"Come back into the office, Ms. Alexander. Perhaps Nell would like a cold drink while we have a chat." I glanced at Nell, who nodded her head imperceptibly and settled onto the couch.

His office was light and spacious. The walls were filled with framed photos of Gruber at various charity events, Gruber accepting an award, Gruber clowning it up at the opening of a new building. Oddly, there were none of the traditional family photos. A huge mahogany desk sat in the corner near the window, dwarfing Gruber when he sat behind it. Sitting there, he looked like a small child in need of a booster seat. I almost felt sorry for him. The feeling didn't last long.

"Why do you find me of such interest, Ms. Alexander?"

"Well, you *have* had a startling rise to fame with all the construction contracts you've been awarded. One might wonder how you got so lucky." He gave me a hard, brief look before answering.

"I'm very good at what I do, Ms. Alexander." I didn't doubt it.

The smile was back and he leaned forward in his chair. "What exactly do you want to know?"

"Mr. Gruber," —

"Philip." I smiled my most ingratiating smile.

"Philip. You own a phenomenally successful company, and yet you hired a known felon as part of your construction crew. You are familiar with Thurman Williams' rather violent record, aren't you?"

"We hire thousands of employees. I'm sure Human Resources did a thorough check on Mr. Williams. But at Hoffman and Gruber we like to give people the benefit of the doubt. If someone has paid his debt to society, we welcome the opportunity to give that person a second chance." I gripped my clipboard and made little scribbles on the attached sheet of paper. "Debt to society," I mumbled. "May I quote you?"

"Of course," he said, but he couldn't hide the accompanying smirk. I wondered how long we were going to play out this little scenario. I was hungry and had the beginnings of a headache. I rubbed my temples.

"Headache?" You have no idea.

"Mr. Gruber—Philip, forgive my bluntness, but there has been some speculation in the community that you were instrumental in getting the mayor elected to office. That your company funded the mayor's campaign in exchange for these lucrative contracts. What would you say to these gossip mongers?" He tossed back his head and laughed.

"I would say they are jealous. Ms. Alexander, you are truly refreshing." Funny, Nick had called me refreshing, too. Only it sounded more like a compliment when Nick said it. The phone rang and Gruber picked it up. After listening for a moment, he hung up and turned to me. "I have a small matter to attend to. If you wouldn't mind waiting for me, I shouldn't be more that ten minutes." He stood up. "Perhaps you'd be more comfortable in the outer office." The guy didn't trust me alone in his office.

'I'm fine here, thanks," I said. I guess he was too much of a gentleman to insist that I remove myself from the premises, so I sat back and gave him a little finger wave as he walked out the door.

All the desk drawers were locked. Damnit. The file cabinet was locked, too, and the little wooden box that sat on the desk. That left the wastebasket. I bent over and began to rummage through it. Used tissue. Eewww. More used tissue. Broken pen, a scrunched up scrap of paper. Quickly I unfolded the paper and discovered a wadded up piece of chewing gum. Way to go, Brandy. That's some mighty fine detective work. My heart was racing as I settled back into the chair. In the next instant Gruber walked in.

"Sorry about that. Sometimes it feels like I've surrounded myself with incompetents." I gave him a sympathetic nod.

"Well, I'm sure I've taken up enough of your time," Mr. Gruber. I started to rise, but Gruber placed a doughy hand on my shoulder, firmly guiding me back down.

"Nonsense, Ms. Alexander. I want to be sure you've got accurate information about me for your article. Not that I doubt you'd do a thoroughly professional job. You graduated at the top of your class at Temple University, with a degree in journalism, I believe. And you've picked up quite a following since you moved to L.A., three years ago, or was that four?" Fuck. What's going on here?

"Have you been investigating me?" He smiled benignly and continued as if I hadn't said anything at all.

"How are your parents enjoying Florida, by the way? And your brother, Paul, isn't it? I hear wonderful things about his club. Although owning a business can be precarious. I just heard of a similar club that was wiped out in a fire. Nine people died. Such a shame." A wave of nausea swept through me and I struggled to my feet. The bastard was threatening my family. Oh God, what have I gotten them into? It was one thing to do impulsively stupid things that landed *me* in trouble. But to drag the people I love most in the world into this. How could I have been so naïve? I stood and put a steadying hand on the back of my chair. I refused to let this slime bucket see he'd gotten to me.

Gruber bent down and retrieved my bag from the floor. He held it in his hand for a moment, rubbing the leather between his index finger and thumb. "This is very good leather. Italian, I believe." He smiled, handing it back to me. I turned to the door, not bothering with the standard goodbye chitchat.

"I'm looking forward to the article in Newsworthy!" He called after me. "You'll be sure to send me an advance copy now, won't you?"

Chapter Fifteen

"Nobody threatens my family and gets away with it. Fucking asshole…Show him a thing or two…fucking jerk." I alternated between quiet muttering and full on ranting all the way home in the car. My headache had gotten worse, and it didn't help that Nell had somehow managed to find the only Swedish Rap station in the universe and was now banging out the beats on the steering wheel.

We pulled up in front of the house. Nell motioned for me to wait in the car while she scanned the area. When she deemed it safe, I climbed out of the Hummer and approached the door just as Mrs. Gentile emerged from her witch's den. She stared unabashedly at Nell who in turn blew her a big friendly kiss. Mrs. Gentile's eyes got very wide for a moment before she retreated inside and slammed her door shut. It was the first time I'd laughed in days.

Nell put in a call to Nick while I changed and went in search of aspirin. I found a bottle of baby aspirin in the bathroom cabinet. My mother says one a day will prevent heart attacks. I popped a large handful of them, then I took a glass from the kitchen cupboard and filled it with some Frank's Black Cherry soda. When I was a kid, aspirin and Frank's soda was the cure-all for all of life's little ailments.

Nell appeared in the dining room holding her cell phone. She drew up a seat next to me and handed me her phone.

"For you."

"Hello?"

"I hear you had yourself a little adventure today." A rush of pleasure swept through me at the sound of Nick's voice. He didn't seem angry. That was a good sign. On the other hand he wasn't exactly jumping for joy either.

"Um, I can explain."

"By all means." He waited for me to continue.

"Well see, an opportunity presented itself and naturally I would have called you" —

"Naturally."

"Yeah, well, you were busy, and like I said there was this opportunity…" Nick sighed heavily. I recognized that sigh. I grew up with that sigh. It was the sigh my mother used to heave right after she'd found out I'd done something particularly fool hardy. Her words, not mine. It screamed, "I'm very disappointed in you, young lady." Her disappointment was worse than being grounded.

"Are you going to ground me?" I asked. He choked back a laugh.

"I thought a spanking might be more in order." I flushed from head to toe.

"Bite me," I growled.

"It would be my pleasure," he replied, his voice dripping with innuendo, "but right now I want you to start at the beginning, and tell me everything you remember from the time you walked into his office until the moment you left."

My bravado abandoned me as I recounted in great detail the events of the afternoon. By the time I had finished describing Philip Gruber, the man had grown cloven hooves and a tail. "I'm afraid for my brother, Nick. I'm afraid for anyone related to me. The guy's a freakin' psycho."

"Stay put. I'm coming over."

I had fallen asleep on the couch and was in the middle of a full-on nightmare when Nick arrived. I awoke to a cool hand on my forehead and some soothing words.

"It's okay, angel. You were just dreaming." Groggily I sat up and looked around.

"How long was I asleep?" Nell shrugged.

"Not so long. You snore."

"I do not!" *Oh God, I snore!*

"I am joshing with you." Oh, some of that hysterical Swedish humor I've heard so much about. Nick lifted my legs and sat down next to me and began absently stroking my calves. He eyed me fondly, and a lump formed in my throat. What with being threatened, chased around with a hatchet, and watching people explode before my eyes, it was getting harder and harder to pull off the "tough girl" routine. Any act of kindness could send me right over the edge. I think he sensed my vulnerability and my need to remain in control, and he cut his eyes away from me.

"Nell," Nick said, "Come here. Now that Brandy's up there's something I want you both to see." He extracted a magazine from his back pocket and placed it on the coffee table. Then he got up from the couch, allowing Nell to take his place. He opened the magazine and waited. Nell and I stared at the contents of the picture for a moment, attempting to focus on the slightly blurry sight that lay before us. Then, simultaneously our brains kicked in and our mouths fell open as recognition dawned.

"Oh, Herregud!"

"Holy Mother of God!" Eeewww!

He was naked. Naked and hairy and giving Curtis Maitlin the time of his life. "He" was Philadelphia Mayor Bradley Richardson. I flipped the magazine over to see the name of it. "Secrets." Boy, you could say that again. "Are these legit?" Nick nodded.

"And hot off the press. It's not even due out until tomorrow."

"Then how did you—never mind." I didn't want to know. "When were they taken?" I asked instead.

"Can't really tell. Maitlin looks pretty young though, late teens, possibly. That could make these shots as old as ten years."

"I wonder who took them."

"They look pretty amateurish. My guess is Richardson had no idea he was being photographed. Maitlin probably set up a hidden camera, or more likely a camcorder and made stills from the original video."

I disappeared into the dining room, allowing time for Nell and Nick to ruminate about this latest discovery. I just couldn't bring myself to look at the magazine with Nick in the room. They were *naked* for God's sake. And *doing it*. What if I started to laugh? Then he'd know how truly immature I am. It was all too embarrassing.

I sat at the dining room table eating peanut butter crackers and trying to avoid eye contact with the photos. Nick brought the magazine in and grinned. "Does this make you uncomfortable, angel?"

"Not in the least." He reached over and flipped it open to "the page."

"Do ya mind, I'm trying to eat here."

Wow. The Morals Police turns out to be a closet, gay porn star. Who woulda thunk it.

Okay, so I'd been half right about the mayor being blackmailed into helping Maitlin. Right crime. Wrong motive. It wasn't information about the slush fund Maitlin was using as bait. It was the pictures of him and the mayor doing the horizontal shuffle. And a few other things I'd never dreamed physically possible. What was the mayor thinking? Talk about your bad career move. I wondered if he even knew about the magazine coming out. Well, he couldn't know about it yet, or he never would have agreed to meet with me. He probably thinks that's the secret I had on him. Which brought up the next question. Who ratted him out to a national gay porn tabloid?

Well, the real question is, who would have the most to gain by exposing, no pun intended, the mayor to a major scandal? Could the mayor's political opposition be so underhanded that they'd go to such extreme lengths to undermine the mayor's campaign for re-election? *Well duh!* And where did Gruber fit into all of this? He financed the mayor's campaign. No doubt about that. And he's a real bastard. No argument there, either. But did that make him an accomplice to murder? My headache was getting worse. I needed chocolate. Now that was one thing I was sure of.

I debated whether to call Bobby. This was big news and he needed to know about it. On the other hand, he'd find out soon enough. He was mad at me, and I didn't feel like getting a lecture about staying out of trouble, or the company I'm keeping or visiting a public official with the intent to blackmail a confession out of him. Since when did he become such a goody two-shoes anyway? The truth is I didn't want him to worry about me, and even if I didn't plan to tell him about what I was up to this evening, he had a way of getting things out of me. In the end I decided to keep my mouth shut.

Eight thirty came entirely too quickly. Nell had left shortly after Nick arrived. I thought she would be coming with us for "back-up," but apparently she was already penciled in to guard some pop star who was playing at the Spectrum. Nick briefed me over and over on our plan. I was to stay at least six feet away from the mayor at all times. I was to keep my back to the wall and make sure I could view all exit ways. If I felt the least bit threatened, I was to leave immediately, and if I couldn't leave for some reason (God forbid a million times—again, my mother's words, not mine) I was to signal for help and he would be there in an instant. No heroics, no unnecessary chances for the sake of getting a confession. Just ask the questions and get the hell out.

While Nick tested out the equipment I phoned Paul.

"I just called to tell you I love you and you're a really great brother."

"Is something wrong with the car?" He asked. "Because you can tell me, and I won't like, get mad or anything."

"No, Paulie. The car is fine, I swear. I just wanted to tell you is all."

"Oh. Well, I love you too, Bran." He paused. "You sure you're okay?" The lump in my throat was threatening to choke me.

"Yeah, I'm fine."

Nick placed the listening device on the dining room table. It was miniscule.

"Are you sure that thing really works?" It looked like a wiretap for a Barbie doll.

"State of the art, angel." He scanned my face. "It's not too late to change your mind, you know." I shook my head. I was going to get the son of a bitch and his little pal too. Nick nodded briefly and then picked up the wiretap and pulled me to him.

"Got to put this somewhere inconspicuous," he drawled, flashing me a grin. Slowly he lifted my shirt. My heart began to beat in triple time as his fingers grazed my belly.

"We could go south," he said, playing with the waistband of my jeans, "or we could put it right about here." I gasped as he slid his hand up my shirt stopping right between my breasts. He lingered there for a moment, resting his palm against the front clasp of my bra. Smoothly he tucked the "bug " inside and slowly removed his hand, but not before brushing his thumb softly against my skin. I felt my nipples go stiff and a soft moan escaped my lips. "Did you say something?" He whispered into my ear.

"No," I squeaked, feeling the flush rise up from my nether regions. "Damn it's hot in here."

"Now for the tape." Nick tore off a piece of tape and began to lift my shirt again. I gently slapped his hand away.

"I think I can take it from here," I said.

"Well, I don't know. This is a delicate operation. You really ought to leave it to a professional."

"I'll take my chances." I took the tape from him and shoved it under my shirt, securing the wire in place. Nick caught my wrist as I began to tuck my shirt back into my jeans, all playfulness gone. He lifted my chin, compelling me to look at him, and there was an edge to his voice when he spoke.

"I meant it before when I said don't take any chances. We don't know what you could be walking into tonight. If you choose not to go there's no shame in it." I gulped. Nick always seemed so in control. If he was concerned, then I should be full on freaking out. No, I'd come this far I had to see it through.

"I can do this Nick. I have to." No other explanation seemed necessary.

"Let's go."

Mayor Bradley Richardson liked to describe himself as "a man of the people." Judging by his zip code I believe he meant "a man of the very rich people." Richardson lives in an old moneyed section of Philadelphia called Chestnut Hill. Chestnut Hill is located along the border of Philadelphia and Montgomery County and is known for its magnificent old homes and sprawling mansions.

Germantown Avenue runs through the center of town. We traveled this route now, Nick at the wheel of a black Ford pickup truck, me staring vacantly out the window, trying not to throw up. A feeling of foreboding settled in the pit of my stomach and refused to budge. Maybe it was the culmination of everything that had happened this week finally catching up to me, or the fact that all I'd eaten in the past twenty-four hours was a pack of stale peanut butter crackers and some baby aspirin. We passed Cosimo's Pizza and I almost asked if we could stop in for a slice. I don't know what it is with me and life or death situations, but they always seem to make me hungry.

At five til nine we rounded Glen Oak Avenue and cruised down the tree-lined street, stopping briefly in front of a beautiful ivy covered three-story home. Set far back from the sidewalk, an enormous cobblestone driveway wound its way through a thickly wooded area that obscured the house from the general public.

"This is it," Nick stated, pulling away from the curb and parking several hundred yards down the block. He cut the engine and unbuckled his seat belt. I reached up to my shirt and fingered the "wire" nervously.

"Testing, one, two, three." I said into the air.

"Don't worry, you're all set. Just walk up to the door and ring the bell. I'm going to double back and position myself off the side entrance. The house has French doors leading out to a back patio. It looks like a tropical rain forest out there so I'll be well hidden."

"How do you know so much about the layout of the house?" I was very impressed, thinking he had somehow managed to obtain blue prints or something.

"I was here for a party once." He shrugged. "Charity event." The man never ceased to amaze me.

I had hoped he was going to kiss me for luck but Nick was in his professional mode, all quiet efficiency and intense focus. I guess under the circumstances I should be grateful he took his work seriously. With ever increasing nervousness I opened the door and shut it softly behind me. I forced myself not to look back at the car for fear that I'd chicken out and dive back in. Taking a slow deep breath I started down the street and up the long winding driveway to the mayor's house.

It was dark when I got to the front door. No glowing porch light to welcome the intrepid blackmailer, only the crescent moon peering out from under a thick layer of clouds. Great. And me without my umbrella. I squared my shoulders and rang the bell. And waited. And waited some more. Then I knocked loudly and waited some more. I was almost to the point of yoo-hooing, when on impulse I tried the doorknob. To my surprise it was unlocked. Should I go in? Would that be rude, considering I *was invited*? Let's see, I'm worrying about appearing rude to a murderer I'm purportedly here to blackmail.

I let myself in and switched on the hall light. As I stepped onto the marble entry, I was awed by the grandeur of what lay before me. A wide marble staircase wound its way to the second floor. Two Grecian urns six feet high stood on either side of the stairs, their estimated value that of the price of a small country. A dim light emanated from one of the rooms off the entryway. Soft, classical music was playing in the background. The music made the quiet all the more noticeable. I began walking towards the room with the light, scuffling my shitkickers along the floor just to make some noise. I would have been petrified if not for the fact that Nick was just outside the French doors, hidden in the bushes, listening to every sound I made.

"Hello," I called out tentatively as I inched my way closer to what appeared to be the library. As I entered the room I noticed a man's arm hanging limply over the arm of a Lazy Boy recliner. "Mr. Mayor, it's Brandy Alexander. We had an appointment this evening." I worked my way around to the front of the chair, positioning myself in front of him. "Mayor?" His eyes were closed, his head tilted slightly forward onto his chest. On his lap was a glass of what smelled like single malt. The glass had tipped over, spilling some of the contents onto his lap. Oh great! He's drunk. Drunk and unconscious. Now I'll never get my confession. I gave him a vigorous shake, hoping to rouse him to consciousness. That's when I noticed the magazine lying at the foot of the recliner. It was torn to shreds, but I could still make out a few essential body parts and the title. Secrets. Well, not anymore. An empty plastic vial rested on the floor a few feet away from the magazine. I picked it up and looked at the label. It was a prescription for anti depressants, but the pills were nowhere to be found. Oh Shit.

I glanced back up at the mayor, who, thanks to my shaking, was now slumped totally forward and bent in half. I leaned over him, wishing I'd paid more attention in CPR class when I did a story on the Red Cross a few months back. Wracking my brains to remember the procedure, I tentatively picked up his wrist and held it between my thumb and forefinger. Okay, no pulse. Not a good sign. I braced myself and tilted his head back. Spittle had formed at the corners of his mouth and was working its way down to his chin. Why hadn't I noticed that before? I mentally went over the checklist. His skin felt cold, he wasn't breathing, no heartbeat and I'm pretty sure he shit his pants. *Oh fuck. Oh fuck. Oh fuck.* "Nick," I screamed. "Get in here. I need you!" I began pacing around the room wringing my hands, trying to digest what had happened. Obviously they'd sent him an advanced copy of the magazine, and he was so freaked out by it he committed suicide. He drank some scotch and downed a bunch of pills and—I stopped, suddenly aware that this scenario sounded very familiar. But why? "Nick!" Where was he? I peered out the French doors, searching the back yard for signs of life. "Nick!" I screeched, panic rising in my throat. I was stuck in a room with a dead guy and I didn't know where Nick was. I reached for the phone to call the police, when someone came up behind me and rested a hand on my wrist. "Oh thank God," I breathed, turning around, but my relief was short-lived. The grip tightened.

"We meet again, Ms. Alexander. How delightful."

Philip Gruber and I stood inches from each other, his left hand still wrapped around my wrist. In his right was a .38 caliber pistol, its cold nose pressed against my side like a persistent puppy. I froze as the blood drained from my face down to my legs, rendering them useless. "What? No hello?" He shrugged. "And here I thought we were pals. How's the article coming along?" Dizzy with panic, I began to hyperventilate. Cautiously I glanced down. Maybe Gruber was known for his practical jokes, and what I'd mistaken for a real gun was actually a life-like water pistol. He'd "pull the trigger" and I'd get soaked and we'd both have a good laugh. "You sure fooled me," I'd say. *Oh shit Brandy, focus!* I found my voice.

"Mr. Gruber I don't know what you think you're doing, but I was invited here by the mayor. I doubt he'd appreciate you manhandling me."

"Oh I don't think my friend Bradley is in a position to appreciate anything at the moment." He shook his head mock ruefully and gestured towards the mayor's inert body. "Shocking turn of events."

"And what's your part in all of this?" The words flew out of my mouth before rational thought had time to catch up to them. Gruber's mouth curved into a tight cruel smile. "You're a bright girl, Ms. Alexander. It will be fun watching you *unravel the mystery."* He said the last part in a Bella Lugosi accent. The man was clearly nuts.

Gruber prodded me with the pistol, towards the couch. He remained standing, one arm draped casually over the back of the mayor's Lazy Boy. He was wearing a brown turtleneck sweater under a designer sports coat, and Dockers. His feet were covered in brand new topsiders. Just your standard Ivy League psychopath. My eyes traveled to the French doors, willing them to open. Any minute now Nick would burst in and rescue me and this nightmare would be over.

"Looking for someone?" I whipped my head back the other way.

"No, I" —

"But of course, your associate, Nick. He did say he'd be right outside if you needed him." He sighed, heaving Armani clad shoulders. "It's so hard to find reliable help these days. By the way, you should have listened to him when he told you not to take any chances." What was going on? The man knew intimate details of our conversation. It was as if he'd been right in the room with us when we'd spoken. The light dawned and I leaned forward, concentrating my efforts on staying alive.

"How'd you do it, Gruber? How'd you wire me for sound?"

"Bravo, Brandy. I knew you wouldn't disappoint me. Remember when you visited me at my office? I had a feeling you were a nosy one. I watched you on the security monitor, rifling through my things. Don't look so surprised. You should figure a person of my stature wouldn't just leave you there to snoop freely. Anyway," he continued, "when I realized you weren't going to go away, I decided to keep a closer watch on you." He tossed me my pocketbook. "Take a look under the flap." Tucked in the corner under the leather flap was a listening device the size of a baby's little toenail. "I'll bet my bug's smaller than your bug. Want to compare?" He strolled over to me, leaning in to grasp the bottom of my shirt with his fingers. He was so close I could smell the Listerine on his breath. The thought of him touching me made my skin crawl. Quickly I reached under my shirt and grabbed the worthless mic and flung it across the room, all hope of rescue gone.

"What have you done with Nick?" I demanded.

"He's—indisposed."

"What do you mean, indisposed?" I shouted wildly. His face twisted into a frightening grin.

"Like I said, you're a bright girl. You'll figure it out."

Oh my God. When I was in Gruber's office he planted the bug in my purse, which meant he overheard our conversations. He knew Nick would be outside the house and he had him ambushed. It was naïve arrogance to think I could outsmart a mad man. I'd been warned; by his college classmates, by Bobby, by the sheer terror in his ex-wife's voice, but I wouldn't listen. All Nick wanted to do was keep me safe and now he was dead. I felt as if I'd been punched hard in the gut. A deep and abiding sadness washed over me and I blinked back hot tears. No way would I give this monster the satisfaction of seeing me cry.

"I should've" — He laughed, interrupting me.

"Shoulda, woulda, coulda. It's all water under the bridge now. Cheer up, kid. It's time to play 'What's My Secret?' Here's how we play. It's very simple really. I've got a secret and you guess what it is." I stared at him, despising every breath he took.

"You're insane." A hand shot out and smacked me hard across the face. I felt a blinding pain as shock mingled with rage and tears welled up in my eyes. My cheek began to throb and swell. He cocked his head slightly, waiting for me to catch my breath.

"Ready to play?"

He was serious. He wanted me to reconstruct the crimes. For every right answer I earned another five minutes of breathing time. Every wrong answer earned me another smack in the mouth.

"So," Gruber started, settling comfortably on the couch. "You've already earned five minutes for figuring out the mayor and I had a special arrangement. I'd finance his campaign and in return he'd award me city contracts. But unfortunately things took a downhill turn when Curtis Maitlin showed up with his private party pictures. Your turn." He smiled expectantly. My head was reeling from the news about Nick, and I had to fight to comprehend what Gruber was telling me. Self preservation kicked in and I opened my mouth and hoped for the best.

"When the first murder took place six months ago," I began slowly, "the mayor hired a cop to pull the evidence on Maitlin. But then six months later he killed again, so you hired Thurman Williams to get rid of John, because he could potentially identify Maitlin. Then somehow you were able to get your hands on Maitlin's original blackmail photos, which eliminated the need to protect Maitlin anymore, so you had him killed too."

"Correctamundo! Tell her what she's won, Vanna." I wasn't about to make the mistake again of pointing out he was crazy, so I just continued to pick my way carefully through the events of the last week and a half, trying to put it all together. It wasn't easy. My head was throbbing and my heart was breaking.

"Ms. Alexander," cooed Gruber in a singsong voice. "The clock's a tickin'." He waggled the index finger of his free hand in a tick tock fashion to illustrate his point. I ventured another guess.

"Maybe the cop was killed because he knew too much, and since you didn't need him anymore it was safer to just get rid of him."

"Right again. You know if this were a real game show you could make a lot of money." No more than five minutes had passed since he'd entered the room, but it felt like a lifetime. Blood was beginning to cake at the corner of my mouth and I licked at it gingerly. My thoughts wandered to my family, my friends, to Nick and I almost burst into a fresh set of tears, but that wouldn't get me out of this mess. I had to keep the conversation going, so I proffered another guess.

"So you and the mayor took care of everyone who could have potentially 'turned' on you. But then someone got a hold of the pictures of Maitlin and the mayor and sent them in to Secrets magazine, which effectively ruined the mayor, so he killed himself."

"Who do you think ratted him out?" He asked almost gleefully.

"His political opponent?" A hard crack across my other cheek sent my head flying backwards and immediately I could feel it start to puff up. At least now I'd be symmetrical. Gruber hopped off the couch and began pacing around the Persian rug. His eyes landed on the empty bottle of pills, and he picked it up and absently began playing with it.

"If I were going to kill myself, I'd do something really spectacular like take a flying leap off of one of my buildings." I watched him toss the pill bottle idly from hand to hand, and as I did, something in the back of my mind slowly wended its way to the forefront. In an instant I had the last piece of the puzzle. Oh my God.

"The mayor didn't kill himself, did he, Mr. Gruber?" His face creased into a broad grin and he patted me on the back. I flinched at his touch but he didn't seem to notice.

"You are one sharp cookie, Ms. Alexander. What gave me away?"

"The pill bottle." He tilted his head, questioningly. "I remembered an article I'd read about your partner. It was an obituary, actually. It said that he had been depressed and he died of an accidental overdose from mixing alcohol and anti-depression medication. You killed your partner and made it look like suicide, and you did the same with the mayor. But why?" Gruber grimaced as if caught up in a painful memory.

"I've got no patience for weak people, Brandy. May I call you Brandy?" He had the gun. He could call me anything he wanted. "My partner was a gutless wonder. We hooked up because he had access to start up money for the company. I was the proverbial 'brains behind the operation.' The risk taker, the mover and shaker. Hoffman was content to remain a low budget company, doing penny ante jobs. But I was going to take this company to the top."

"So you started a slush fund for the mayor in exchange for a guaranteed pay off when he got elected. But Hoffman disapproved, I take it."

"Exactly. You know, you seem to have a real head for business. Under different circumstances I'd be recruiting you for my company." He sighed. "C'est la vie. Anyway," he continued, "Hoffman made some noises, yada, yada, yada," he rolled his hand over and over to fast forward the passage of time, "and I realized he'd become a liablility. So I did what any good businessman would do. I dissolved the partnership."

I looked at him as if for the first time. He seemed to have absolutely no concept of right and wrong, only what was to his advantage or disadvantage. Gruber was a man without a conscience, which made him as dangerous as a man could possibly be. He began speaking again but I was only half listening. I was desperate to find a way out of the God forsaken library. "It's a wonder Richardson got elected in the first place," he was saying. "The man had the personality of a sponge. And what a whiner, boy, I'll tell you. First he begs me for my help with Maitlin and then he complains when I do something about it. He was just so damn squeamish about all the killing. I would have knocked him out of the loop a long time ago, but I had to wait until that last big city contract was signed, sealed and delivered. After that, Bradley was expendable. But I had to make it look like suicide."

"*You* were the one who sent those photos to Secrets. You made it look like the mayor killed himself over the public exposure, and then you shredded up the magazine and left it under the chair, as if he'd torn it up in a fit of rage." The man was brilliant. Crazy as a loon, but brilliant.

"Ya know I like you, Brandy. I really do. You've been a good sport and I wish there were a better pay off for you, but you're going to have to die." Without warning he yanked me off the couch by my hair. Pain shot up my neck and I screamed in surprise.

"Oh, you're going to have to be a lot more quiet than that if we're going to get out of here unnoticed."

"Where are you taking me?" I asked thickly.

"If I told you, it would spoil the surprise." He reached into his jacket pocket and produced a roll of duct tape. Deftly he bound my hands together in back of me and placed a strip over my mouth. Then he wrapped his hand tightly around the back of my neck and led me out the door.

A black Audi was parked around the other side of the house. Gruber opened the back door and threw me unceremoniously inside. I landed on the floor and he quickly tossed a blanket over my prone body. As I struggled to right myself, he issued a gruff warning to lie there and behave myself or else he'd cut my fucking head off and mount it on his wall. Remembering the goat's head, I opted to behave myself.

As the car started to roll away from the curb I stretched my legs out, my body vibrating with pent up adrenalin. I wanted to bang my feet hard against the side of the door, kick out a window, anything to get out of there. I hated being tied up. Hated it more than anything. It made me crazy. I lay there gulping hot air, tears and sweat co-mingling on my face. Oh Jeez, my parents will be so bummed when they find out I'm dead. And Paulie, and Johnny and the twins. And Bobby. We finally put our past and all the bitterness behind us and then I have to go and get myself killed. Fucking typical. And then my thoughts turned to Nick, and I cried silent tears for someone I barely knew but who had come to mean so much to me. Maybe it was the injustice of it all, or maybe it was the point beyond hysteria where you suddenly feel invincible, but I knew I would not go gentle into this damn goodnight. I was going to figure a way out of this stinking mess or die trying.

After about twenty-five minutes I heard the crunch of gravel under the tires as the car slowed and stopped. Gruber cut the engine and pulled the blanket off of me. "We're here," he announced in that bizarre childlike singsong. I wanted to belt him one, and I would have if my hands hadn't been strapped behind my back. I was so beyond reasonable thought it wasn't even funny. I struggled to sit up and peered out the window.

We were parked next to a plywood and chain link fence, which ran the length of a city block. On the fence was a large rectangular sign. I could barely make out the words in the darkness. Gruber flicked on the high beams momentarily so that I could read the printing. FUTURE HOME OF MEMORIAL SPORTS COMPLEX, and under that in only slightly smaller letters, HOFFMAN AND GRUBER CONSTRUCTION.

"It never fails to give me a thrill," he commented, dousing the lights.

I cast a furtive glance around, searching for signs of human life. We were parked in the middle of a major metropolitan city, for Christ's sake. Where was everyone? I didn't have time to ponder the question, because at that moment Gruber yanked open the back door and hauled me out by my elbow. I lost my balance, stumbling and landing hard on the gravel surface. My chin hit the ground and started to bleed. Bits of stone and glass ground into my knees and I whimpered in pain. He pulled me up, a look of annoyance crossing his face. "You haven't said one thing about my building. You are very self absorbed, you know that? Now pay attention, you might learn something."

It was hard to keep up with his mood swings. He changed from southern gentleman to east coast Mafioso in a heartbeat, and I couldn't decide which one was creepier. As he guided me towards the construction site, he slung a companionable arm around my shoulder and I flinched at his touch. His gentleman mode was definitely creepier.

Cement mixers and other heavy equipment littered the unpaved parking lot. The building, a gigantic state of the art oval shaped structure looked very near completion. It was all steel and glass, about ten stories high. It must've cost over three hundred million to build, with a good-sized portion going to my host for the evening.

"Just think, Brandy, when this place is completed it will be able to seat twenty thousand sports fans. Imagine your friends, comfy-cozy in their luxury boxes, knocking back a couple of brewskis while rooting for the home team. Doesn't that sound like fun?" I nodded, my mouth still covered in duct tape. "Now, I don't want you feeling all left out because your friends will be having fun without you," he continued, a maniacal note lacing his voice. "I've thought long and hard about how I can include you in the festivities, and I think I've come up with a darn good solution." What the hell was he talking about? If the man had *his* way, the only festivities I'd be participating in was pushing up daisies at Forest Lawn. "Brandy, our time together has been fun, but I really am going to have to bid you adieu fairly soon. The trouble is, what to do with your body? And then I got to thinking." He rubbed his gun softly along my cheekbone, edging me towards the cement mixer. "I shoot you, then I hack you up in convenient disposable pieces. After that I toss you in the hopper, where, with the flick of a switch I grind you into pulp. Tomorrow morning when the dry cement is mixed with water in the cylinder for the paving of our new parking lot, you will be added to the mix. So you see, you'll live on in the very pavement beneath our feet."

A great swooshing sound filled my ears as my legs buckled beneath me. He hauled me back up, laying a hand on the back of my head and pushing it forward until he was sure I wasn't going to pass out. Wiggling out of his grasp I began to make incoherent noises through the duct tape.

"Come again?" He ripped the tape off my mouth, leaving my lips swollen and sore.

"I want my fifteen minutes," I shouted wildly, hoping to throw him off course.

"Your what?"

"My fifteen minutes. I earned it back at the house when we were playing that game. You may be a lot of things, Gruber but I never thought of you as a welcher." I was grasping at straws here, taking a gamble that his ego would supersede his need to kill me on the spot.

"Christ, you're a feisty one." There was definitely an admiring tone in his voice. He cast his eyes towards his watch as if trying to decide if he had anything more pressing to do, and glanced back up at the site. "Oh, what the hey." He grabbed my arm and steered me towards the building. "The view from the top is fantastic!"

It was absolutely imperative that I stay calm. I settled for not throwing up on my shoes. My chin was throbbing, my shoulders were aching and I couldn't feel my wrists anymore.

"Could you please take off the duct tape?" I asked. "It's not like I'm going anywhere. You've got the gun."

"Point well taken, but no."

Gruber punched in the security code and we entered the building through a back door. It was humongous inside, with a concourse that ran the length of the building, and video walls and monitors so that fans wouldn't miss a minute of the action. There were twenty concession stands, tons of restrooms, and a special "members only" area for those willing to shell out the big bucks for exclusive dining rights. Gruber explained all this to me as he urged me onwards and upwards. "The escalators aren't running right now," he apologized, "so we have to walk up four flights, but after that we get to take the elevator." I climbed the stairs with difficulty. My knees were bruised and starting to swell and I added them to my mental list of injuries. Two swollen cheeks, a fat lip, a bloody chin and I suspected that my hands would be falling off any moment now, due to lack of blood flow to the wrists. Tears of frustration began to make their way down my face and I tried to rub them off on my shoulder. Gruber smiled benignly at me. "I know how you feel. I get all choked up just looking at the magnificence of it all too." He made a sweeping gesture with his hand to encompass the room. "Well, your fifteen minutes are almost up and we haven't reached the top yet. Let's see a little hustle in your step."

We stood in one of the offices on the top floor of the complex, overlooking the street below. The only thing standing between us and an eight-story plunge over the edge was a waist high iron safety railing that stretched across what would eventually become windows. Ten-foot panels of tempered glass lay stacked nearby, awaiting installation. A cold breeze blew in through the opening, scattering the dirt and debris that littered the concrete floor.

Gruber maneuvered me over to the railing and leaned forward, exhaling deeply.

"Take a look at this," he said. "Hoffman and Gruber construction as far as the eye can see." He pulled me closer to the edge and I shut my eyes tightly, guarding against the nausea that was sure to betray my fear of heights. "You know," he continued, oblivious to my lack of enthusiasm, "one day they may consider changing the name of our fair city to Gruberdelphia. It's got a nice ring to it, don't you think? I'm kidding, of course," he added, chuckling at his own joke. I wasn't so sure he was joking.

While Gruber ruminated over his constructural achievements, I took this time to try and figure out how to save my own life, but I was fresh out of ideas. Any minute now he would snap out of his ego driven reverie and implement his plan to chop me up like stew meat. And then I heard something. A faint mewing followed by a tiny scratching sound. He must have heard it too, because he leaned back from the rail and gazed off in the direction of the noise. We heard it again, more distinctly this time. I followed Gruber's gaze, and there under a pile of two by fours lay a black and white kitten the size of a large man's hand. My heart lurched and automatically I began walking towards it. Gruber put a restraining hand on my arm. "Do kittens make you feel all warm and tingly, Brandy?" Before I could respond, he turned and pointed the .38 in the direction of the pile of wood. Oh my God. The bastard's going to shoot the cat. And in that instant blind rage took over. Maybe I couldn't save myself, but I'd be Goddamned if he'd kill that baby.

"Nooo!" I screamed, catching him off guard. As he turned I bowed my head and rammed him in the gut as hard as I could. The gun clattered to his feet and I scrambled to kick it out from under him, but he was quicker and had the advantage of two working arms. He bent to pick it up and then casually advanced on me.

"So, you like it rough, do you?" He raised his arm and smacked me with the full force of his swing. I crashed sideways to the ground, hitting my head on the concrete floor. Pain wracked the side of my face and I rolled into a fetal ball, trying to protect myself as best I could. Gruber stretched out a foot and dealt me a vicious kick with the pointed toe of his designer shoe. I flipped onto my stomach, but he caught me right under my breast. The sickening crunch of breaking bones filled my ears as white-hot heat seared through my ribs. The pain was unbearable, and I cried out, tears streaming down my face. He lowered the gun to my head, spitting out the words in one furious sentence. "I would shoot you right now, but then I'd have to haul your worthless ass down to the ground floor." Thank God for small favors. With my last ounce of strength I lashed out with my boots, catching him in the shin. He stumbled and reeled back against the safety railing, knocking the gun out of his hand. It skittered across the floor and slipped under the guard rail. Gruber stared back at me, pure, unadulterated loathing etched on his face. He lunged forward. He was going to rip me apart with his bare hands.

"Step away from her." The voice was low and commanding. And oh so familiar. Nick stood at the entrance of the office, a .38 trained at Gruber's heart. Gruber stepped back, his eyes never leaving Nick's.

"Nick," I cried, fresh tears gushing forth. I tried to stand but the pain was overwhelming. He reached me in seconds and bent low to speak to me. "Can you stand up?" I shook my head, no. "You're a dead man, Gruber." He raised his gun again and this time cocked the hammer. Gruber smiled.

"Touché, Mr. Santiago, touché." In one fluid motion he saluted Nick and, placing both hands on the safety bar, vaulted over the railing and was gone.

Chapter Sixteen

I arrived home at three a.m. after a pit stop at Jefferson Hospital for two cracked ribs. The doctor who taped me up told me I was lucky. Had they been broken they could've punctured my lung. She said I'd hurt like hell for a while but I'd survive, and she gave me a prescription for painkillers. Gruber wasn't quite so lucky. He landed face down on the sidewalk, dying on impact. *"If I were going to kill myself I'd do something really spectacular like take a flying leap off of one of my buildings."* The master controller to the bitter end.

"I thought you were dead," I sobbed as Nick cradled me in his arms. I leaned against him and he let out a breath, shifting slightly. I looked down at his arm. There was a gaping hole in the sleeve of his jacket, its ragged edges soaked with blood. I nearly gagged at the sight. "What happened?" I whispered.

Thurman Williams had been hiding in ambush when Nick arrived at the mayor's house. Nick sensed something was wrong and he turned a split second before Williams pulled the trigger. The bullet caught him in the arm and lodged there.

"When Williams came over to check on his handiwork, I let him know he didn't quite finish the job. Vicious little asshole." Nick shook his head. "It took me ten minutes to lay him out. Trouble was, it laid me out too. Luckily, I woke up first. It's amazing how persuasive I can be when I'm holding a gun to someone's head. He told me where I'd find you and then, poor guy, he just passed out again." I didn't want to know what kind of help Nick gave him to that end.

"Where is he now?"

"I left him handcuffed to a wrought iron fence. Then I called the station to let your cop friend know where I was headed."

The sound of sirens screamed in the distance. I tried to raise myself up but the pain was excruciating. Nick gently unwound the tape from my wrists and massaged them until the blood started to flow on its own. I touched his arm. "Does it hurt much?" He grimaced. "Well, let's just say it doesn't tickle." I laughed as relief flooded through me. Then I cried and kept on crying until I heard my name being called, and suddenly I was lifted up and Bobby was holding me, helping the paramedics get me onto a gurney. "The kitten," I wailed through a flood of tears. Please, somebody help him." I was babbling incoherently and I just couldn't stop crying. After that, I passed out and didn't wake up until I hit the emergency room.

"Is Nick alright?" Bobby peered at me through a mist in his deep blue eyes.

"He's fine. He got fixed up and he's down at the station making a statement. Jesus, Brandy." Uh oh. I recognized the beginnings of a marathon lecture. Fortunately, some plain clothed cops came in at that point and began to interrogate me. I answered them as thoroughly as I could, but just breathing was an effort at the moment. They backed off when Bobby promised to deliver me to the police station personally, in the morning.

The hospital wanted me to stay overnight for observation, but I'd had enough of being told what to do. Bobby took me home in a squad car. He even put the lights and sirens on because I asked him to. As he helped me into the car I heard a small purring sound emanating from the back seat.

"Looks like someone wants his mommy." He reached over the seat and lifted up a tiny bundle of black and white fur. True to form I started crying again.

"Are you gonna be doin' this all night? Because I gotta tell ya, I need my beauty sleep."

I was laid up for the next couple of days, which gave me a lot of time to think. What would have happened to me if Nick hadn't come along when he did? If Gruber hadn't jumped, would Nick really have pulled the trigger? Would I have wanted him to? I honestly think the answer was yes, and that scared me more than anything.

My ribs were starting to heal and my face had taken on a sort of jaundiced hue, which was a step up from the blue and purple of the previous day. A little foundation and you could hardly tell I'd been beaten within an inch of my life.

Bobby had taken me home that night and stayed with me. He helped me to change out of my dirt-encrusted clothes, cleaned my knees and used a washcloth to wipe the dried blood from my chin. I'm sure I would have been mortified, had I been halfway cognizant, but as it was, I was totally whacked out on Vicodin and don't remember a lot of the details.

Bobby wouldn't let me go near a mirror, which was probably a wise move, as my body couldn't take another shock to the system. He carefully tucked me in and turned on the nightlight. The kitten was perched on the pillow next to me. I named him Rocky, after my favorite Philadelphian.

"I'll be in the next room if you need me." Bobby turned off the overhead lamp and laid the palm of his hand against my cheek.

"I don't want you to go," I whispered, suddenly afraid. He ended up sleeping all night on a chair next to my bed. I wanted him right on the bed beside me, but my ribs groaned in protest, so I settled for holding his hand until I fell asleep.

I made the morning, midday and evening news, not just on local stations, but nationally, as well. My boss in L.A. called to congratulate me on "breaking the story," and then she asked if I'd given any more thought to the "on air nose job" segment we'd discussed. "It seems like perfect timing, what with your recent injuries and all."

"Why stop there, Gail? Why don't we do an upbeat spot on vivisection? I'm sure lots of viewers will tune in for that one."

"Maybe this isn't the best time to talk about it." *Ya think?* Once I was through with the pain meds I was going to have to do some serious re-evaluating.

Paul and the gang came over with a huge bouquet of flowers and a nice big box of chocolate truffles.

"This is a hell of a way to get out of wearing that bridesmaid's dress," Franny sniffed. "If you didn't like it you could've just told me."

"We *did* tell you," Janine and I chimed in together.

Vince Giancola stopped by with a foot long hoagie from his dad's deli, and Johnny consumed more than half of it. "What happened to your new diet?" I asked, eyeing my quickly diminishing food. He threw me a disgusted look.

"Have you ever known cauliflower to keep body and soul together? These are stressful times, dollface. I need the meat!" Even Mrs. Gentile showed up with a casserole. It tasted like it was left over from last Thanksgiving but it was the thought that counts.

The only conspicuously absent person was Nick. Okay, so I got him shot, but we had some good times too, didn't we? I debated whether to call him. Maybe he'd just decided I was more trouble than I was worth. The thought of not seeing him anymore made my stomach hurt, but I owed him my life, and if nothing else I wanted to let him know how grateful I was. I finally plucked up the courage to call him, but all I got was his voicemail. "Uh, Nick, it's Brandy. Alexander," I added. Oh God, like he couldn't figure that out. "I just wanted to see how you were feeling and to say thank you for saving my life. And um, okay then, I'll talk to you soon. Unless you don't want to. I mean, I'd totally understand. So, uh"… *Oh WHY couldn't I just shut up?* "Okay, bye." What a colossal geek. No wonder the man is avoiding me like the plague. He probably thinks geeky is contagious. If I'd had the time I would have dug a great big hole and climbed in, but I had to get ready for Franny and Eddie's serenading party.

In predominantly Italian South Philly it is the custom for the groom to serenade the bride the night before the wedding. It's like a gigantic block party. They cordon off the street and all the neighbors come out to witness the event and partake in massive amounts of food and alcohol consumption.

Franny stood at the bedroom window, looking down on the crowd below. Her parents had insisted that she "come home where she belongs for a proper send off." I could tell by the look on her face that she was embarrassed to death by all of this. She would have much preferred being in on the action, eating crab cakes and drinking champagne, than to be stuck up in a tower like Rapunzel, waiting for Eddie to belt out his rendition of "Fly Me to the Moon." At least she wasn't standing on the sidewalk freezing her butt off.

Someone had started a fire in one of those big metal trashcans, and I made my way over to it to warm up. Uncle Frankie was there with Carla. She was wearing a faux leopard skin coat and white go-go boots, with this funky Russian cap. She looked like a good-natured Cruella DiVille. Frankie had his arm around her, and when I walked up to them he opened his arms to encircle me as well.

"Don't you ever scare me like that again." I wasn't sure but I think my big, macho uncle had tears in his eyes.

"Believe me, I don't plan on it."

"Where's Bobby?" Carla wanted to know.

"He had to work late. He should be here any minute." She gave me a sidelong glance.

"What?"

"Nothing," she shrugged. "It's just that you're getting pretty chummy with him again, that's all."

"We're friends, Carla. But thanks for worrying about me." I kissed her on her heavily made up cheek.

"Hey, anyone want a crab cake?" Frankie took off in search food, and then a bunch of Franny's cousins started singing "Goin' to the Chapel," acappella, and Carla drifted off to join them. On the other side of the street Paul, Kenny and Taco had set up a bandstand and were wiring it for sound. I tried to focus on the festivities but somehow my heart wasn't in it. It was time for my pain medication, and I was feeling tired and achy. My emotions were still pretty raw and I just wanted to go home and curl up in bed with Rocky, who, by the way, turned out to be a Rockette. My house is only a few blocks away, so I decided to walk home. I didn't want to spoil anyone else's fun by asking for a ride, and I figured a little "alone time" would be good for me.

As I rounded the corner three squad cars were parked outside the house. Two uniformed cops, guns drawn, came around from the side of the building, holding a short well muscled man in handcuffs. Bobby led the pack, his expression grim. Oh, what fresh hell is this? Curiosity beat out the stone cold lump of fear in my stomach, and I edged closer to get a better view. The man in custody looked up, his drunken eyes darting back and forth. I recognized those eyes. "Get him out of here," Bobby said, his voice tight. He turned to me. "I drove by your house to see if you needed a ride over to the party and I caught him climbing up the trellis. He was carrying this." I knew what Bobby had in his hand without even looking. "Who is he?" I asked, almost too numb to care.

"His name is Luis Gomez." AKA Hatchet Man.

"But Gruber's gone." Jeez, this guy must have a really strong work ethic. He was going to finish the job even if his employer was too dead to pay him.

"Ah, Brandy, there's something you should know." I didn't like the sound of that.

"What?"

"Gomez didn't work for Gruber."

"How do you know that?" Bobby hesitated, clearly embarrassed. Well, tough. "Spill it, DiCarlo."

"Last time I checked, he's my brother in law." *Oh, fabulous.* Marie DiCarlo's crazy-assed brother, out to avenge his sister's honor. Apparently the genius thought this up all on his own, so I could rest easy knowing that all the would-be Brandy stalkers were finally laid to rest. Bobby felt terrible and asked if there was anything he could do to make it up to me. Gazing into his deep blue eyes, I could think of a few things, but nothing that wouldn't require a trip to confession in the morning. I sighed deeply.

"Nope, I'm good." Before he left he did a quick sweep of my house and yard and made me promise to call him if I needed anything. I promised, knowing that what I needed he wasn't free to give.

Rocky was sitting on her little pillow beside the stove as I walked into the kitchen. She stretched out one tiny paw to greet me, and I scooped her up in my arms, rubbing her soft little white belly with my nose. She purred contentedly and promptly fell asleep. I envied her.

I would have to get a carry-on box for her for the plane ride to L.A. It was hard to believe I'd be leaving the day after tomorrow, and by the end of the week I'd be back to reporting on monster truck rallies and Thanksgiving diet tips. *Wow. I am freakin' indispensable.* I placed the kitten on her pillow and ripped open a package of chocolate cupcakes. I was feeling restless and depressed. I guess it was to be expected after all that had happened.

The answering machine blinked two messages. I pressed the button as I sank my teeth into the cupcake. No ripping off the bottoms, this time. I wanted the whole damn thing.

"Hey, Brandy Alexander." I never dreamed the sound of my own name could give me so much pleasure. Then again, I had to consider the source. "It's Nick. Santiago," he added after a beat, and I could hear the sweetly mocking laughter in his voice. It warmed me all over. "Call me."

Message number two was from my parents. My mood had lifted considerably after listening to Nick's call, and I dialed my parents with a light heart. After a round of the usual questions about my health and welfare, they frankly shocked the hell out of me.

"Brandy, honey, your dad and I have decided to live in Florida year round. We're selling the house."

"You're what?"

"We love our life down here, and we figured with you kids gone it's foolish to hang on to the place." They said a bunch more stuff after that, but I'd stopped listening after they told me they were moving. I made all the appropriate "happy noises" and then I hung up and cried myself silly. How could they sell the only real home I'd ever known? L.A. never felt like "home" to me. Not once in the four years I've lived there. Now, some strangers would be parading around in *my* house, with *my* friends, eating *my* TastyKakes, living *my* life! *Unless...*

I called my parents back. "Mom, about the house..."

About the Author

Former Philadelphian Shelly Fredman firmly believes in what she once read on a bumper sticker: "Reality is for people who lack imagination." She splits her time between writing, teaching elementary school, consuming mass quantities of chocolate and enjoying the many characters that manifest themselves in her head (in the non-clinical sense). Author of the young-adult novel Creeps, she is currently working on a sequel to No Such Thing as a Secret. Shelly resides in Santa Monica, California.